A
Deadly
Chapter

Also available by Essie Lang

Castle Bookshop Mysteries

A Deadly Chapter
Death on the Page
Trouble on the Books

A Deadly Chapter

A CASTLE BOOKSHOP MYSTERY

Essie Lang

NEW YORK

Published in the United States by Crooked Lane Books, an imprint of The Quick Brown Fox & Company LLC.

Crooked Lane Books and its logo are trademarks of The Quick Brown Fox & Company LLC.

Library of Congress Catalog-in-Publication data available upon request.

ISBN (hardcover): 978-1-64385-576-9
ISBN (ebook): 978-1-64385-577-6

Cover illustration by Teresa Fasolino

Printed in the United States.

www.crookedlanebooks.com

Crooked Lane Books
34 West 27th St., 10th Floor
New York, NY 10001

First Edition: March 2021

10 9 8 7 6 5 4 3 2 1

To Lee,
My sister, my best friend.

Chapter One

S helby Cox woke with a start. She wasn't sure what had penetrated her sleep but when she looked at the clock, she saw it was a good thing something had. She had a bookstore to open, and her alarm clock was faulty. Maybe she'd better skip breakfast and grab a protein drink to take with her. There certainly wasn't time to stop at her favorite shop, Chocomania, for her usual latte and a truffle—the breakfast of champions.

She dragged herself out of bed, not sure why she was so tired and had slept so late. That was so unlike her. It had been an early night. Zack Griffin, her boyfriend, was out of town and she hadn't wanted to spend Saturday evening in a restaurant by herself. So, she'd spent it at home by herself. Of course, her cat JT had kept her company, even daring to dip his paw in her glass of red wine. The look of disgust he'd bestowed upon her guaranteed it would never happen again.

This morning, she stuck her head out the door, then stepped out onto the upper back deck of the houseboat she rented, wondering if she could get away with wearing a light sweater but then thought better of it. The shuttle ride over to Blye Island would be a chilly one no matter what the thermometer showed.

A small motorboat sped by, leaving a wake behind it. She could feel a slight motion as the craft gave the houseboat and dock a wide berth. A fisherman, Shelby thought, and it looked like he was heading back to shore. Another indicator of just how late she'd slept.

Shelby heard a sound somewhere down at the dock level, something she couldn't quite describe. A thunk? Maybe that's what had woken her, she thought as she wandered to the side railing. Although this was her second year living on the houseboat, she still wasn't too sure what to expect with the changing seasons. Maybe some ice had broken loose from under the dock and worked its way next to her houseboat. No, that didn't sound right for May but, if so, it had to be the last piece of the season. She was fascinated by the ever changing river and felt, once again, that she'd made the right decision moving back to her home town of Alexandria Bay in Upstate New York.

She shielded her eyes from the low level of the sun and focused on a dark object wedged between the houseboat and the dock. Something dark, rounded, and floating.

It couldn't be a body. Not again. That was just her fanciful mind.

Her own body felt cold inside and out even as she tried to convince herself it was a foolish thought. She went back inside to grab her cell phone from the bedside table, planning to take a closer look. A scratching at the door and fierce meow alerted her that she'd locked JT outside. She remedied that, grabbed her long, worn sweater that doubled as a robe, and then ran down the inside stairs of the houseboat. Out on the dock, she knelt down for a closer look. It was indeed a body; someone with gray hair. That's all she could make out since the body was facedown. She thought it was a man, though. She sure hoped it wasn't anyone she knew. Another wave hit the dock, and she saw what had made the noise. A small log seemed to be wedged there, one end tipped up and hitting the edge.

She tried to steady her hand but still had trouble punching in the shortcut on her phone to the local police office. When Shelby had explained what she'd found, she walked to the end of the dock and sat on the bench of a picnic table, near the parking lot, hugging herself to warm up, waiting for the police to arrive. She had no desire to be near the body or even add her weight to the houseboat that tried to lock him in place.

She heard the siren followed by a screeching sound as the Alexandria Bay police black-and-white SUV made a quick stop in the parking lot behind her. When Chief Tekla Stone's footsteps sounded loudly behind her, Shelby looked around but didn't say anything, only pointed to the houseboat. Shelby watched as the chief made her way slowly along the dock and stopped at the post near the end where the houseboat was tied up. She crouched down, removed her cap, and leaned over to try and see beneath the dock. But she didn't try to move the body.

The thought flitted through Shelby's head that maybe she should go over and grip the back of Stone's jacket, just in case she might start to tumble in. The chief was her Aunt Edie's age after all, and had the gray curls to prove it. When Stone looked back at her, Shelby realized what a foolish idea that would have been.

The chief stood up with great effort, giving a hint of her advancing age, then put her cap back on, pulled her cell phone out of her jacket pocket, and made a call. When she finished, she retraced her steps and sat down beside Shelby.

"He's dead all right. Are you okay?" For a minute it looked like she might touch Shelby's hand but seemed to decide against it and leaned back instead.

"I'm fine, I guess. It was just such a shock. I thought it might be a large piece of driftwood or something, and I was worried it might damage the houseboat. But a body. . . "

"Do you know him?"

"It is a man, then? I couldn't tell. I mean, I didn't really get a good look at him. I hope it's no one from town." Shelby shivered, and Stone put her arm around her shoulder. For comfort or warmth, Shelby wasn't sure.

"Huh. We'll just have to wait for Doc Rivers before we can pull him out for a good look. You might not want to be here for that. There's no telling how long the body has been in the water or what shape it's in." She turned and looked closely at Shelby. "Why don't you go over to your Aunt Edie's for now. I'll come and get you when we're done here."

"But I have to get over to the castle to open the store."

"I suggest you give your good friend Matthew Kessler a call and ask him to hang a sign on the door saying you're delayed."

Shelby didn't miss the sarcasm in Stone's voice when she talked about Matthew, but it no longer came as a surprise. Some relationships were destined never to improve.

She looked down at her pajamas. She couldn't very well walk to her aunt's house wearing those, and her car keys were still in the houseboat. Chief Stone seemed to realize the same thing.

"Where are your car keys? I'll bring them to you. Also, your purse."

"On the kitchen counter. Thanks. Don't let JT out. Please."

Stone looked back at her.

"The cat."

Stone nodded and walked back to the dock, letting herself into the houseboat. When she returned, Shelby asked, "How will I be able to tell you if I know him if I'm not here when you pull him out?"

"I'll take a photo if he's not in bad shape. Now, you head up there, and I'll be over just as soon as I can."

"Do you think it was an accident?" Shelby didn't dare mention the M word: murder. Not after what had happened last fall.

"Too soon to say. Now, go."

Shelby nodded and took one last look at the houseboat. From where she was sitting, everything looked normal. The sun was glittering off the wind chimes she'd hung at the back corner; there was little to no breeze so under normal circumstances she probably could have sat on the upper deck for her morning espresso.

Maybe this was all just a bad dream and she was still in it. Only it was real, all too real.

Chapter Two

S helby had debated phoning her Aunt Edie first to make sure she wasn't still in bed. She knew it was Trudy Bryant's day working in the main store, so Edie might just be treating herself to a slow morning. When she pulled up in front of the old family house, she realized how ridiculous that thought had been. Edie didn't take it easy, now that her knee was finally healed. In fact, Shelby was unsurprised to see her aunt squatting and digging in the flowerbed beside the front steps. And, she'd probably been at it for hours.

Edie looked up from her gardening when Shelby called to her, pushing back her straw hat which allowed a swath of gray hair to fall across her forehead. She took in Shelby's expression, and also her pajamas, all in one glance.

"What's going on? This doesn't look good. Is something wrong? Or are you just locked out of the houseboat?"

"No, nothing like that. Chief Stone basically told me to get lost after I found a dead body wedged between the houseboat and the dock." Shelby sank down onto the bottom step.

"What are you talking about? A dead body? Who? What happened? And why at your place?" Edie stripped off her gardening gloves and hurried over to sit beside Shelby. With a small groan, she tucked her long, billowing green skirt under her, and put her arm around her niece.

"That's a lot of questions, and I don't have any answers. The chief said it was a man, but he lay facedown in the water, so I couldn't tell if it was anyone I knew."

"Well, let's get you inside, and we'll talk after a cup of tea. And, I'll bet you need some breakfast, too, that's if you can eat. You stand up first and give me a hand, please."

Shelby did as she was told and followed Edie into the house. She sat at the kitchen table watching her aunt go through the familiar motions of filling the kettle, then pouring some hot water into the teapot, and, finally, adding the loose tea. No tea bags in Edie's house.

"Can you eat a bit?" Edie asked after they'd taken several sips of tea.

"I don't think so." Shelby looked over at the stovetop and saw the baking sheet of fresh scones. They smelled so good. "Well, maybe I could manage a scone."

Edie smiled and chose a couple, and set some butter and a small pot of jam on the table.

Finally, after a couple of mouthfuls, Shelby said, "It was awful, Aunt Edie. The body, not the scone. I mean, it's not like I haven't seen dead bodies before, but this one was at my house. And, if it turns out to be someone I know, it will be even worse, if there is a worse for the dead."

Edie reached across the table and touched Shelby's arm. "I can't imagine it, but at least you know this is in good hands, don't you?"

Edie looked so earnest that Shelby offered a small smile of reassurance. "Of course I do, and don't worry, I'm not getting involved. I've learned my lesson."

"I hope so."

"Besides, it was probably just an accident. Maybe some drunk fell in after a night on the town." Shelby glanced at the clock hanging on the kitchen wall. "I'm getting antsy. I wonder if the police are finished yet. I'm really anxious to get over to the island."

"Patience, my dear. It won't ruin our business if the store doesn't open for a few more hours."

"I beg to differ, dear Aunt. It's Sunday, so we only *have* a few more hours of being open for the day since we close up at four. I'd like to get over and check for messages at the very least." Shelby's fingers drummed the table top as she stared out the window. "I'm going over. I have to be doing something. Chief Stone knows where she can find me. I can't add any information about what happened anyway. I was asleep all night, so I didn't hear or see a thing until I was awake and out on the deck." Shelby felt a shiver slide down her spine, but she wouldn't let her aunt see the thought affected her. Otherwise, next thing, Edie would probably be trying to tuck her in for a nap. Shelby tried to smile and leave the uncomfortable memory behind her.

But Edie was focused on Shelby's clothing. "You're planning to go in your PJ's? I mean, not that they're not cute."

Shelby groaned, looking down at her pink-and-white polka dot pajama bottoms and fuchsia T-shirt top. She'd forgotten she was still wearing them.

"I could lend you something—a skirt, a top?"

Shelby couldn't figure out how to politely refuse, although she couldn't really see herself in one of Edie's long multicolored skirts or a tie-dyed T-shirt. But as long as Zack didn't arrive back in town unexpectedly, she guessed it would be all right. Hopefully, no one from town would come in and as for the staff at the castle, well, she'd just have to grin and bear it.

"Come with me and have a look," Edie said, leaving the kitchen without a backward glance.

Shelby followed her upstairs, noting that Edie seemed at ease on the climb. That was a relief, anyway. Once in the bedroom, Edie opened the closet doors and told Shelby to make her choice.

"Sandals are on the shoe rack to the right," she added, before she went back downstairs.

Shelby somewhat hesitantly pushed some clothes aside to make it easier to sort through the skirts. There were only four, but they were all bright. She pulled out a paisley number and then looked for the least colorful top. Then she tried on the pale pink, V-neck T-shirt and the skirt. She figured, if she pinned the waistband, the skirt would stay up. Maybe Edie had a belt she could borrow that would make the top seem less voluminous.

When she felt put together, Shelby rejoined Edie in the kitchen and twirled to show off the outfit.

"That looks super on you," Edie gushed, pushing her newly permed gray curls back from her face. This time she'd opted to forgo the usual patch of bright color she had applied to her locks that usually draped across one side of her face. "Maybe you'd like to keep it?"

Shelby quickly shook her head. "Uh, no thanks, Edie. I appreciate the offer, though. Now, I'll drop the car off in my lot before catching the next boat over to the island, and take a quick look at the dock. Who knows, they might be finished with that part of the investigation. Thanks for the breakfast and the wardrobe."

"Call me when you hear something, anything," Edie said and gave Shelby a quick hug.

After Shelby had locked her car back in the parking lot, she stopped at the edge of the dock but was disappointed to see crime scene tape dangling off the front of the houseboat and two men scouring the area. She had been holding onto the final shreds of hope she might be able to duck inside and change. No sign of the chief, though.

Shelby hurried off to the main dock, hoping to make the next tour boat. She'd definitely missed the shuttle run by Terry's Boat Lines, which the Heritage Society had hired to take staff and volunteers over to Blye Island an hour before opening time. Otherwise, they had been issued passes to use the tour boats that the larger cruise company ran at other times of day.

When she arrived at Blye Castle twenty minutes later, she managed to be the first to slip off the boat, hitching up the long, flowing skirt, and walking at a fast trot up the stone stairs to the front door. She took a moment to compose herself before opening it. Nobody seemed to be paying attention, so she slid inside and quickly made her way to Bayside Books, nestled in the front right, 300 square feet off the castle. She unlocked the door and had almost made it inside when she heard Chrissie Halstead rushing up behind her.

"Wow, are you channeling your aunt today, Shelby?" Chrissie was the acting Volunteer Coordinator for the castle site, although Shelby figured the "acting" part of the designation had been forgotten by this point. From what she'd heard, no one else seemed anxious to assume the role, but with Chrissie's job as PR person for the Alexandria Bay Heritage Society, Shelby wondered how she had the time during high season at the castle to manage both.

Shelby headed inside and held the door open for Chrissie before answering. "I had to borrow this outfit because I couldn't access my houseboat. Long story. And, I couldn't make it over here any sooner either. I hope it hasn't been a busy day so far?"

"We haven't had a full boatload of tourists come through yet today but I have great hopes about this afternoon." Chrissie leaned against the door frame. She'd recently had her blonde hair cut in a bob that ended just below her ears. Shelby was still getting used to it. She thought it looked great, but in her mind, Chrissie used to have this debutante air about her, from her shoulder-length blonde hair to her neutral toned pumps. And now, suddenly, Chrissie looked the part of a fun-loving gal from the flapper era.

"By the way, I heard that a body was found in the Bay this morning," Chrissie continued, oblivious to Shelby's scrutiny.

Shelby groaned inwardly. She didn't want to get into this conversation, but if she didn't tell Chrissie what she knew, Shelby worried her feelings would be hurt when she found out exactly where in the water the body had been found. And she did like Chrissie.

She worked through the store opening routines while she explained. "I was the one who found the body. It was wedged between my houseboat and the dock, which is why I couldn't get back inside to get dressed. The police were busy there, so I was sent to Aunt Edie's to get out of the way, in my pajamas no less, and, therefore, this outfit. And that's all I know about the body, except that it was a man."

Chrissie gasped. "You found him? That must have been horrible. I can't imagine what I'd do if I found a body. Although it's not your first time finding one, is it? Still, I'd imagine it never gets easier. Are you okay? I mean, shouldn't you be back at your aunt's resting or something?"

Shelby grimaced. "No, I'm fine. It was gruesome but that was a few hours ago, and I'll be okay if I don't dwell on it."

"I can't believe what's been happening around here lately. Do you know, that's the third body in about a year? Oh, of course you know. Silly question. So, any idea who it is, or was, I mean?"

"Nope."

"So, maybe no one from around here? One can hope." Chrissie had started fingering the zipper on her stylish sweater. She looked, as she always did, like she was ready to step into any PR photos that might need taking.

"I couldn't tell. He was facedown, and I haven't heard anything further from the police."

They both looked at the door at that moment as it flew open. Chief Stone managed to fill the space, even though she was shorter than Shelby and on the thin side.

"I hope I haven't interrupted any gossip," she said, walking over to them. She snapped her police baseball cap off her head and dropped it on the counter.

"Nope," Chrissie chirped, glancing quickly from Shelby to Chief Stone. "I've got to get back to work. Nice to see you, Chief."

Stone nodded at her then focused on Shelby. "I see you decided not to wait for me."

"I did wait, but then I was worried about missing too much business."

Stone eyed her from top to bottom. "Your aunt's influence is beginning to show on you." She barely hid a smirk.

Shelby sighed and touched her ponytail, hoping it at least looked professional. "Only for one day. Did you find out who the man is?"

"Do you have any coffee?"

"I just got here, so I haven't made any yet. I'll do it right away. It'll only take a few minutes to brew." She ducked into the back room and was back quickly.

"Well, he didn't have any ID, so we don't know who he is, but I did get the photo of him." Stone pulled out her cell phone and Shelby took a step backward without realizing it.

"He's not in bad condition, so he must have gone into the water possibly only a few hours before you found him. But, of course, he's dead. Just take a deep breath and then have a look." Stone tipped her cell phone toward Shelby. "Please."

Shelby did as she was told. She took the cell from Stone's hand and took a look, but her hands started shaking so badly, she dropped the phone.

Stone looked like she was about to burst a blood vessel in her neck, but she quickly scooped up the phone and then took hold of Shelby's arm. "What is it? Do you know him?"

Shelby couldn't stop shaking, so Stone stuffed the cell in her pocket and put both hands on Shelby's shoulders.

"Look at me, Shelby. Good. Now, take a deep breath and slowly let it out. Good. Now, go around and sit down on the stool behind the counter and talk to me."

Shelby did as she was told, trying to gain control of her emotions. When she felt she could do so, she said, "I'm okay. It was just a shock, that's all."

"So, you do know him?"

"Not really, as in I can't tell you his name or anything, but he was in the store yesterday early afternoon and we did talk."

"What did he say?"

"He began by reminding me he'd been in the store last fall. It didn't really ring any bells until he said he'd been looking for a woman. I can't remember who it was he'd wanted to find. When he told me her name, it hadn't sound familiar." Shelby slumped a bit but then straightened her back, taking another deep breath.

The chief looked toward the back room and sniffed the air. "I think our brews are ready, and they might help."

Shelby nodded and went to get the coffee, bringing back two mugs filled to the brim. She handed one to the chief.

Stone nodded her thanks and took a tentative sip. "Go on. What did he tell you about her? Why was he looking for her?"

"He didn't say why, but he said she loved books so he figured she might have been a customer."

"So, he thinks she lives in the Alex Bay area?"

"I guess. He did say something about her having moved here about seven years ago. I know he'd also checked at the main store and some others in town back in the fall. That was it."

Stone started pacing, careful not to slosh her coffee too much. Shelby tracked the few drops on the floor, making a note to clean them after. "But he didn't tell you his name or where he was from?"

"No, he didn't, either time. He was very nice though, friendly, and, it seemed, eager to find this woman. After all, he did come to town twice and asked about her both times. She must have been important to him."

Stone stopped her pacing and stood, looking at Shelby who could tell the chief's mind was racing.

As was Shelby's. She suddenly remembered, "He did show me a picture of her."

"Really? You didn't think to start with that? Sorry, I'm just a tad testy," Stone admitted. "So, anyone you've seen before?"

"No, but I remember he said it was taken about fifteen years ago, maybe even longer, and he guessed that she had probably changed her hair coloring and style. I tried to visualize it, but that didn't really make a difference. I mean, she still didn't look familiar. It wasn't a very clear picture of her to start with, and she was just one in a group of six people, and she was scrunched in between two big guys, in what looked like a staged photo."

"What do you mean by staged?"

"You know, posed. Sort of formal, not at all casual or relaxed. Like maybe for an official photo in a newsletter or something."

"Hm. We didn't find any picture on his body."

"Well it was last fall when he showed it to me."

"Huh. Maybe he was trying a different tactic this time." Stone didn't look convinced, though.

"Oh," Shelby said with a start.

"What?"

"I'd been thinking, when he was here in the fall, that there was probably a romance involved. And something reminded me of that after he left yesterday." Shelby sighed. What had reminded her of that? Something he'd specifically said? She didn't think so.

"Huh. That was based on something he said?"

"No, just my mind spinning out a story about a long-lost love that he was finally trying to track down." Shelby felt her face flush and wished she hadn't mentioned anything about it. She looked down at Edie's skirt. She just felt so disoriented today. "I mean, why else would he be searching for someone for so long?"

Stone gave her head a slight shake. "Well, I guess that's something. One more thing, has anything else come to mind about earlier this morning? Any sounds of a car or a boat? Or even footsteps on the dock?"

"I've actually been trying not to think about it, but I'm pretty sure I told you everything."

"Okay." Stone reached out and squeezed Shelby's arm, which came as a total surprise to Shelby. "I'll touch base with you later."

"Uh, Chief? Do you know how he died?"

Stone sighed and stuck her baseball cap on her head. "It looks like he hit his head on something hard and blunt when he fell into the water. Now, he could have slipped beside the riverbank and hit his head on some rocks as he slid in. Or, he was clobbered beforehand. But I'll leave that decision to the coroner."

After the chief left, Shelby poured herself another cup of coffee. It sounded like this might be murder, another one so soon. Shelby shivered and forced herself to think back to the morning's discovery while she drank her coffee. She had told the chief everything. She started to think back on her encounter with the man the afternoon before but felt another chill. Best not to spend too much time with the thought until she'd had time to accept it.

She didn't have time to think about it anyway as, at that moment, a family of four, including twin toddlers, entered the bookstore. The mom, who looked to be around Shelby's age, smiled and grabbed the hand of the little girl while the dad did the same with the boy.

"Just let me know if I can help you find anything," Shelby said then finished her coffee before getting down to store business, taking a look at the report of Saturday's sales and deciding what needed to be reordered. She also gave Edie a quick call, filling her in on Stone's visit.

Her call was interrupted by the arrival of another young couple with a toddler in tow.

"We heard you'd opened the shop," the woman said. "It was closed when we arrived, and I was disappointed. I'd so been hoping to get in here on our visit to the castle. I love looking around bookstores."

Shelby warmed to the woman's enthusiasm although she noticed the man seemed less keen and the child would probably have been happier at a playground.

"Just take your time browsing. I'm happy to answer any questions you may have." She looked at the toddler. "I have a coloring book and crayons if he'd be happier with that."

"Oh no, don't worry about Mikey. My husband is anxious to escape, I'm afraid, so the two of them can go wander outside." She waved at her husband, who smiled at Shelby, the relief on his face palpable. He picked up the child and, with a nod, made a fast exit.

While her customers browsed, Shelby worked on some shelf talkers, colorful cards on which she wrote recommendations for a couple of new arrivals she'd just finished reading. By the time she'd secured them to the proper shelves, the woman was standing back at the counter with two books. The family of four had left without buying anything.

"I've so enjoyed looking around. I always try to buy one book about the area we're visiting and a newly released mystery as a treat. You have a good selection of both."

"Thank you for saying that. Where are you from?"

"We're from Boise, Idaho, and we've been visiting my husband's family just outside Clayton. I wanted to do a boat tour of the castles before we left. I'm so glad I chose Blye Castle.

It's well worth seeing. Especially since it has a bookstore," she added with a smile.

Shelby beamed. Her feelings exactly. When she'd first moved back to Alexandria Bay, she'd seen all the usual tourist sites, including the two larger and better-known castles in the islands—Boldt and Singer Castles. While they'd both been amazing and quite different from each other, she felt that Blye Castle was where their bookstore belonged. Where she belonged.

When the customers had gone and she was once again alone, Shelby busied herself changing one of the display areas. By four o'clock, she was ready to close up shop and head home. She ran to the boat, determined to catch it before it shoved off, then stood at the railing, enjoying the wind and sun on the short ride back to Alexandria Bay.

She tried not to think about how much she missed Zack. His job as a Coast Guard Investigative Service agent had taken him out of town again, filling in at the office in Buffalo for three months. He tried to get home to Alex Bay whenever possible, but his hours were often irregular at best. She'd been hoping he'd have the weekend off, but he'd called on Friday with the bad news. How she could have used a major hug from him today.

Ah well, at least she had Sunday dinner at Edie's to look forward to. After the day she'd had, she needed a bright spot. And of course, there would be a delicious meal with her aunt along with Matthew Kessler, caretaker at the island, who just might have some ideas. His job, which involved the care of the gardens and lawns surrounding Blye Castle, required that he live in a separate cottage on the island year-round. She looked forward to their weekly meals together, as much for the company as for the pleasure of eating Edie's mouth-watering roast beef and Yorkshire pudding. It was also heartwarming to see the bond between the two of them. Although Edie didn't talk much about it, Shelby knew it ran deep.

Chapter Three

Shelby headed straight home when she got off the boat, grateful to be allowed back on her houseboat, and quickly changed. As much as she appreciated Edie's generosity, Shelby was much more at home in her own clothes. Edie had told her not to bother washing the items before returning them and so, with a quiver of guilt, she piled them into a bag then set out on foot.

She could hear laughter as she climbed the front stairs. Edie and Matthew, having a good time as usual. She wondered for a brief moment if she should just turn around and slink away, leave them to a romantic evening, but she had been invited and she was hoping that Matthew had heard something about the body and the investigation. Of course, she assured herself, it was only natural that she should be a bit curious.

She knocked before walking in and finding them relaxing in the living room.

Shelby lifted the bag of clothes. "Thanks for these, Aunt Edie. I'll just leave them in the hall."

"That's just fine."

"It smells delicious," Shelby said, as she came back in and gave Edie a hug. "It's rare to find you just sitting before a meal, though. Usually you're a human dynamo in constant movement in the kitchen.

Matthew chuckled. "Blame it on me. I thought she deserved a bit of a break after cooking all afternoon. And how are you doing after your upsetting start to the day?"

Shelby noticed the glasses in their hands and guessed there was whiskey adding to the cheery noise level.

"Yes, Shelby. Was it a rough day for you?" Edie asked, grabbing hold of Shelby's hand before she could move away and sit down.

"I'm better now than earlier, that's for sure," Shelby answered. "I still can't believe there he was, wedged in between the houseboat and the dock. I don't think I'll be able to walk that dock again without looking down and checking the water."

"I'll bet," Edie answered. "And then to find it was actually someone you knew."

"You knew him?" Matthew sounded surprised.

Shelby shrugged. "Not really knew. He stopped in the store yesterday and he'd also been in last fall. I wonder if you might have seen him wandering around the island either time? I imagine the Chief showed you his photo."

Matthew shook his head. "She did, but it didn't ring any bells. If I had met him, it probably wouldn't have stayed with me anyway, unless there was a reason to remember him or if I'd spoken to him, which I know I didn't."

"Edie, do you happen to remember an out-of-towner coming into the bookstore last fall and asking about a woman who would have moved to town about seven years earlier? It would have been just a couple of weeks before we closed down the island location for the winter."

Edie thought about it for a minute or so. "No, I don't. It could have been on my day off. This was the same man?"

"Yes. I'll check with Trudy, in that case," Shelby said, making a mental note. "I wonder what happened to him? If it was an accident, then it could have happened anytime yesterday afternoon after he'd been in the store, but if he was murdered, that's entirely another matter. I mean, the island is so busy during the day, surely a murder couldn't have taken place there. So, it must have happened here in the village. But where?"

"Hold on," Edie jumped in. "Who says it's a murder?"

"The chief said it could be rather than a simple case of his losing his footing and falling in the river. I guess he had a bump on his head, which makes it questionable although that could have happened if he hit his head when falling."

Matthew gave it some thought. "If he'd been hit by someone, it probably would have led to a wound being in a different location from one if he just happened to lose his footing and slipped down the slope. Huh. Another murder. I was hoping we'd seen the end of those."

"Another murder." Edie echoed and took a sip from her glass. She looked suddenly pale, but Shelby thought it might just be the contrast to the bright gem tones she was wearing—an emerald tank top with a purple shirt doubling as a sweater.

"Maybe. But what are the chances?" Shelby asked Matthew.

"I think we all thought that when the last murder occurred. Anyway, we may be jumping to conclusions."

"Why do you say that?"

Matthew looked serious, but Shelby could hear some playfulness in his voice. "Because Chief Stone hasn't accused me of murder and we know how she loves to do that."

Edie gasped and then started laughing. Shelby joined in, too. It felt good to be a bit silly after all the tension she'd felt building up since the morning. She was also secretly pleased to hear Matthew being so blasé about Stone's obvious distrust of him and, as he said, her usual readiness to blame murders on him. Shelby knew that Edie must feel relieved, too.

Shelby watched Matthew as he watched Edie enjoying the final sip of her drink. He looked far more relaxed than when she usually saw him on the island. Of course, he was always working at those times. He seemed to fit into Edie's cozy living room décor, sitting in the Lazy Boy recliner, the sleeves of his blue plaid shirt rolled up to his elbows, and his gray hair, which always somehow looked in need of cutting, curling from behind his ears. It was his face though, that Shelby watched. His blue eyes looked almost dreamy.

The mood broke when Edie stood up and shooed the two of them into the dining room while she dished out the meal.

Over dinner, Shelby tried to steer her mind away from what had happened, but it wasn't easy.

"I can tell you're thinking about what's happened, aren't you?" Edie asked.

"I guess. It's hard to get it off my mind but I was also wondering about this mysterious woman he was looking for. Is she in Alexandria Bay, and if so, who could it be? Has he been looking for her all these years or did he just start? And, probably most importantly, did she have anything to do with his death?"

"Do you remember what he said about her?"

"He showed me a photo that first time, but she didn't look familiar. Of course, she was part of a group and was scrunched in between others, and it was taken quite a while ago. He mentioned a name, too, but I can't remember it. I do know it didn't sound familiar at the time. Of course, I hadn't been living here very long, so I had no idea who might have moved here seven years before. Can either of you think of anyone?"

"Not offhand," Edie said. "Does that ring a bell?" She looked at Matthew.

He shook his head. "I'm not really into the social goings-on in Alex Bay, as you know."

"Hmm," Shelby said. "I'd be interested to know though if anyone comes to mind."

Shelby finished the last enjoyable bite of the traditional Sunday prime rib roast on her plate then turned to Edie. "On a happier note, I knew you'd want to know what's happening with the upcoming murder mystery event."

"What's that?" Matthew asked.

Edie looked at him. "Have you not been listening to any of our conversations over the past several weeks? Shelby's been involved in the planning, on behalf of the bookstore, for a couple of months now."

Matthew tried to look apologetic. "I try not to eavesdrop."

Edie harrumphed. "We're co-hosting along with the public library. It's a day-long event, which includes two panels of authors in the morning, book signings in the afternoon, and a murder mystery dinner."

"That sounds like fun," he said, although he didn't sound like he believed it. "So, where's it being held?"

"The morning events will be at the library, the signings at the main store, and the dinner at the Black Fox Bistro."

"And just who all will take part in this?"

Edie waved her hand at Shelby who took up the explanation. "We've been advertising it all around the county and on Facebook and some other social media, hoping to get the word out to an even wider audience. Registration is almost full. There are a lot of folks from the Bay area coming, of course. And we, or should I say, Nora Dynes at the library, has invited six authors. Two are from Buffalo, two Canadian, one is local, and one is from New York City. They all sound excited about it, at least according to Nora."

"Huh. Don't know her, but I guess it sounds like a good idea."

"Well, of course it does," Edie said, crossing her arms on the table and leaning on them. "It's a win-win for everyone involved."

"So, who's writing the dinner mystery?"

"Nora has taken care of that," Shelby supplied. "She knows a writer who's written several. And the authors will be taking on some of the acting spots."

"Are you playing a role in the murder mystery," he asked Edie, obviously amused.

She straightened up and sat back in her chair. "We're in discussions."

"In discussions? As in, my people will contact your people?" he asked, a chuckle in his voice.

"You scoff, but I want you to know, if I make my acting debut, I expect you to be there to see it." Her gaze pinned him to his spot. "And, I'd like you to go as my date."

Matthew quickly changed his demeanor to one of total seriousness. "Only if you're not playing the victim. I'd hate to be abandoned partway through the evening."

Edie threw her napkin in his direction. "You're incorrigible."

Shelby felt a happy glow, enjoying their banter. She hadn't known that Edie had been approached for the play, but she did know that it promised to be an evening to remember. Now, if she could just get focused on her part of the long event to-do list. She realized she kept putting it off and wasn't really sure why. Maybe she'd get to it tomorrow.

*　*　*

Zack called as she was crawling into bed, thoroughly worn out. She brightened when she heard his voice.

"How are you?" he asked. "I heard what happened today."

"You did? Of course, the cop grapevine or some such thing. Well, it didn't start out to be my best day, but it's a far worse one for the dead guy."

"I can hear that you're still upset, and that's not surprising. I wish I was there." His voice was low and soothing. Shelby could feel herself melting, as usual.

"I second that wish." She paused and thought she heard him sigh. "Well, Chief Stone is on it, and that's what I'll concentrate on."

"Did you know him?"

"No, not really. He was from out of town, but he'd come into the store a couple of times, and although we spoke, he never mentioned his name. Or if he did, I forgot. He came in once in the fall and then again the day before I found his, uh, his body. He was asking about a woman both times, the same woman. He said she moved here seven years ago and he was looking for her."

"Anybody you know?"

"I'm pretty sure not."

"Well, as you say, Stone is on it, so I hope you're able to put it out of your mind. Especially tonight and get a good sleep."

"Believe me, I'll try." She crawled into bed and JT jumped up a few seconds later.

"And I'll try to come home next weekend. I'll call later in the week when I know better, if not before. You be sure to call me if you need to talk."

"All right," she agreed as they hung up. She tried to imagine the kiss he'd ended the call with, actually on her lips.

She was happy he'd called even though she knew it would be almost next to impossible for her to get in touch with him later in the week as he'd suggested. He was a busy guy.

She did hope at least that, after hearing his voice, her dreams would be of him.

Unfortunately, they weren't.

Chapter Four

Tuesday morning, as she got ready for work, Shelby thought back to what she'd accomplished the day before. Exactly nothing. She'd been looking forward to the day off, to try to put some distance between herself and what had happened on Sunday. However, looking back, she realized her day had been sort of a haze and she hadn't even done any housework, not that she counted that as a great loss. She'd spoken to Edie several times on the phone, knowing that each call Edie made to her was one of reassurance for them both. Still, as she grabbed her usual latte at Chocomania on Tuesday morning, she wished she'd dropped in the day before also. Erica was in the back of the shop, doing some chocolatey things, Shelby supposed, and Rainbow wasn't too talkative; not that Shelby felt all that comfortable with the new part-time staffer. She left without speaking to her friend, vowing to return the next day with plenty of time to wait around, if need be, for a chat.

As she headed up the stone pathway to Blye Castle, she noticed some activity off to her left, in the direction of the grotto. Two men and one woman were poised with binoculars trained on the upper branches of nearby trees. Usually the staff and volunteers at the castle were the first people on the island.

She wondered who the people were and how they'd gotten over to the island. Her curiosity got the better of her, and she veered from the path, crossing the lawn toward them when she heard Matthew call out to her. He came scurrying over to her as she paused.

"You shouldn't go over there," he said, nodding in the exact direction she'd been headed.

"Why not? Who are those people? What's happening?"

"According to Chief Stone, they're local birders from the Thousand Island Bird Watchers' Society," he explained, holding onto her elbow to redirect her back to the castle.

"And what's that all about?"

"Of course you'd want to know," answered Chief Stone, who approached them from the other side of the lawn. She stopped in front of them and looked from one to the other.

Neither Shelby nor Matthew said a word.

"All right, I'll tell you this much. We found his car and there's no evidence of foul play. But an eagle feather was found in the jacket pocket of our victim, and the birding society has agreed to search for the eagle nest. There aren't many of them in this region. We have birders on two other nearby islands actively searching. We're trying everything we can in order to determine where the body went into the water."

"Wow, that's an unusual clue. So, you think . . ."

"If we find the eagle, we'll find where our victim has been and, if we're lucky, where he was killed. Although, I don't mind admitting, it's quite a long shot. I'd think that if there was an eagle nest on the island our friends here would have tracked it down many months ago."

Shelby had wondered if there would be a connection to Blye Island since the man had visited there the day he died, but hearing this further news still gave her chills. "So, he could have been killed on this island. And are you thinking it was a murder then? Couldn't he have just missed his footing while looking at eagles, if that's what he was doing?"

"We have reason to believe he was indeed murdered."

Shelby stared at the chief, waiting to hear more. The chief stared back, lips in a tight line.

After several seconds of standoff, Shelby finally said, "Huh. I guess I'd better head to the store and get ready for opening."

Stone nodded. "Good idea. And I'm sure you have something to do also, Mr. Kessler."

Matthew smiled, although Shelby could tell it was forced. "Of course," he said and walked with Shelby to the castle.

"That was really weird, right?" Shelby asked.

"What, that it's a murder or the bit about the eagle feather?"

"Both, I guess, although I think the eagle feather is the winner in that contest."

"I haven't heard of anything like it before, but I do know eagle sightings are not as common here as farther along the river. Also, I do believe it's an offense to take an eagle feather."

"Really?"

They'd reached the front door of the castle, and Matthew held it open for her. "Yup. Google it. Well, I've got to check on an upstairs window that seems to be warping. See you later."

Shelby watched as Matthew made his way to the staircase, before heading over to the store to get it ready for what she hoped would be a busy day. She got the coffee started and then shelved some books, taking time to turn the occasional book cover out, to better display the work.

She paused to take a good look around the store. She did this occasionally to try and see what impression the store might make on customers as they entered. The pale green—correction, willow green—walls, combined with the numerous large windows and newly acquired ferns, gave the store a bright and natural feeling of welcome. There were bookshelves in spaces without windows, some high enough to require a stool, and other shoulder-high ones that stood in the center of the floor. The first was the show-case for new arrivals and always an attention grabber.

On the opposite side of the store, two white wicker chairs were placed as a lure for shoppers to stay a bit longer and take their time browsing through books. The light from the window behind them made it the ideal place to do so. And the small wicker table nearby gave them a place to stack extra books they might want to consider.

She loved this place. It felt so inviting every time she walked in. Not that she didn't feel the same way about the main store in Alexandria Bay. It's just that this was a smaller version, a cozier version, and her own territory. She supposed that had a lot to do with it.

By break time, her curiosity got the better of her once again, and Shelby headed back to the spot where she'd seen the birders. Only they weren't there. Instead, a man and a woman she didn't recognize were taking measurements and photographs. She walked closer, hoping to get close enough to hear what they were saying to each without being noticed. That's when she spotted Matthew, apparently doing the same thing. She hurried over to him.

"What's going on? They've found something obviously. Is this where he was killed?"

"Apparently. Those there are state police, so I guess the Chief found something and called them in for extra help. From here, it looks like there was a struggle around that area. Some bushes have been trampled, and there's blood on them, according to one of the birders. I haven't heard anything official, though, just some comments from the searchers. Uh-oh, we've been spotted and are about to get lectured."

Shelby turned around to see Chief Stone striding toward them. Again.

"I take it you know what's been found. It does look like a struggle of some sort took place there and it may, in fact, be where the murder was committed. So, until we have more facts, I want you both to keep quiet about this, understood?" Her glare hovered on each of them for a few seconds. "And Shelby, no asking questions about any of this. Got it?"

Shelby nodded.

"Yeah, right," Stone muttered as she stomped over to the crime scene.

On the way back to the store, Shelby considered what she knew about the crime so far. She'd seen the victim early Saturday afternoon. He'd been in the store, and now he was dead. There wasn't much more to know than that.

She was actually happy when three women of varying ages wandered into the store, forcing her to abandon all thoughts about the murder. After they left, each with a book, Chrissie Halstead walked purposefully over to the counter.

"Have you come up with any ideas for the Victorian weekend we're planning? It's only a little over a month away, you know. And it will be our most exciting event of the summer season here on the island." Chrissie straightened her blue jacket as she glanced around the store. Shelby wondered if it was real leather. Either way, it looked very classy with Chrissie's moss green straight-legged pants.

"I'm sorry, I haven't really, not with everything else we've been planning. And now, with all that's happening, I think I'll have Laura tackle it, if she agrees. She'll be in all day tomorrow so I'll check with her then. Is that okay?"

"Sure thing. Just let me know and I'll figure out when she and I can talk. I'm counting on you all dressing in Victorian garb and, of course, you'll have a big sale going on, too, won't you?"

"Of course," Shelby answered, returning Chrissie's goodbye wave. She also wondered why she even needed to take part in the event discussion. All the decisions about the bookstore had already been made, it seemed. It would be good to involve Laura, though. It would help her to feel part of not only the bookstore, but of Blye Castle.

Shelby had just finished restocking one of the shelves in the mystery section, and was trying to give some thought to the special island event coming up, when Chief Stone walked into the store.

"A fresh pot of coffee's on and should be ready momentarily," Shelby said, pleased to beat the chief to the punch.

Stone grimaced. "I'm that obvious, am I?" She took her hat off and wandered over to sit down hard on a chair.

"Predictable, maybe. About coffee at least," she hastily added.

In fact, in Shelby's opinion, the chief was not only predictable but also, at this moment, looking very fatigued. The investigation might be taking its toll. After all, Tekla Stone was the same age as her aunt Edie, late sixties, and she had to be missing out on sleep when trying to get a jump on any murder investigation. When she had moved to the Bay, Shelby had been told there were hardly any murders in the area. In fact, the chief had boasted there had been only one in her long tenure with the police. But between last year and now, this was the third. Shelby wasn't superstitious, but she wondered if she had somehow jinxed the place by moving here. She gave herself a mental head slap. *Ridiculous thought.*

Stone seemed to have ignored the coffee comment.

"I wanted to tell you we've identified the victim. His wallet was found in the bushes close to the tree with the nest. Here's the picture from his driver's license. See if it rings any bells. I've already contacted the police in Fulsome Falls, which is where he's from." Stone pulled out her cell phone and took a few seconds before finding the black-and-white photo. "That's out Massena way. I've been there, a bit bigger than Alex Bay but just as friendly."

"His name is Nathan Miller," she said as she showed the photo to Shelby. "This is the man who was in your store Saturday afternoon?"

Shelby nodded her head. "Oh, definitely, although that is a driver's license picture and you know how notoriously bad those can be."

"And, he was here last fall, both times asking about a woman?"

"Yes."

Stone sniffed the air.

"I'll grab that coffee," Shelby said. "Do you think I could get a copy of that photo?" she asked from the back room.

"And just why would you want that?"

Shelby heard the steeliness in Stone's voice. *Tread carefully.*

"I just thought if I looked at it now and then, some details might eventually come back to me. That's all." *Maybe.*

Shelby delivered the coffee to Stone and tried to keep a neutral look on her face. *No plotting going on here.*

"All right. I'll forward it to you. But, right now, I'd like you to concentrate on coming up with that name Mr. Miller asked you about. You just keep on thinking back on it and see if anything comes to mind." She took a long sip of the coffee after blowing on it. "Good coffee, as usual."

"Have you talked to any of the staff in some of the other stores in town?"

"Of course. We've covered them all, and it appears he stopped in at your main store and then next door at Felicity's gallery. He also talked to the sisters at Driftwood and Seawinds. And, of course, we've checked in at the library. We're still trying to locate anyone else he may have visited."

Shelby thought for a brief moment that a small smile might have twitched Stone's lips. So she dared to ask, "And none of them had more information than what I gave you?"

"I didn't say that, and I'm not about to share what they told me. But I will say, nobody has remembered the mystery woman's name. So, keep on it. Please. I'd better get on with my investigations. Thanks for the coffee."

The chief had almost reached the door when Nora Dynes came rushing in.

Nora looked startled and then seemed to regain her composure when the chief nodded briefly to her and continued out the door.

"I hope this is an okay time for our meeting," she said, looking back at the door. She'd tamed her short curly brown hair by sticking a straw hat with a small brim on her head, which she left in place now. Shelby pegged her at about forty-five years old but that could be way off. Nora came across as being a very private person despite her ready smile, so Shelby doubted she'd ever get friendly enough with her to find out her real age.

"Yes, this is just fine," Shelby answered, although she'd forgotten the library volunteer was coming over to discuss the "murder mystery night" the bookstore and library were co-hosting later in the summer.

"That was the police chief, wasn't it? What was she doing here? And what's going on outside on the lawn? I couldn't help but notice the police and all the commotion." Nora moved closer to the window and leaned into the pane facing the side yard.

"I'll bet it has something to do with that body found beside your houseboat, doesn't it?" Nora continued, answering her own question. "I mean, how many things do the local police have on their plate at one time?"

"How did you know about the body?"

"The whole town knows." She reached out and patted Shelby's arm. "That must have been quite a shock for you. I had heard it was nobody from the Bay area, so that's good anyway." Nora busied herself pulling a couple of file folders out of her bag.

"That's true, but it's still distressing."

"Oh, of course, I didn't mean that it's any less of a tragedy, only that none of our neighbors are directly affected."

Someone will be. "Can I get you a cup of coffee before we begin?"

"I'd love some, thank you," Nora said, settling into one of the two wicker chairs placed in front of the side windows. "One sugar, no milk, please."

Shelby brought two mugs out of the back room and sat in the chair opposite, before getting up to grab a pad and pen. She was pleased that, apparently, Nora knew how to plan an event. She'd taken control right from the first meeting and, better yet, followed through on her own suggestions, meaning Shelby had been off the hook so far. Which also meant she hadn't done much about the event on her own and was now feeling a bit guilty.

"Now," Nora said, sitting forward and pulling her iPad out of her bag along with a file folder, "this is what we've got so far." She held her iPad out to Shelby to read. "Location, date of course, authors, the play is being written as we speak, a lot of publicity in the works, but, I think, we can do even better with that."

She paused and pulled some papers out of the folder, explaining, "I much prefer having paper copies of the visuals. Have a look at the brochure. Did I miss anything? Have you had any new ideas since our last meeting?"

Shelby had been trying to concentrate, picturing what they'd been going over the past few months. She decided to bypass Nora's last question. "It sounds about right to me. Have all the extras for the murder mystery been recruited? I know my Aunt Edie was saying she was thinking about it."

"I'm pleased to hear that. I asked Julie. You remember her? She's another library volunteer—short, petite, bright red hair— she's in charge of filling in the gaps. Last I heard, she had most roles accounted for, and those she'd spoken to, who had agreed, were really excited about it."

Shelby gave a fake shudder. "Not on my to-try list."

"That's because you like working in the background, Shelby. I sensed that about you right away."

"You did? How?" Shelby tried to think back to the first time she had met Nora and was pretty sure it had been in the office of the librarian Judy Carter. It had only been the three of them, and nothing sprang to her mind that accounted for Nora's comment. Maybe it was the way she had come across. She used to be far more uncomfortable meeting new people but she'd thought that, after a year, front and center meeting new people every day in the bookstore, she'd changed and now appeared more relaxed and friendly. Maybe not. Should she be concerned, she wondered.

"Well, for one thing, I thought you'd want to lead on this project, it being a money-maker for your business and all. So, although I've had a lot of experience in fundraising and putting on such projects, I would have been happy to have you make the decisions. I hope you know that. However, I am pleased to have taken on that role." Nora slid her iPad back into the

39

briefcase along with the file folder, and so missed the perplexed look on Shelby's face.

Was that a dig at her?

"So, to summarize, Shelby," Nora said, looking directly at her, "you will be in charge of the store signings. That's all right with you?"

"It is. I think it makes the most sense, also because I'm still not overly familiar with the town and its people." She was determined to salvage a bit of her pride. "I'm so impressed with the thought you've given to it and all the details," Shelby admitted, thinking, too, that a little praise can go a long way.

Nora's smile was wide as she stood, leaning over to pick up her briefcase. "There can be a lot of downtime at work when we have several volunteers on hand, so I take advantage of it. Plus, I have all those books as resources. Now, if you think of anything else, just let me know, and we'll plan to meet again, next week maybe?"

Shelby nodded and followed Nora to the door and remained standing there, holding the door open for a small group of seniors who came wandering in, and Shelby found herself answering their questions for the next twenty minutes, leaving her little time to think about theatrical murder mystery nights or the real thing.

Chapter Five

Wednesday morning, despite the surprising heat of the rising sun, Shelby felt a chill at the sight of the crime scene tape still up as she was walking along the pathway up to the castle. She couldn't see anyone in that immediate area, though, nor did she hear any voices. Surely that meant they were finished investigating the area. She hoped the tape would come down soon. She'd seen far too much of it since starting to work at the castle the previous year.

One year. She rolled the thought around in her mind, amazed that she had moved to Alexandria Bay from Boston the previous February, and so much had happened in that time. When she came to take over the running of the bookstore from her Aunt Edie, who was recuperating from a knee replacement, she thought it would be for a few months. In fact, at first she'd only taken a leave of absence from her job as an editor at a small regional publisher, and had sublet her apartment in Lenox. Within a few months, though, she'd found out she was actually a co-owner of Bayside Books, which she would be in charge of at the seasonal location in Blye Castle, and that her mom, who, she'd been told, had died when Shelby was three, was still alive and had, instead, abandoned her husband and daughter. Shelby had run through a gamut of emotions over those months—apprehension, anticipation, excitement, bewilderment, along with hurt and anger. Then, of course, there had also been love.

She'd been unwilling to admit at first just how hard she'd fallen for Zack Griffin, but now he seemed so much a part of her life, she couldn't imagine it without him. Thinking of Zack resulted in a sigh, as she thought about how much she missed him and hoped he'd be home for the weekend. He said he'd try. That would have to do, for now.

Shelby was in the back room later in the morning, trying to make space for some book returns she'd pulled from the shelves, when she heard the tiny bell above the front door. She stuck her head around the curtain. "I'll be right there."

She left things as they were and hurried out. She was surprised to find Hilary Miller there. "Hi Hilary! Great to see you again. It's been months since I saw you at your showing at Felicity's art gallery. That was such a great show."

Hilary nodded but didn't smile. "It was, thanks. But I'm actually here with the police chief."

"Chief Stone? Why?"

"My dad, uh, you see, my dad is . . . was . . . Nathan Miller."

It took a couple of seconds for that to sink in. "I'm so sorry," Shelby said as she hurried over to Hilary. She wasn't sure what to do, though. She finally reached out and patted Hilary's arm.

"I never made the connection," Shelby explained.

Hilary shrugged. "That's okay. Why would you? We only met that one time. I asked the chief to bring me over here to the island to where, uh, it happened."

"That must be so upsetting for you."

"It is, but I just felt I had to see it, you know?"

Shelby didn't, but she nodded anyway then looked toward the door. "Where's the chief?"

"She had something to check on." Hilary brushed back a strand of her long blonde hair that had strayed from her black headband, across her cheek.

Shelby noticed she wasn't as brightly dressed as that first time they'd met at the art showing. Pink and orange had been her color combination back then. Today, her choice was black leggings and top, probably a good indication of how she was feeling.

"I haven't been here on the island before if you can believe it. I'm sure everyone in Upstate New York has. I did want to have a look at your store at the same time." Hilary's voice sounded as lackluster as her outfit. "Felicity has said so many good things about it and you."

That surprised her but it also pleased her.

"I'm really sorry for your loss, Hilary." Shelby wasn't sure what else to say. There was no way she was mentioning she'd been the one to find the body, just in case Hilary hadn't already been told. She was afraid that horrible image would show in her face.

Hilary nodded. "Thanks."

The door opened and Chief Stone wandered in. She looked from one woman to the other before speaking. "Anytime you're ready to go back to the mainland, Miss Miller."

43

Hilary took a deep breath.

"I'm ready." She looked back at Shelby but seemed at a loss for words.

"You take good care of yourself, Hilary." Shelby gave her arm a squeeze.

Hilary nodded and headed to the door.

"Ah, Chief, do you mind if I ask you something?" Shelby asked and waited until Stone had a few words with Hilary and had stepped back inside the store. "Ah, when do you think the crime scene tape is coming down?"

Stone was instantly alert. "Why? You itching to get back there and nose around?"

"No, nothing like that. Really. It's just, there's been so much of it around here in the past while. It's . . ."

"Unnerving? I get that. I'll take care of that myself before I leave the island today." She wandered over to the local authors shelf. "I see you still carry Loreena Swan's book. Is there much call for it?"

"It does do well with tourists who want to read up on island history, but that's about it."

"I'll bet that author Savannah Page's book is still a hot commodity around here, though? Do people still ask about her death?"

Shelby really wished they'd move away from the topic of the two recent murders but answered the chief's question anyway, "There was last fall, of course, just after it happened, but I'm not sure what it will be like these days. I'd think it's not as fresh in readers' minds."

"Just as well. Remember to let me know if you recall anything more about Mr. Miller." Stone stared at Shelby for a couple of moments then left, leaving Shelby feeling unsettled. She was grateful when noon rolled around.

Shelby had just finished washing out the mugs when Laura Watson, her new part-time staffer, arrived. This was Laura's first summer season with Bayside Books, having been hired as a part-timer in February. A retired practical nurse, she was a quick learner when it came to the book business and had certainly helped ease the strain in both stores, even though she'd been hired during the slow season and the castle store was only now beginning to get busy. But Shelby was confident they'd made the right choice in hiring her.

"Hi, Laura," Shelby greeted her employee then focused on a young couple who had followed her through the door.

Laura smiled and then turned to the customers. "Just let us know if we can help you with anything," she said then slid out of her jacket as she disappeared into the back room.

Nicely handled, Shelby thought. Yes, Laura was fitting in very well.

By the time she returned to the room and pulled up the stool behind the counter at the cash, Shelby was busy with the couple, making suggestions about books from the local section. After they'd made their selections, paid, and left, Shelby said to Laura, "Thanks for bringing in our first customers of the day."

"My pleasure. So, a slow morning." Laura pulled off the elastic holding her shoulder-length pale brown hair and carefully reworked it all back to the way it was when she'd walked in the door. The amount of gray streaks had Shelby pegging her to be around sixty, but her trim body looked to be that of a much younger woman. Shelby wondered if all the physical demands of her former job were responsible for that.

"Well, it's been busy, just not with customers. I do have something I'd like to discuss with you before it does get busy. I'd like to get your input on an event that's coming up, a Victorian period weekend that's happening in the castle and on the island, and we're expected to be a part of it. They try to put on something special each season."

"Sounds interesting. What's it all about?"

"Chrissie Halstead is organizing a weekend with a Victorian theme as part of the July 4th celebrations. By that she means costumes, events in the castle and on the grounds, and a book sale in the store. I really don't have time to work with her on this as much as she'd like, what with the murder mystery night coming up with the library, so I was hoping you'd represent the store on the planning committee?" She watched carefully for Laura's initial reaction. She didn't disappoint.

"That sounds like a lot of fun, and I'd love to be a part of it. I can think of a lot of things we can do."

Shelby breathed a sigh of relief. She'd been pretty sure that Laura would do it, but she had also been hoping for enthusiasm, and there it was. "Great. I'll let Chrissie know and she can bring you up to speed."

She looked at the wall clock.

"I think I'll take a lunch break, if you don't mind," Shelby said and grabbed her small insulated lunch bag that held the tuna sandwich she'd made that morning. She wanted some time alone to clear her mind before getting back to the realities of the day. She couldn't get the visit from Hilary out of her mind. It was hard to connect the fact that she knew the daughter of the man whose body she had found.

As she stepped out of the store, she grabbed her jacket and was glad she had when she sat at one of the picnic tables down near the water. She looked around for another spot that might get her out of the wind but stayed put, zipping up her jacket. She was close enough to the Sugar Shack to hear they were doing a lively business.

She was trying to resist the temptation to wander over and get an ice cream cone for dessert. But summer wasn't even here yet and the Sugar Shack was just too close, so Shelby knew she should start curbing her impulses right away. It looked inviting, though, with its brightly painted wood walls, it's red tin roof, and those alluring signs showing ice cream flavors plus a variety of candy.

She pulled her lunch out of the bag and her thoughts flew back to the previous spring when she'd shared a tuna sandwich with Zack for the first time. He'd dropped in unexpectedly, not really to see her but because of the ongoing murder investigation. She didn't know what had possessed her to offer him half of her sandwich, but she had. He had accepted it and sat on the bench beside her to eat. It was the first time she'd felt that relaxed with him and, in hindsight, was probably her undoing. She had to admit, he'd been on her mind ever since then.

On her way back to the store she deliberately detoured over to the spot where Nathan Miller had been murdered. She tried to see it as Hilary must have earlier and felt even sadder.

"Oh-oh, this is not a good sign," Matthew said as he sauntered over.

Shelby shaded her eyes from the sun with her hand and watched as he approached. "Why do you say that?"

"It means you're taking an interest in what happened here and, as we know, that never turns out well."

"That's not really what I'm doing. I just met the victim's daughter, and I was trying to imagine what it must have felt like for her, looking at this spot."

"Why would you do that? No one can possibly imagine exactly what someone else is feeling. We all have our own perspectives when it comes to that. And you know, it's a slippery slope from what you're doing to finding yourself investigating the murder. And you also know what Chief Stone would say about that, not to mention your aunt."

Shelby sighed then laughed. Matthew was good for the soul. "I do know, and those are the best incentives to steer clear. But before I do, have you heard anything new?"

Matthew shook his head and glared at her from under the brim of his usual NY Yankees baseball cap. "Seriously?"

"Okay, maybe we'll just forget that question. How about, what's new on the island?"

"Not much. Same old boats with the same old tourists, day in and day out."

Shelby grimaced. He sounded so defeatist, or else he was teasing her. Sometimes she couldn't tell. "You don't get much of a break, do you?"

He chuckled. "I'm quite capable of hiding out in my little house when I need to. And then there's Sunday dinner at your aunt's. That's a special break for me and one that I look forward to all week."

"Yeah, me too. Guess my own break is over for now, though," she said, after a glance at her watch. "See you later."

She walked slowly back to the castle, thinking about what Matthew had said. She wouldn't get involved this time. It didn't concern her.

Besides, where would she even start?

Chapter Six

S helby left the store with a feeling of anticipation. She had a dinner date with her friend Taylor Fortune and her baby daughter, Olivia. Taylor would be back to work at the store on a part-time basis as soon as her maternity leave was over. But this evening, her police officer husband, Chuck, had to work late, and Shelby had offered to bring some take out from the Black Cat Diner for a girls' night in.

Shelby arrived just as Taylor was finishing burping Olivia after a feeding. She wasn't used to being around babies, but there was something special about Olivia that grabbed at her heartstrings. She offered to hold her while Taylor transferred their food to serving dishes, even though Taylor said Olivia would be fine in her playpen.

"This is so good," Taylor said with a huge smile after taking her first bite of the grilled shrimp and peppers skewers. "It feels like a long time since I've had anything somewhat special."

Shelby grinned. "This is special to you?"

"Oh, you bet. Anything I don't cook is special. Of course, I can't complain. Chuck takes over in the kitchen quite often."

"Special isn't his forte either?"

"Something like that." Taylor smiled again, leading Shelby to once again think how young she looked, although she was six years older than Shelby. It was her blonde hair and the pixie cut, Shelby decided. And the carefree smile—still there although a bit more tired looking these days.

"So, what is new in your life, Shelby?"

"Well, Zack is still out of town, so nothing exciting, that's for sure. I think you're the one with more to report these days."

"If by that you mean the eating and sleeping habits of Olivia, then you're right. But by no means would I classify any of it as exciting, although I will admit, I wouldn't trade all of this for anything."

Shelby smiled. "It shows."

Taylor brightened "Really? Huh, I thought that the only things showing these days were the bags under my eyes and the extra weight that still hasn't departed."

"Just because I know so much about pregnancy and child-birth, I will predict that it will all be taken care of soon."

"I like your prediction. If only you were clairvoyant. Speaking of which, if you were, you might find solving murders a lot easier."

"Hey, I did not bring the topic up, I want to point out. In fact, I would not have said a word." She took a sip of sparkling water.

"Well, Chuck isn't talking about it, and I am curious. After all, I do work on the island, or I will again soon."

"Okay. But I don't really know that much. The body I found at the houseboat was the same man who'd been in the store that afternoon. And, he had stopped in last fall also. He was asking about a woman he said moved here about seven years ago. He had a photo of her but it wasn't very clear. But he did say she loved books and reading so was asking at both stores and it turns out, at the library, too."

"That's the only time you've seen him, when he was asking about her?"

"Right. Odd, don't you think?"

"For sure. It's too bad he didn't say why he was looking for her, or did he?"

"Nope."

"What about her name?"

"He mentioned it, but I guess I wasn't paying too much attention because it wasn't familiar and I've since forgotten it."

"So, what are you going to do?"

"Well, it's no surprise that Chief Stone wants me to stay out of it but, after all, I talked to the guy, and I found his body. I think I owe him something."

"Of course you do," Taylor said. "Oops, Olivia is getting restless. I'll just get her."

Shelby finished the final bit of her supper as Taylor re-entered the room.

"You've got a bit more to eat," Shelby said. "Why don't I hold her for you?"

Taylor handed over the baby. "Thanks."

Shelby tried to look like she was confident and knew what she was doing, although she was terrified she'd drop Olivia. She resorted to bouncing her on her knee while trying out some baby talk. She noticed Taylor grinning as she ate. When she'd finished, Taylor took the dirty dishes into the kitchen, closing the door behind her as she rejoined Shelby.

"Let's take the rest of this sparkling water into the living room and just relax for a while before it's time for Olivia's bath. You're welcome to stay and join us. It's quite an experience. She loves her baths."

"I'd like that as long as I don't have to be the one to bathe her."

"Aw, you have to learn some time."

"No, I don't. Not until it's absolutely necessary."

"Ah, so you are thinking you'd like children at some point."

"Yes, I would. But I'll ease into it." Shelby couldn't get over how easy Taylor made it all look, like she'd had several children before this. She knew Taylor was the youngest child in a family of three children so not much practice there, but maybe she'd done a lot of babysitting.

"Now," Taylor said, "you were saying about this woman?"

"That's basically it. I don't have any other information about her so I'm asking around to see who might have moved here around seven years ago."

"You know, with those parameters, I could be that woman."

Shelby stared at her then remembered. "That's right. You'd once told me you moved here just before marrying Chuck and that was . . ."

"Seven years ago, this past March."

"I missed your anniversary?"

"You did but don't worry about it, so did we." She chuckled. "We were just so tired and thought next year we'll make up for it."

"Well, Happy belated Anniversary." Shelby saluted her with her glass. "And you do fit the parameters of the mystery woman—moved here seven years ago, and loves reading books. Are you sure you're not on the run from a distinguished looking man in his seventies?" She gave a wicked smile.

"Only if he were an attorney with news of an inheritance and then I wouldn't be running."

"Hah. But maybe you might know who the woman is. Can you think of anyone who may have moved here about the same time?"

Taylor gave it some thought. "Not really. I had a job waiting for me at the hospital. I was a social worker in a previous life, you know."

"I didn't. And why did you leave the field?"

"Burn out. I thought a change of location would help, but it didn't. But I met Chuck because of the job, so it was a good thing, then, after a couple of years, I quit. But back to your question, it took me some time before I started meeting people who weren't hospital staff. By that time, I wasn't so new to town and didn't know if anyone else was. Sorry."

"No problem. I've only gotten started asking questions." Shelby paused, trying to keep a straight face as she added, "But you understand, I do have to add you to the suspect list."

Chapter Seven

S helby woke before the alarm went off the next morning but took an extra few minutes to stay in bed, patting a lazy JT, who was in the process of a full stretch, all paws pushing against Shelby's arm. She finally decided to get her day going and checked outside to see if it would be warm enough to enjoy her morning espresso on the upper deck. It sure felt like it. That was a good sign, she decided.

She willed herself to go to the railing and look down at the dock where she'd first seen the body. She stood there waiting for the chill to finish snaking down her spine and then she took a deep breath, settling into her favorite chair.

She breathed deeply again, enjoying the feel and smell of spring, a good omen for the weekend, she hoped. Her wishes were confirmed when she heard Zack's ping on her phone. Fortunately, she had already put her espresso cup on the small table before she read the text saying he'd be driving home Saturday morning. She let out a small whoop which startled JT as he was about to step out on the deck. He ran back inside and scurried down the stairs. Shelby followed him inside and got ready for work, pulling on some clothes without giving it too much thought, trying to keep her excitement in check. She decided a final look in the mirror was necessary to make sure everything matched or at least didn't clash.

She ran downstairs and fed JT, grabbed a bagel for herself, and left while still munching on it.

She had to wait in line at Chocomania, a good sign for Erica and not a problem since Shelby had enough time left for schmoozing before heading to catch the shuttle. When it was finally her turn, she checked to make sure no one had lined up behind her, then placed her order.

"By the way," she led casually, "I was just wondering if everything is now up to code with your electrical wiring?"

Erica looked over from the latte she was making and grinned. "Unfortunately. I sort of wish it hadn't been when the inspection was done a couple of weeks ago."

"I would imagine so. Then there would have had to be a follow-up inspection, right?"

"At the very least, and they would certainly have to keep coming back until I had everything fixed."

"That is seriously devious. But it could have been a good way to keep talking to a certain ruggedly handsome firefighter, I'd say."

"Wouldn't it? But seriously, I am really pleased no violations or problems were found on the spot check. Besides, since Adam called the next day and asked me out, I needn't go in for subterfuge. I'm seeing him anyway."

"So, how many dates is it now?"

"Only three, but who's counting." Erica placed Shelby's coffee in front of her. "What about your hunky guy? When's he coming home?"

"I got an email this morning saying he's coming home tomorrow for the weekend."

"That's good news. Wait a sec. I need an opinion." She dashed into the kitchen and was back in a flash with a dark chocolate truffle cradled on a piece of wax paper. She held it out to Shelby.

"Oh, yum," she said, eagerly popping it into her mouth.

Erica waited, arms folded across her chest, eyebrows raised in anticipation.

"A hint of citrus, maybe lime?"

"Yes, you got it. What do you think?"

"Amazing, as always." Shelby licked her lips, exaggerating the movement.

"Thank you. You are my primary tester, you know. Well, maybe number three."

"Three, how did I get all the way down there?" Shelby asked, pretending to be offended.

"Well, there's me and then there's Sharon in the kitchen, and Rainbow. Staff always get first dibs."

"Huh. Maybe I could get a part-time job here. No, I take that back, I couldn't cope with the extra pounds."

The door flew open, and three noisy teens charged in and over to the counter before Erica had a chance to answer.

Shelby picked up her latte, gave Erica a small wave, and left, knowing it would be added to her tab. She needed to remember to settle that next time she came in.

As Shelby tried to maneuver through the door, both hands full, one with her latte and the other hanging onto her bag, she almost backed into Felicity Foxworth, who was trying to hurry through the door to get inside.

"I'm so sorry, Shelby. I don't know where my mind is. I wasn't paying attention. I hope you didn't spill your drink."

"I'm okay, Felicity. I should have been more careful. Why the hurry?"

"I have to be at the gallery early today. I'm meeting with a custom jewelry designer from out of town. I haven't seen you in your main store in a while." Felicity grabbed Shelby's elbow and moved her over to the side, out of the way of more customers. She looked in the window and patted her black hair back into place before turning back to Shelby.

Since Felicity seemed to have forgotten about her rush, Shelby glanced at the clock to make sure she had time for a short talk. "I've been too busy on the island since we reopened to do more than just drop by and pick up supplies. I hope all's well with the gallery."

Felicity's art gallery, Gallery on the Bay, was next door to Bayside Books, and although Shelby seldom went into the neighboring shop as a customer, she did know the owner quite well after all that had gone on with the earlier murders.

"Oh, it is, it is, but you know," Felicity leaned in a bit closer, "I'm in a bit of a tizzy about that poor man who was found at your houseboat."

Not at, rather beside. "Why's that?" Shelby thought she was the one who should be in a tizzy, having found the body.

"Well, I remembered him well from the time he came into my gallery last fall. He was very polite and kind of attractive. It really rattled me to hear about his death, especially when I found out he was Hilary's dad. I quite like her and I've had a lot of success with her paintings after the showing just before Christmas. You remember it. In fact, I had her bring in some more artwork not too long ago. It's such a shame, she's so young to go through losing a parent."

Shelby nodded. She could relate to that.

"He asked if I knew a woman who'd moved here about seven years ago. His description didn't fit anyone I knew, nor her name, although he did say she might have changed her name and even her looks. I found that all very odd. And of course, I've forgotten what that name was."

"That's about all I know, too. He asked the same questions, showed the picture, and mentioned her name. But it didn't ring any bells."

"Well, it did make me stop and think that I haven't really been on top of things like newcomers lately. I mean, I realize when someone new moves here, if I have something to do with them, like you. But other than that, if our paths don't cross, there are no triggers to the memory. I used to be so much more involved with the community, you know, the Welcome Wagon group and all."

"Did he stop in your store again last Saturday?"

"Not as far as I know, but I wasn't in the store that afternoon. I was in Watertown, meeting with an artist about getting some more of her paintings into the store. I'm doing a lot of ordering and building up my inventory for when the tourist season really kicks in, you know. By the way, that must have been ghastly for you, finding the body. How are you feeling?"

"I'm doing fine now, Felicity. Thanks for asking. I'd better run or I'll miss the shuttle."

"Oh, for sure. You take care now."

Shelby nodded as she left, then paused farther down the street at the bookstore, wondering if Trudy was in. It was still closed, and she realized, belatedly, that was as it should be. It wasn't even 9:00 AM after all. She'd call later because she wanted to know if Nathan Miller had been asking Trudy any questions, too. Now that she had a picture of him, she'd be sure to show it to Aunt Edie and see if it jogged anything in her memory as well.

On the shuttle ride over to the island, Shelby thought again about having seen him in the bookstore Saturday afternoon. *What was so special about the woman? And did she have something to do with his death?*

She was still pondering the question a couple of hours later when Hilary Miller entered the store. Shelby was surprised to see her.

"I'm sorry I left so abruptly yesterday," Hilary began. "You know, sometimes when I'm talking or even thinking about him, it's like I can't breathe."

"Don't worry. I understand totally. I'm guessing you stayed in town overnight?"

"Yeah, at the Lavender Hill Inn. The owner is really thoughtful and so nice. And she makes the best cheese scones I've ever tasted. But I think I'll head home later today. I did want to just wander around a bit first and I wanted to touch base with you again. I understand Dad visited you here in the store a couple of times. The police told me he'd been trying to find a woman but I have no idea what that's about. Although I live in an apartment in the attic of his house, we didn't spend an awful lot of time together. He'd been busy doing some consulting work even though he's officially retired. And he was always involved in a lot of volunteer activities. Unfortunately, being an artist doesn't pay all the bills so I work part-time at a local art supply store. Our schedules were often totally different."

"And what about your mom?"

"My stepmother, Giselle. She's really devasted. My real mom died when I was twelve, and he remarried a couple of years later. Giselle and I get along really good, well mostly," Hilary said, almost as an afterthought. "I don't think it's really sunk in yet. Maybe it will when I get back and make the funeral arrangements. I'm hoping the chief will release his body later today." The tears started to flow, and she turned away. Shelby held a box of tissues out in front of her and Hilary grabbed a couple.

"I'm sorry."

"Don't be," Shelby said, feeling slightly uncomfortable. "Now, is there anything I can do to help?"

Hilary looked surprised. "I don't think there's anything, but thanks." She paused, as if considering what she was about to say. "Well, I guess there is. You're absolutely certain you have no idea who that woman is? It must have been awfully important finding her. I just wish I knew so I could talk to her. You don't think she's responsible for his death?" Hilary's right hand was worrying the zipper of her jacket. Shelby resisted the urge to reach out and steady it.

Shelby had been wondering the exact same thing, but thought it best not to mention it. "I'm sure that Chief Stone is covering all the bases. She's really smart and dogged, so you can feel assured she'll find out what happened."

"I sure hope so. I hope this wasn't one of those random attacks and the murderer never gets caught." Hilary shivered and crossed her arms as if trying to keep herself warm. "I don't think I could handle that. I need to know who and why. I mean, wouldn't you?"

Shelby nodded. "I'm sure I would, but there's so much more involved in an investigation than just asking some questions. Like I said, you can have total confidence in the police chief."

Hilary's smile was hesitant but warm. "Thanks. It's good to hear you place so much faith in her. I guess I'll do just that. By the way, can you recommend a funeral home in town that I can use to handle the details from this end?"

"Not offhand, but I'll ask my Aunt Edie. She'll know. Can I email you?"

"That would be great. If you happen to think of anything you feel I should know, I'd appreciate you calling." Hilary pulled a business card out of her wallet. "Here's my card."

Shelby took her card and looked at it. "I love this. What is the painting?"

"It's one of the older houses in Clayton. You probably didn't see all the pieces I brought in to Felicity. I mainly do landscapes but once in a while, something else, like an old house with lots of character, grabs my attention."

"Do you sell online also?"

"I'll sell anywhere I can," Hilary answered with a small embarrassed laugh.

Shelby reached for one of the store cards. "Here's mine. If you have any more questions or need anything, please don't hesitate to get in touch."

Hilary leaned over and gave a surprised Shelby a quick hug. "Thanks again. And, I know it's asking a lot, but if you think of anything else or hear anything, I'd appreciate you telling me. I'll be in touch."

Shelby watched as the girl wiped tears from the corner of her eyes before leaving the store.

Shelby felt her eyes watering as she walked over to a nearby shelf and turned a book right side up. There must be something she could do to help Hilary.

Something that didn't involve getting on Chief Stone's bad side.

Chapter Eight

Shelby left the store a couple of hours earlier than usual the next day. Although Laura was part-time, she was happy to do extra hours until Taylor came back from maternity leave. Now was a great time for her to learn the book business, and with fewer customers so early in the season, she could play with the computerized inventory and wander around the shelves to check out the books individually. It all seemed to be working out smoothly.

Shelby also had to admit it was liberating to have a few extra hours to herself. Although there was always paperwork related to the business that she could be doing. Not today, though. She wanted to talk to some of the staff and volunteers in the castle to see if any of them had more details to add to what she knew about Nathan Miller's visit to the island. And after that, she wanted to talk to Trudy at the main store and find out her impressions or anything she'd remembered from her encounter with Nathan Miller. Did he mention to her that he was looking for the mystery woman and had he added anything else? And then, her final stop would be at the library to see what anyone there could add to the story.

As Shelby walked into the main hallway, she spotted Mae-Beth Warner walking purposefully toward the staircase. Shelby quickened her pace in order to touch Mae-Beth's arm just before she started to walk up.

"Do you have a couple of free minutes, Mae-Beth? I'd like to ask you something, if you don't mind."

Mae-Beth turned around, and her usual smile grew wider. "Why, Shelby. For you, I do. I haven't seen you in a few days. How are you doing after all that upsetting business?"

"That's what I wanted to talk to you about actually," Shelby admitted. She glanced around and saw that no one was in the vicinity of the indoor water feature, so pointed in that direction. Mae-Beth followed her over and they sat in the two wicker chairs positioned at one side of the fountain. The backdrop of large, drooping ferns and short palm trees gave the area a tropical look and feel. To Shelby, it was the most relaxing place in the castle.

Mae-Beth was the unofficial staff person in charge of volunteers, even though the title officially belonged to Chrissie Halstead. Mae-Beth was the person everyone went to with questions or problems, or just to experience her warmth and concern. Probably because Mae-Beth was a true motherly type.

"I heard all about it," Mae-Beth said. "What a terrible thing for you to find the body. Again." She shuddered.

"Yeah, it was. So, I'm just trying to put together some of the pieces about why he was here at the castle. Do you remember seeing him? Was he asking any questions of anyone in the castle?"

"Chief Stone asked me the same question and showed me his picture. I don't recall seeing him at all the day he died."

Mae-Beth shook her head, and a few gray curls rearranged themselves. Shelby liked the permed look that Mae-Beth was sporting this spring. It made her look younger and seemed to have added a bounce to her step as well as her hair. "It's really such a shame. I hope his death wasn't tied into the castle in any way."

"Well, he seemed to have a purpose in mind and it wasn't the castle but rather the bookstore he was interested in. He asked me if I knew of a woman he was looking for. It sounded like he thought she might have moved to the Bay years earlier. I couldn't come up with any suggestions for him, though. I understand he'd asked in town, too."

"Really? Unrequited love, maybe?"

"I'd wondered if it might be something like that, but it doesn't sound like it. He was married."

Mae-Beth chuckled. "That doesn't seem to make much difference these days, but he looked to be an older man so you'd think he have some common sense. And why wait until now to search for her? He could obviously live without her."

"It seems that way. Well, thanks for taking the time to chat with me." Shelby stood, but Mae-Beth remained seated.

"I wonder if any of the volunteers might have spoken to him," Shelby said. She wondered if she should ask any of the volunteers some questions, but she was pretty sure Mae-Beth would know if anyone else had encountered Nathan and his questions. And of course, the police would also have checked.

Mae-Beth confirmed that. "I'm sure the chief asked them. Did the man tell you how long ago this woman he was looking for moved here?"

"He said seven years ago."

"Seven years, you say?" Mae-Beth mused as she pushed herself up out of the chair. "I'm pretty certain that's when Alice Jones moved to town. I remember it because I needed a very special dress for my sister's fiftieth wedding anniversary, so I went to the Style Shop, of course. They really do have the best selection when it comes to upscale clothes, unless you want to drive into the city. It was Alice's first day at work, and I spent as much time filling her in on the town and its people as she did finding the right dress for me. Yes, seven years it was. She's really nice, but on the shy side. I haven't really learned much about her over the years, but I do enjoy talking to her whenever I go shopping, or more often than not, browsing."

"Do you happen to know where she came from?" *Fulsome Falls perhaps?* But Shelby realized that she had no idea where the mystery woman had lived before. Nathan had not said.

Mae-Beth thought a moment. "No, I can't say I recall her ever mentioning it. I did at one point ask her why she chose Alex Bay though, I do remember that, and she said it just seemed like such a quiet, pretty place. I thought to myself, she obviously hadn't been here during the Thousand Island River Run in June, if that was her impression." Mae-Beth laughed and glanced toward the stairs.

"I guess I should get on with things. I'm glad you're doing okay, Shelby. Maybe we can have some tea one day on your break. You know I keep the kettle at the ready in the so-called staff room."

"I'd like that," Shelby said and watched Mae-Beth retrace her steps to the stairs.

She liked Mae-Beth, who was a friend of Edie's, and probably a few years older, Shelby suspected. She knew Mae-Beth had been volunteering a long time at the castle, after retiring from her day job. What that was, Shelby realized, she didn't know. Now that needed to be rectified. Here she'd been trying to get to know everyone a bit better and fit into the community. How had she missed getting to know Mae-Beth better before now? They both worked in the castle, after all, although they didn't bump into each other very often. She heard the warning whistle from the boat and shrugged into her jacket as she hurried out the main door and toward the dock.

Back on the mainland, she went straight to the main store and was pleased to see Bayside Books was having a busy afternoon. Trudy nodded at her as she wandered in, then walked over to her when she'd finished talking to one of the customers.

"It's nice to see you in here today. Do you need some books or supplies for the castle?"

"Not today, but I did want to ask you a few questions about Nathan Miller."

"Ah, the dead man. I heard you'd found his body. That must have been so dreadful, Shelby. I hope you're all right now?"

"Yes, but I did want to find out some more about Nathan's visit to town. Felicity said he'd been in the art gallery. Did he stop in here, too?"

"He did stop in but only briefly. He said he was looking for someone who he believed had moved here about seven years ago. But it was busy in here, and I didn't have time to talk at that point. Then he asked how well I know Alice Jones at the Style Shop because he'd been told she moved here about seven years ago. I didn't think it right that I talk about someone like that, so I said I knew who she was since she was working at one of the few women's shops in town, but that I didn't really know her to socialize with. He thanked me and left."

"And, how well *do* you know her?" Shelby absently straightened a couple of books whose spines were pushed too far back on the shelf next to her right arm.

"Alice? I didn't lie to him. I don't know her very well. I only see her when I'm shopping, but we don't really talk, other than about what she has for sale. She doesn't share much information about herself, and she tends to keep to herself. I asked her to join the Book Club Babes Plus One at one point, but she said she didn't have much time or interest in reading. Let me tell you, I had to bite my tongue so I wouldn't ask her what she did with all her time because I'm pretty sure she hadn't joined any other activity in town. But I told myself it was really none of my business and she had the invitation if ever she wanted to join."

"That's the sort of impression I'm getting about her. She keeps to herself."

Trudy was scanning the bookstore while they talked and Shelby watched her. Her shoulder length gray hair looked like she had a stylist on call, which was all part of her polished look. Shelby knew she had been an office administrator at one point in her life, and that period seemed to have imprinted. She and Edie had been friends since childhood, but what an odd pair they made. Shelby snapped back to attention as Trudy answered.

"You're asking questions? Do you think she could be the mystery woman?"

"I really have no idea at this point. The time frame works, but from what I've heard from others, until she's willing to share more details about her life, who knows? I wonder if Chief Stone has questioned her."

"From what Edie tells me about your dealings with Tekla Stone, you'd likely be taking your life in your hands to ask her about Alice."

Shelby smiled ruefully. "Tell me about it."

* * *

Shelby left the bookstore feeling fired up enough to pay a visit to the Style Shop and talk to Alice Jones in person, if she was working today. She needed to get a feel for the woman and, maybe if today was a positive day, meaning if she was in a talkative mood, Shelby might get some answers. She went over in her mind the things she wanted to ask as she made the four-block walk to the store. She had been in it once before after she'd just arrived but decided it was more a good place to shop for gifts for Edie than for her personal shopping. She wasn't sure who had served her that day. It could have been Alice. She hadn't been paying much attention. Nor had she been at the stage where she was looking to make it a permanent move to the Bay, therefore, she hadn't been looking to meet many of the people in town. She inwardly cringed at the thought of how reserved she'd been at that point while now she *wanted* to make friends.

Of course, there was that all-important friendship with Zack. Uh-oh, there he was, creeping into her thoughts again.

She reached the store, realizing she hadn't really formulated any questions. Talk about a wandering mind. The bell over the door tinkled as she walked in, a feature most of the stores in Alex Bay seemed to favor. The woman standing behind the counter appeared to be several years older and about the same height as Shelby, but she was stylish enough in her choice of clothing to accentuate just the right curves, a look Shelby had been attempting to achieve for a while now. Maybe she should put herself in this woman's hands after all.

She put on a smile as she headed across the store floor, glancing around to see if anything in particular caught her eye. Yup, a red and purple scarf. She made a beeline over to the display and gently felt the fabric. Very soft, lightweight, perfect for any season and it would look terrific with several of the tops Shelby wore most often. She casually glanced at the price tag. This was also a reason she didn't shop at the Style Shop on a regular basis. But, oh, the scarf had that wow factor. She picked it up before she could change her mind and walked to the counter.

She read the woman's nametag as she passed the scarf to her. Alice. Good beginning.

"This is such a fabulous scarf," Alice said, carefully folding it between tissue paper and transferring it to a bag. "And believe me, with the amount of wear you'll get from this, it will more than pay for itself."

So she noticed that look of panic on my face. Shelby tried for a look of nonchalance as she pulled out her wallet. "You're right. I really love the colors. I know I'll make good use of it."

Once she'd paid and had the bag in hand, Shelby introduced herself. "I'm Shelby Cox, by the way. I'm part-owner of Bayside Books."

"I know. I've seen you at the store in the castle. It was busy, so I'm sure you didn't notice me. I'm Alice Jones."

"Nice to meet you. I haven't lived here very long and still find there are so many people I haven't yet met. Have you been in Alex Bay long?"

Alice hesitated a fraction of a moment. "A few years."

"Oh, fairly new, too, then. Where did you live before?"

"In the Midwest. Maybe I can interest you in a top to go with that scarf?"

Shelby was taken off guard at the direction of the conversation. "Not today, but I will be back. Thanks for your help. I know I'll love the scarf." Maybe it was a good time to leave rather than appear too nosy.

Next time she could really get down to business.

Chapter Nine

S helby had just flicked off the lights and was climbing the stairs to her bedroom ready to call it a night, when her cell phone rang. She'd stuck it in the back pocket of her jeans in order to free her hands to carry a book and a glass of water, both of which she deposited on a stair and pulled out the phone. Her heart beat a bit faster when she saw it was Zack followed by a momentary dread that he was calling to say there had been a change of plans.

"Hi there. I hope you're not calling with bad news," she answered.

She heard his chuckle and she smiled. "It's only bad news if you want to be alone tonight. I decided to drive back early, and I'm now standing at the end of the dock. I thought I'd better give you a call rather than a scare by knocking on your door."

Shelby let out a whoop in answer and ran to the door, switching the lights back on. She met him halfway along the dock and almost literally fell into his arms. After a long, deep kiss, he pulled back and rather breathlessly whispered, "That was well worth the drive."

*   *   *

The next morning, Shelby eased out of bed, determined to let Zack sleep in after his tiring drive. *And night*, she thought, with a smile.

She quickly and quietly showered and dressed, then fed JT, who finally came downstairs after having opted to stay curled up in bed next to Zack. She looked up from setting his bowls on the floor to see Zack walking toward her, hands outstretched to grab her own and help her to her feet. His arms slid around her and he kissed her, then asked, "Coffee ready?"

She chuckled. "Yes, although I thought you'd sleep longer." She poured them each a cup.

"I was tempted, but I wanted to catch you before you went into work today. We're on for dinner tonight, at my house?"

"Sure, but wouldn't it make more sense to cook here. You can't have much in the way of groceries on hand."

"That's what stores are for." His blue eyes twinkled even more than usual. That's what had first attracted her to him, what she thought of as his crinkly eyes, which made it look like he was always smiling or, at least, finding the humor in whatever was happening. "While you enjoy spending time in your own store today, I'll hit the grocery store and stock up for the feast tonight. I also have a couple of things to do at the office," he added.

"A feast, is it? You must have missed cooking."

He nodded. "But also I want to make it special. Any requests?"

"I'm always blown away by your meals so it's up to you, chef," she answered, filling their coffee mugs. She was suddenly aware of the hominess of this all. She could get used to it, she realized.

"Good. Thank you for the coffee, and for last night." He held her gaze a few extra seconds and she felt her cheeks warming up.

"My pleasure. Would you like some breakfast?"

Zack eyed the clock on the wall. "How about we do that tomorrow when you go in to the shop later. I think you'd better head out soon if you want to make the shuttle."

Shelby followed his gaze. "Yikes. Where did the time go? You're right. Will you lock up here?"

"Sure thing. See you tonight."

They shared another long kiss and then Shelby, after checking that JT was eating, headed out.

* * *

Shelby had to admit, she was having a tough time concentrating on her customers for the first hour or so. Her mind kept drifting to Zack and just how tingly all over she'd felt when he had arrived the night before. She had never felt that way about anyone before and, she had to admit, it was exciting although still a little on the scary side. She knew she was far more committed to the relationship than she'd been willing to admit. And having him out of town was certainly an effective way of bringing it all to the forefront.

The phone rang, startling Shelby, and after taking the call from a customer wanting to know if her special order had come in, Shelby decided she'd better focus on the store and customers for the rest of her shift.

Just after her short lunch break, an older man came in. Shelby thought he was probably in his late seventies. He used a cane and wore glasses with the thickest lenses she had ever seen. He walked up to the first shelf on his left and was practically nose to book, looking at the titles. After several minutes of making his way around the perimeter of the store, he finally approached the counter.

"Good afternoon, miss," he began, leaning on the countertop. "I was hoping you'd have some large print books in stock and, in particular, ones that deal with this area."

"It sounds like you want non-fiction, right?"

"Oh, absolutely. It's hard for me to read these days, and I want to be learning something new at the same time. Might as well make the most of the challenge," he added with a chuckle.

Shelby smiled. "Well, I'm really sorry to say we don't have any large print books at this location but I know there are a few at our main store in Alexandria Bay. I could call and ask what's on hand, if you'd like."

"No, don't trouble yourself. I'll just stop in there when I get back on shore." He took a minute to glance around the store. "I like this place. It's very welcoming, and I'm sure you must be doing well with it."

That seemed an odd comment. "Well, I enjoy working here. I get to meet so many people who are visiting the area. You're not from around the Bay, are you?"

"No, no. I'm just visiting my daughter and her family. Maybe you know them, the Johnstons on Mackinaw Road?"

"I don't think so, at least not by name. But maybe I would know them by sight. Being a small town, you keep bumping into residents all the time and not getting more than a chance to say hi. I haven't lived here very long, so I'm still learning names and faces."

He nodded. "Well, it's a good place to live and bring up a family, is all I can say." He looked around behind him before asking, "Do you have any audio books by any chance? I'm also trying to get used to listening to stories."

"No, none here, I'm sorry again and I can't even say if there are any in the main store. Where are you from?"

"Oh, a small town you've probably never heard of. Fulsome Falls?"

Shelby almost dropped the bookmarks she was putting out on display on the counter. "Really? Did you happen to know Nathan Miller?"

"Of course, I did. We were on the museum board together for several years until I had to cut back on my evening activities. Not able to drive at night, you know. He was a nice man, a gentleman as we used to say. I was sorry to hear of his passing. It happened around here, didn't it?"

Shelby was really alert now. *Why is he asking?*

"Um, yes. Had you seen him much lately?"

"Not at all, as a matter of fact. That was a long time ago that I knew him. But I know he was keeping busy in the community and doing a lot of volunteer work. Although I seem to remember there was a bit of a problem with one of the boards he sat on. It was all hushed up pretty quick and I can't remember any of the details and as they say, it's all water under the bridge by now. It's probably more like ten years since I've seen him, although they all fly by so quickly, I have a hard time keeping track of what year it is." He leaned towards her as he lowered his voice. "Of course, I don't usually admit that. They'd have me admitted to the dementia ward for sure."

He chuckled and straightened up. "Of course, folks in Fulsome Falls are getting to be of a certain age. Not many young folk stay in town. Better jobs in the bigger cities. And since there's no real falls, no waterfall to be exact, there's not anything touristy about the area. Do you know why they call it Fulsome Falls when there are, in reality, no falls of any size or shape?"

Shelby shook her head, amazed he was sharing so much with her.

"Neither do I. In fact, no one admits to knowing. Now, it's been real nice talking to you but I've got to get a move on. I still want to see the outdoors here before heading back to shore. I know the gardens are quite amazing, even this early in spring. You have a good day now."

"Thanks, you too."

Shelby was smiling as she watched him stop just outside her door and start talking to one of the volunteers. She'd bet it would take him a while to get out into the gardens. Someone else from Fulsome Falls. Small world. But did it mean anything?

* * *

"I grilled some salmon and veggies and made a green salad to go along with them," Zack said as Shelby shrugged out of her jacket and hung it up in her closet. "Hope that sounds good," he added.

She'd been thinking about him on the way home, and it wasn't the meal that had been on her mind.

78

"My favorites." She was pleased. "What's up?"

"I missed you, that's what."

"Well, I missed you too. That's why I switched my days off with Laura. I don't have to go in tomorrow so please, please don't say you're leaving early in the morning." She knew she looked pleased with herself and was even more so as his smile widened.

"I won't say that. In fact, I'm really happy you did that. We can do something, whatever you like."

"Good, I'll give it some thought," she answered with what she hoped was a suggestive smile.

Zack kissed her again. "We need to talk, but first, let's eat."

That got her wondering as Zack brought their plates in. He sat and watched her closely while she took a bite. When she smiled and made a small appreciative sound, he started eating.

After her final mouthful, Shelby said, "That was totally delicious. Thank you so much."

She meant it, too, although she'd barely tasted it. Her mind had been playing with the phrase, "we need to talk" ever since Zack had said it. That had always meant something negative to Shelby. Her dad said, "We need to talk" and they moved away from Alexandria Bay to Boston; "we need to talk" and they had to sell their large house, too big for them really, but it had become home, and move to a smaller more affordable apartment; "we need to talk" and he'd told her about the cancer that had taken hold of his body and his future, only to be cheated by a car crash.

What did Zack need to talk about? Was he breaking up with her? Surely not after last night and this wonderful meal.

Maybe he too had a terminal illness? She felt sick to her stomach at that thought. She couldn't stand it anymore.

"I need you to tell me what we need to talk about," she said, leaning toward him. "It's really driving me crazy."

Zack looked surprised, but when he saw the serious look on her face, he reached for her hand. "I'm sorry, I shouldn't have phrased it that way. It's nothing bad, at least I hope it isn't. Let's leave the dishes where they are and get comfortable on the sofa."

She sat and, after a few minutes, he joined her, a brandy snifter in each hand.

"This is supposed to be a celebration of sorts," he said as he passed one of the drinks to her. He settled beside her before continuing, "I've been offered a promotion."

"That's exciting, Zack. How wonderful for you. Congratulations! You must be very pleased."

His smile was more quizzical than anything, she thought.

"There's a catch, isn't there?"

"It comes with a permanent move. I've been on temporary assignment here in Alexandria Bay for a couple of years now."

"I didn't know that it was considered temporary." She felt the room go slightly off kilter.

He shrugged. "I guess it never came up in conversation. I'm sorry, I should have made a point of telling you."

"Okay, so what does this promotion mean?"

"I've been assigned to Boston as soon as I finish my stint in Buffalo."

Boston. Shelby felt like she'd been hit by a semi-trailer. She didn't know what to say. She just stared at him.

"I wanted to let you know right away. I just found out about this yesterday."

He reached for her hand and gently rubbed the back of it.

"Huh. I don't know what to say, Zack."

"You could say you'll miss me."

"Of course I will." *More than you can imagine.*

"That's good, really good because I have a suggestion. I'd like you to consider moving with me."

"To *Boston*?"

"That's right? That's where you grew up, isn't it? It should be a good fit for you. But if you're not quite ready, and I understand that, I don't want to rush you into anything. We could always try making a long-distance relationship work. I'd come here whenever possible and you could visit me, a lot. It's only a six-hour drive. That's not really very far at all."

Shelby put her drink down on the coffee table and stood. She started pacing, not sure what to say, and not wanting to let him see the tears in her eyes.

"Shelby?" Zack sounded worried.

She stopped and faced him but remained standing on the other side of the coffee table.

"Zack, I can't imagine you living there and me here, but you have to realize, I've just started settling into my new life. I'm part owner of the store and I finally have more of a family. And, I have friends here. I can't imagine leaving it all. Not now." *And certainly not back to Boston.*

She could see that what she'd said hurt him, but it was all true. And she had to be honest about it.

"Look, I know it's a lot to take in, and maybe I should have eased into it but I want you to promise me you'll think about it, okay? Really think about it."

"Oh, I will, of course." *How can I think about anything else?*

He walked over to stand beside her and turned her to face him. "Good. I get it. That's all I can ask at this point. But I don't want to lose you, Shelby."

"I don't want to lose you either," Shelby said in a small voice just before Zack kissed her.

Chapter Ten

S helby was a bit wary Sunday morning, wondering how put off Zack was by their conversation the night before and if he was just being polite when he said he understood. Okay, she knew he was disappointed, but she dreaded that he might be deeply hurt and that it would somehow affect their relationship. She lay still for several minutes, letting the evening replay in her mind, wondering if she felt any differently about it all this morning. She didn't think so. She was filled with dread bordering on panic. She glanced at the clock on the bedside table and decided she needed to get up and moving rather than daydreaming, unless she was on the way to figuring out a solution, which she knew she wasn't right now.

Shelby slid quietly out of bed, dislodging JT, who had finally given in gracefully to allowing Zack to occasionally share the bed. Grabbing a long wraparound sweater out of her closet, Shelby tiptoed downstairs with JT close on her heels. She quickly fed him and then made herself an espresso, worried that it would wake up Zack but also hoping it would.

They'd done the dishes and cleaned up his kitchen after their talk the night before and then made their way back to the houseboat, detouring for a walk along the water at Scenic View Park. Neither one of them seemed to feel the need for a lot of talk. Shelby had tried to concentrate on the moment. Here she was, with her guy, under a magical full moon, and she refused to let any disturbing thoughts about what they'd recently discussed lodge in her brain. Fortunately, JT sat waiting at the door. He'd disappeared just before they left for Zack's and she still managed to worry he might not come back to her, especially if she was gone overnight.

As they got ready for bed, Zack did allude to it by saying he promised he wouldn't mention it again that weekend. Shelby was grateful and curled up in the crook of his arm. She just hoped he remembered that this morning and stayed clear of The Topic, as she now thought of it.

Her final thoughts that night were about how lucky she often felt, she thought she should pinch herself. She couldn't believe how easily Zack had slipped into her life. So, this was what love felt like. She'd had a couple of false starts before, but nothing like this. She couldn't bear the thought of him moving away permanently, she knew that, but she also couldn't go with him, not now anyway. A long-distance relationship seemed the only solution, but would it be enough, for either of them? She knew what the six-hour drive to Boston meant and how easy it was *not* to make the trip. She shook her head, not wanting to dwell on that now. She'd give it some serious thought once Zack had gone back to Buffalo. Maybe she could be more clear-headed about it then.

A part of her mind was warning her not to get too hung up on it right now. After all, she didn't want any negative thoughts that would ruin the time they had together. But try as she might, it was all she could think about as she made herself an espresso. That's what often happened, her mind would go straight to the worst-case scenario and hover until she was proven right. Or wrong, which she was hoping would happen now.

She decided she wanted him awake and made more espresso, one for each of them, heading upstairs and opening the door to the deck. Zack woke at that sound and eyed the espresso appreciatively. He followed her outside and gave her a quick kiss before taking his cup.

They each sat enjoying the sun that peeked from between heavy clouds.

"It looks like we're going to get rained on at some point today," Zack commented, checking the sky again.

Shelby nodded, feeling a bit disappointed. She'd hoped they'd be able to do something outdoorsy, maybe some exploring in the afternoon.

"Of course," he continued after waiting for her to say something, "we could play tourist, weather be damned."

"Say what?"

"Well, what do tourists do when they come here, aside from hopping on boats and going to the islands? There's a lot going on in the Bay area. What haven't you seen or done since you've been here? What do you want to see or do?"

"I'm not sure." She turned to him. "If I knew that I'd probably have done it by now." She offered a small grin.

Zack's eyebrows rose. "Is that so? Well, I guess you'll just have to place yourself in my hands then. Are you game?"

Shelby pretended to give it some serious thought. "I guess."

"I guess! Oh, you will regret your lack of enthusiasm. Let's get dressed and start with breakfast at Riley's."

Shelby followed him back to the bedroom, feeling a little lightheaded. Once they'd gotten ready, he pulled her into his arms for a long, deep kiss. She felt breathless and elated when they finally parted.

"That was nice."

"It sure was." He pulled her closer again, but she realized they might not make it out of there in time for breakfast if they kept at it.

"Let's save something for later."

Zack grinned.

By the time they reached Riley's on the River, it was fairly crowded, but they were lucky to get a table for two by a window and were ready for the coffee the server offered. They made a big production out of reading the menu to each other, finally agreeing on French toast with crème fraiche for them both. As they waited for their food, they sat making small talk about the town, fingers entwined, his thumb rubbing hers.

They were into their second cups of coffee when their order arrived. Shelby took a bite and a look of total delight spread across her face.

"So good," she managed to get out before taking another bite.

Zack did the same and nodded.

"Do you remember our first dinner here?" he finally asked as he was enjoying his final mouthful.

"I think I do," she said in a teasing tone. "Actually, I remember our official first date, which was here, and also the first dinner we ever had, which was before that, when you wanted to check up on me, or so you said."

She held up her hand as he was about to answer. "But, in hindsight, I think it was just as much about you wanting to see if I'd uncovered anything useful for your own investigation."

"Uh, yeah that may have been a secondary motive, but mainly it was to make sure you weren't getting into trouble. As you ended up doing, I might add."

"Oops, yeah. But I sort of solved that one, didn't I?"

"Excuse me?" He put his fork down and leaned towards her, adopting a stern look. "You almost got killed along the way is how I remember it."

"But you didn't let that happen. You wouldn't let that happen, would you? You take good care of me." She stopped, suddenly realizing where the banter was leading. She was an independent, capable person who wasn't looking forward to moving anytime soon, and reminding Zack of his importance in her life wouldn't help that cause.

Zack seemed to realize the turn her thoughts had taken. "What do you say we finish up and then go play tourist?"

After they left the restaurant, they walked to the wharf, watching the river with the freighter traffic and other smaller boats making their way along. The amount of traffic seemed to have increased recently with the spring weather, at least doubling in the past week or so. She looked beyond the boats to Boldt Castle, always so mysterious looking and yet so inviting. So *close and yet so far*. Would that be what happened to her and Zack?

"I can't get enough of this view," he said.

Then don't move. She hoped she hadn't said it out loud. When he didn't respond, she breathed easier. "Let's walk."

He held her hand as they headed back into the center of town, window shopping their way to the end of the business district and looping over to the next street, and finally heading back in the direction they'd come.

"Have you been to the Heritage Museum?" he asked.

"I stopped by early last spring, just to see what information or displays they had about the castle, but not since then. I wonder if they're open today?"

They wandered over and were pleased to see the "Open" sign hanging in the window.

They slowly walked past the displays running along one side of the interior before being drawn to the large windows overlooking the river.

"There it is again," Zack said.

"It won't go anywhere," Shelby answered then realized what that might have sounded like to Zack or had she just imagined she'd put an emphasis on the word 'it'?

Before she could decide if she needed to do some explaining, an older man approached them, introducing himself as Wally, the volunteer on duty and asking if they had any questions. That was just the prompt Zack needed. Shelby enjoyed Wally's enthusiasm as he answered Zack's inquiry about the wooden boat building business of decades before. Shelby had to admit it added greatly to the romance of the area. And just looking at the large display of boats and people strolling along the shore watching the annual boat races transported Shelby to that scene, if only for a few seconds.

As they made their way back to Shelby's later that afternoon, they walked hand-in-hand, stopping to admire the signs of spring that were blossoming all over. Shelby had decided it was her turn to treat Zack to a meal. So, with great trepidation, and with the help of a cookbook Edie had long ago given her, she put together a colorful pasta and pesto dinner, complete with hits of bright red grape tomatoes.

She wasn't sure if she should be flattered or annoyed at Zack's praise of the food, if he was laying it on just a bit too thick. At least, she figured, it was a start.

"I'm really sorry to have to be leaving tonight," Zack said after finishing an after-dinner coffee. "If it wasn't for my early morning meeting, I'd stay." He pulled Shelby into his arms and held her long after their kiss had ended.

Shelby crossed her fingers that he wouldn't mention his move again before he left, and he didn't.

"I'll call you as soon as I can."

"Text me when you get home, okay? Just so I know you arrived safely."

His smile widened at her words.

Chapter Eleven

First thing Monday morning, Shelby headed to Chocomania. She felt restless and needed to talk to someone. She'd awakened down in the dumps, missing Zack already. She was also not looking forward to dinner at Edie's, the one that had been postponed from Sunday. She would try hard not to talk about Zack's news. She had to deal with it herself first, before she broke it to Edie, to have come to her own decision. But she did need to talk it over with somebody.

Erica smiled. "This is very early on a Monday, for you."

"I'm working today for Laura. She took over for me yesterday."

"Uh-huh. I hear you had a visitor. Good weekend, huh?"

"In some ways." Shelby looked around at the only other customer, a young mother with a baby in a stroller, sitting with a coffee at a table on the far side of the room. "Do you have a few minutes? Can we talk?"

Erica studied Shelby's face as she answered. "Let me make us a couple of lattes and we'll sit as long as I can. Rainbow isn't in until 11 AM."

"How is your new employee working out?"

"She's great. Her years as a part-timer at various franchises in Syracuse gave her some super barista skills. I wish I could offer her more hours, though. I know she needs the work. She's interviewing for a few hours a day at Driftwood and Seawinds. If she gets it, she plans to do a lunch hour or two shifts here and then work there."

"I can't imagine the sisters taking in help. They *are* that store, after all."

Erica nodded. "True, but they're getting older. I think it will be good for them to have someone younger there who can do the lifting as well as being good at talking to customers. And Rainbow is certainly a good talker."

"I hope it works out in that case," Shelby nodded and went to choose a spot to sit.

She was pleased to see the mom finishing her coffee and heading for the door. Hopefully she'd have time enough to tell Erica what had happened and get her opinion. Not that she wished her a slow morning.

Erica joined her, placing the lattes on the table and then clearing away the used dishes from the just vacated table, before sitting down to join Shelby.

"What's up?" Erica asked, watching Shelby over the rim of her mug.

Shelby sighed. "It was great to see Zack and spend all that time together, but he did drop a bombshell. He told me that after this assignment is over, he's being transferred to Boston."

"Boston?"

"Uh-huh. And he wants me to go with him."

Erica gave a small whoop. "But that's a good thing, isn't it? Why don't you seem excited? I mean, I'd miss you terribly, but it's Zack we're talking about and I know you're nuts about the guy."

Shelby sighed. "I am, I admit it. But I just settled in here and I have responsibilities to the bookstore, to my aunt. I have a whole new set of friends. It just feels right to be here, like I've finally found both family and home. What am I going to do?" She thought she must sound pitiful.

"I see your point, and I'm not really the one to offer advice. After all, I'm not in love and I've never lived anywhere but Alexandria Bay. We would all miss you, of course. Me, in particular."

That warmed Shelby's heart to hear.

"Have you told Edie?"

"Not yet. I wanted to sort out how I feel about it all first."

"Do you love him?"

Shelby sighed. "I think so."

"Well, it's hard to find the right guy, so you don't want to lose him. On the other hand, your own priorities are also important. What about a long-distance relationship, for the time being anyway? And when you're certain about the love part, then make the final decision."

"That makes a lot of sense, on the one hand. On the other, long distance can be very hard on a relationship, or so I've heard. If neither of us are sure about how deep a commitment this is, what's to keep us together?"

"I'd say you've got part of your answer as to how you feel about Zack right there. You don't want this to fail, right?"

"Right. But I don't want to jump into anything either. We've known each other only about a year."

"So? A year, a month, a week . . . if it's the real thing, you want to be working on it. Look, I know you like to take the cautious approach and are, how do I put this, slow to let others into your life, but this is different, I think."

"You sound very sage. Romance novels?"

"Hallmark movies." Erica pointed at Shelby's mug. "Another?"

"Thanks, but I'm sure I should be on the shuttle by now." She glanced at her watch. "Yikes. I have to run. I do appreciate the ear."

Erica gave her a quick hug. "That's what friends are for. I'm here whenever you want to talk some more."

Shelby nodded, hoping the tears gathering in the corners of her eyes weren't obvious.

How can Zack expect me to leave this?

* * *

By noon, Shelby was ready for a lunch break. It had been a busy morning, which surprised her. She hadn't done a Monday shift since the days when she'd first started at the main store. If this were a regular pattern, she wondered if she should try to make new arrangements for the workday. What, she wasn't sure. She should ask how Laura felt, of course. She was the primary part-timer at the castle, for now. Taylor was still out of circulation being a full-time mom, and wouldn't be back to her part-time job until the fall. Trudy was needed in the main store with Edie. Cody was a great help, but only on weekends, and then, usually in the main store. Was it time to hire yet another part-timer or should Shelby split the Monday shift with Laura. She knew that Edie would object. She'd been the one to insist Shelby take the day off, saying she could not keep up the pressure of working seven days a week. And, she'd been right.

That was something they'd have to talk over at dinner that evening. When had life become so complicated?

* * *

Her thoughts about the Monday shift hadn't changed by the time she reached Edie's house. It had continued to be a busy day. She'd made a quick detour home and fed JT, then practiced some power walking, up the hill to Catherine Avenue. She knocked on the front door and walked in without waiting for an invitation and found Edie pulling a roast out of the oven.

"Perfect timing," Edie said, without turning around. "I was glad when you called to suggest we do supper tonight." She looked around at Shelby. "Matthew and I missed having you as part of our usual Sunday evening, although you did have a darned good excuse."

Shelby groaned inwardly. And there you have it. Edie would most definitely miss the Sunday suppers if Shelby moved away. She decided to come clean if it came up again, but put a smile on until then.

"I'm glad you were available. But you know, this won't be purely pleasure."

Edie raised her eyebrows. "No? What's up?"

"It's the shifts at the store, Mondays in particular. I couldn't believe how busy today was, and to think that Laura handles the entire day on her own while she's still learning the ropes. That is, if today's a typical Monday."

"That is interesting. The reason I suggested you take Mondays off in the first place was because that used to be the slowest day of the week. But if it's changed, you're right, Laura can't handle it all on her own. Not yet, anyway. I'm surprised she didn't say anything about it, but of course, I take her to be someone who doesn't complain, just adjusts. Now sit and we'll get started before this cools off too much."

"Can I help with anything?"

"No, just sit."

Shelby sat at the kitchen table next to the window and felt the stress starting to leave her body as she gazed at the garden Edie loved so much. The backyard was a generous size with a variety of shrubs hugging the fence. Shelby had no idea the names of anything out there, except for the tulips and daffodils that added so much color to the scene early in the spring. Of course, Edie had many more varieties of blooms in various stages of growth, and the two tall Japanese Cherry trees, another name she *did* know, were just finishing their colorful display.

Tucked in closer to the house was the sitting area with patio stones, wicker outdoor chairs, and two small tables, while an ornate iron bench was tucked next to a stone garden that had been built up as a focal point. And the gardens in the front yard were just as eye-catching. Shelby often marveled at the number of people passing by, who would stop and enjoy the view, often pointing out something special to each other before moving on.

Shelby knew the gardens at the house were part of the reason Edie wouldn't even consider selling and moving into a smaller place, maybe even an apartment. And she couldn't really blame her aunt. Of course, it was the family home and had been since Shelby's great-grandparents had built it in the 1920s.

Edie served the slice of roast beef and Yorkshire pudding that she'd dished out on each dinner plate. "I know how much you love this, so I thought, there's nothing that says I can't make it two days in a row."

Shelby chuckled. "And it sure helps that it's your favorite, too."

"There is that."

Shelby eyed with appreciation the mashed potatoes and broccoli but decided to try the Yorkshire pudding smothered in gravy, first. "Delicious. I do appreciate you doing this, you know."

Edie's mouth was full, so she just nodded. They continued eating in silence until Edie brought up the topic of the store again.

"Do you have any suggestions?" she asked Shelby.

"I've been thinking about it. Either we hire another part-timer—then again, we don't know when Taylor will want to get back to work and even what shifts she'll be up for, and we *are* holding the job for her. Or, Laura and I split Mondays as well as her regular half-days that she does with me working also. Ideally, I'd like Monday mornings off so I can get through my chores, and they are aptly named. But I'll give her first choice and maybe on the other days, we can experiment with my taking a part-day off. That should give us both some variety."

"Do you think she'll agree?"

"I can only ask. But I have a feeling this arrangement might suit her better. She knows the business pretty well, I think, but I'm not so sure she feels she does."

"That's not surprising. It does take experience to give one confidence. Well, if you're sure you can handle the extra hours also, I'll leave the asking and arranging to you, all right? Just let me know what's decided."

"Happy to do so."

She helped Edie clear the table, feeling slightly guilty about not having mentioned the topic of Zack, even though she hadn't yet reached a decision. Edie cut them each a slice of pecan pie with a scoop of vanilla ice cream on the side, then casually asked as she set them on the table, "So, what's new with Zack?"

So, there it is, the opening.

"Zack. Hm. We had a great weekend even though he had to leave last night in order to get to an early morning meeting. Speaking of which, we had a busy day playing tourist yesterday. So, I plan on doing a bit of housework when I get home tonight, to catch up." *Stop delaying it.*

She watched as Edie ate another forkful, obviously enjoying it. "He did have some news, though."

"Oh? Not another secondment?"

"No. A promotion."

"Well, good for him. I'd always thought of him as being a hard worker and I'm sure he's heading for bigger things in the Coast Guard."

"Probably. And, it is good for him, but there is a problem. It means he'll have to move to Boston." The pie suddenly tasted off, and Shelby took a long gulp of water.

"Oh, my. And, I guess, he's proposing a long-distance relationship. How do you feel about that?"

"I don't know how I feel about anything. His alternate suggestion was that I move to Boston with him."

"Oh, my." Edie put down her fork also and just sat looking at Shelby.

At that moment, Shelby wanted nothing more than for Zack to call and tell her it had all been a mistake or a joke, maybe a test of how much he meant to her. But if that were the case, she would have failed.

Chapter Twelve

S helby had been hoping to catch up on the sleep she'd lost over the weekend, but Tuesday morning, she felt even more tired. JT gave her an imperious look before jumping off the bed. Apparently, he'd been bothered by how restless she'd been. She just couldn't turn off her mind. She kept going over the final part of her conversation with Edie.

Edie had been very methodical in going over the pros and cons of a long-distance relationship versus a move. She'd never questioned the fact that Shelby and Zack were in love even though Shelby wasn't even certain of that. Did Zack love her? Was that even necessary for her to make the move with him? Yes, it was. The thought had hit her at some point when they were talking although she wasn't quite ready to admit it to anyone yet.

Edie had been quick to assure Shelby that she could manage the stores, with Shelby in the role of a long-distance partner; she had even said that, as much as she loved having Shelby around, she had a lot of friends, and they made sure she wasn't lonely and wouldn't have to tackle things alone. She had done it before, after all. And they could have visits, often she hoped. In fact, they would just have to decide to do that.

The thought crossed Shelby's mind as to how such visits had never taken place when she and her dad had lived in Boston, but she didn't interrupt her aunt.

Edie assured her she'd even hire another part-timer.

But Shelby had seen the sadness in Edie's eyes as she eventually said it was Shelby's decision to make, and that she'd respect it and support her. That hadn't helped even an iota.

She tried to shake the unwanted thoughts out of her mind now as she hurriedly got ready for work. When she arrived at the shuttle, Laura was already on it. They were working the morning together, but Shelby was taking the afternoon off. This was her chance to quiz Laura about Mondays.

"Yesterday was an eye-opener for me. I hadn't realized how busy a Monday could be. Are they always like that?"

Laura smiled. "They weren't at first, but the last couple of weeks have been getting more hectic."

"You should have told me."

Laura shrugged. "It's been okay, and I knew to call the main store if I needed anything answered. Don't worry about it."

"Well, just so you know, Aunt Edie and I are considering how we can juggle the shifts to make everything more fair, but we wondered first if you have any suggestions?"

"Not at the moment." She grabbed at her straw hat as a wind gust threatened to snatch it off her head.

"Well then, how would you feel about doing a split-shift on Mondays? You could have your choice of morning or afternoons, 10 to 2 or 2 to 5, what do you think?"

"I like that idea, and it really doesn't matter to me which time frame, but maybe I'll take the mornings, if that's okay."

"That sounds good. Actually, I was hoping you'd say that. I've got to get my housework done some time," Shelby said, with a lopsided grin. "Maybe we could split another day on a regular basis, too. How about Wednesdays or Thursdays, with me taking the afternoon off to make up for the Monday?"

"That sounds good to me. It doesn't matter to me, so you can just decide at the beginning of the week which day you prefer, if that's better for you. I'd just like a couple of days' notice, please."

"For sure and that's great. I'll let Edie know."

Shelby looked out the window at the river, feeling pleased that at least something had been settled. She hadn't been paying any attention to how choppy it was that day. She looked up at the sky. At least there weren't any storm clouds in sight. She'd also forgotten to check the weather before heading out in the morning. Where had her mind been? She knew the answer to that, of course.

When they arrived at the castle, Shelby and Laura went through the opening routine and had just finished dusting and tidying when the first customers walked in the door. Shelby hadn't even heard the boat whistle sounding as it approached the dock. Where was her mind? Maybe she should be letting Laura handle the money for the next few hours.

*   *   *

Later in the morning, Shelby grabbed her ringing cell phone before it disturbed the customers standing right beside the counter.

"Shelby? It's Hilary."

"Oh, hi. How's everything going?" She signaled Laura to take her place and headed to the back room. She felt a bit guilty at not having given any thought to Hilary and her dad all weekend.

"I guess all right. I'm still trying to come to grips with my dad's death. Murder just seems something so far removed from his life, our lives. I mean, he's just a regular guy. I don't understand. I've been going through Dad's life, at least the paper part of it. He'd always kept meticulous records. So, I was hoping maybe there was a clue as to what was going on in his life."

"And did you have any luck?"

"Do you have a few minutes to talk, or is it busy there?"

"It should be all right. Laura is here and can handle customers. Was there something that bothered you?"

"Not really, just surprised me. Like, I knew he was working with a consulting firm but, I guess, I'd never taken the time to ask him about it. But it turns out, he's been doing some work with the Alexandria Bay town council. I called his boss at the firm and he said Dad would visit there at least every second week."

"That changes things. If he was here a lot, he would know someone here who might have a better of idea of everything, including the identity of this woman."

"That's what I was thinking. I've found some receipts in his Council files and it looks like he stayed at the Edgewater Motel whenever he was there."

"That's good to know. Do you happen to know who his contact was at the office?"

"I do. It's right here somewhere. Just a second, I'm going to put you on speaker."

Shelby could hear Hillary shuffling papers and then she was back on the line. "His name is Roman Sykes, and he works in the zoning branch."

"Good. He might know something helpful. I wonder if Chief Stone knows about this."

"She hasn't gotten it from me. Do you think I should tell her?"

"I do, just in case she's not aware. It could be just the clue she needs. And besides, if she finds out you know and kept it to yourself, or worse yet, shared it only with me, she'll be ticked off."

"I hadn't thought about that. I'll give her a call. Uh, do you think I could meet up with you tonight?"

"You mean here? Sure, why don't you come to my place? Should I do anything before you come? Check on anything?"

"I want to show you what else I've found and maybe we can put our heads together and come up with a game plan."

Game plan. Hmmm.

"Okay. I'll text you directions. Anytime is fine for me. Just give me a heads-up, okay?"

"Thanks, Shelby. I was hoping you'd be okay with all this. I'm not being too much of a bother, am I?"

"Of course not. I'm happy to help."

"Great. I'll see you later then."

Shelby was wondering what other information Hilary could have that she wanted to share in person. It had to be more details about her dad's consulting job. She was curious to see just when it had all started and how it might tie into his search for the mystery woman. And even though it looked like this woman hadn't been his main reason for being in Alex Bay, it still begged the question of her identity. Of course, none of it might tie into his murder. She could understand Hilary's need to know, though, and it sounded like she really needed a friend right now. And Shelby knew all too well what that was like. She had been in a similar place when her father died.

Chrissie Halstead came rushing through the door, driving all thoughts of the phone conversation from Shelby's mind.

"What's up, Chrissie? You look excited." Her cheeks were flushed and her new bob was in slight disarray like she'd been outdoors.

"Oh, I am." She looked around the room. Laura now stood in the far corner helping two women looking through the mystery section.

Chrissie grabbed Shelby's arm and steered her over to a corner, talking in a whisper. "They caught the thieves."

"You mean, the ones who've been stealing from the castle?" Shelby had almost forgotten about last fall's crime spree. Mainly smaller items had disappeared over a period of time but some of them had been quite valuable. Chrissie had been in quite a state about it all, and that was *before* the added drama of a body having been found in the castle last fall.

"Yes, of course. What other thieves are there?"

"Of course. I'm just amazed they've finally been caught. How did it happen?"

"Chief Stone kept checking back with the pawnshop in Clayton and, finally, one of the items, an antique magnifying glass, I told you about it, was brought in. And the shop owner knew the person who brought it in. Is that dumb or what?"

"I've heard that if it wasn't for dumb crooks, the police wouldn't solve too many crimes."

"That's great for us. So, they brought this guy in for questioning and he admitted to doing it, with his girlfriend, over a period of about four months, last summer and fall. Can you believe the nerve? They thought if they didn't try to pawn it right away, they'd be in the clear."

"That's really good news," Shelby said. "I'm pleased for you."

"Me too, and now that we have the extra security system installed, it should never happen again. I just thought you'd want to know. I've got to go back to the mainland and have a chat with the executive director and the chair of the board. I'll finally get them off my back."

Shelby was smiling as Chrissie left the store. One mystery solved.

*   *   *

Hilary arrived at Shelby's at 6:30 PM that night.

"Are you planning to stay overnight in town again?" Shelby asked as Hilary removed her jacket and hung it on a coat peg next to the door.

"Yes, I've already booked in at the same place. I don't want to make that drive when it's dark and it's actually a treat to get away, even for one night. Everything is driving me crazy right now. I'm sorry, I'm a bit early." Hilary looked around the room. "This is so cozy. You must love living on a houseboat."

"Oh, I do. Would you like a tour?"

"Absolutely."

Shelby was pleased to see how animated Hilary seemed. She'd been dreading what could easily have turned into a very depressing evening, although it still might, she warned herself.

"We'll go upstairs first," Shelby said, leading the way. "This is my bedroom, not large but all the windows let in a lot of light. And through that door I have access to the upper deck. At the front, I have space to barbecue and for a fold-away table and chairs. I usually leave a lounge chair up all times just to take advantage of nice weather on the spur of the moment. And in the back, I have a bistro table with chairs and the perfect view of the sunset, and sometimes a partial sunrise also."

Shelby had opened the door for them to move out onto the back deck.

"This is so wonderful. I can't imagine living like this. But I'd like to try it sometime." Hilary took one last look at the river before they headed back down to the main level.

"As you can see, I have a compact but open kitchen with a small dining area, and of course, this living space. And the bathroom is tucked behind the stairs. It really has everything I need."

She realized once again how much this felt like home especially since she'd brought her own furniture when she moved to the Bay from Lenox, Massachusetts. The loveseat, two slipper chairs and black floor lamp fit in well with the layout. She'd chosen the new glass table because it was airy looking and, better still, it could pull out to seat four. Not that she'd had that large a dinner party at the houseboat yet, but it was in the back of her mind. Some day, she hoped.

The walls were painted a muted gray-blue to tie in to the outdoors, and thanks to an agreeable landlord who had no objections to any of her decorating plans. She'd chosen some roller blinds that, although pricey, gave her a combination of privacy and light, when she extended them only partway. It was that bright airiness that had sold her on renting the houseboat in the first place. She hadn't even stopped to wonder what living on water would feel like, but she'd soon found out. It didn't take her long, just one major storm, to find her sea legs. And she was extremely proud that no seasickness had been involved.

JT had taken his time coming back downstairs. He wound his way around Shelby's legs and then sat, staring at Hilary.

"Your cat has amazing coloring and such a penetrating stare."

"He does. I'd love to know what goes on in that brain."

"I'm sure he figures out a way to let you know when he feels it's necessary."

Shelby laughed. "You know cats, I see. Now what can I get you—Tea, coffee, wine?"

"I'd love some white wine, if you have it."

"I do. Just make yourself comfy and I'll be right back."

Hilary sat at the kitchen counter and waited until Shelby sat down next to her, their glasses of wine placed in front of them. "I wasn't quite sure if this was something I should be sharing but I can't figure out what, if anything, it means. It's so weird that I'm worried it's tied into Dad's death." She pulled a folder out of her bag and handed it to Shelby.

After glancing through four sheets of paper, Shelby finally said, "What am I looking for on these bank statements?"

Hilary held out her hand for them and put them in order of date on the counter between them.

"If you look at this one, dated last July, there's an entry for a two-hundred-dollar deposit." She pointed to it. "I found that entry every month for the past three years. That's as far back as his statements go. Then, look at August." She pointed to it. "No two-hundred-dollar deposit and none after that. I may be trying to make too much of this but, at this point, anything unusual is ringing little bells."

"Is there no indication where it came from?"

"I couldn't find any. And Dad was a meticulous record keeper."

"What about a bond that's finished paying out, or an annuity or something? I'm not a good person to talk to about banking. I try to keep mine as simple as possible."

Hilary sighed. "Me too. But if it were a bond or something official, there should be a record of it somewhere. Like I said, Dad kept those kind of things and I went through them all. None fit this entry. You think I'm way off, don't you? Grabbing at straws?"

"I think you're desperately hoping to make sense of what's just happened and maybe you're looking for everything to have an answer or fit, but it might not. I can understand how you feel, though."

"Can you?" Hilary sounded exasperated. She gave her head a small shake. "I'm sorry, this isn't even your problem to begin with. I know you're just trying to keep things in perspective. I always go flying off the deep end."

Shelby watched as a variety of emotions flashed across Hilary's face. Frustration, anger, grief. Finally, she said, "Look, why don't we make a timeline of what you've learned. It might highlight something you haven't thought of yet."

Hilary brightened. "Good idea. Do you have some paper?"

Shelby went around to the other side of the kitchen island and pulled a pad of paper out of a drawer, along with a pen. With Hilary's help, they listed what she'd found in the bank records, and then wrote down the dates of Nathan's visits to Alexandria Bay that they knew had to do with his consulting job.

"There's something else to add," Shelby suggested. "Last fall, near the end of September, is when I first met your dad. He came to the store and asked about that woman, and he also visited some places in the village, asking the same things. We need to double-check if those were days he was already here on business or if he made specific trips to town to ask about her."

"Okay," Hilary said, adding that to the chart. "That was one of the business trips he made, so he was already here. It wasn't a special trip just to find her."

"Right." Shelby continued to study the timeline. "So why, after all this time of working in the village, did he start asking around about the woman last fall? Why not before?"

Shelby tapped the paper with her pen. "The only other things that align, almost, are the final payment into his bank account and his asking about the woman. I mean, the deposits stopped in July and it was September when I first saw him. Not that it helps in any way to know this."

Hilary finished off her wine. "Maybe it doesn't make any sense, but maybe we're just missing more information. What if you talk to Roman Sykes, you know, at the town council offices? Since they were working together, he might know something about her. Surely Dad would have asked him first. And if not, maybe she's not important, but he might know what is."

"You want me to talk to him? He might be more forthcoming with you, since you're Nathan's daughter." Shelby knew that made sense but she did want to talk to him, too. "Why don't we do it together? Maybe tomorrow before you head back home? I work until noon, if that's not too late for you."

"That would be great. Thanks, Shelby. I appreciate this."

"That is, if Mr. Sykes is able and willing to see us." Shelby worried that he might already have a full agenda.

"If he doesn't, then I'll come back another time. We won't let this drop, right?"

Hilary looked so hopeful. Although she had some misgivings, Shelby nodded. "Right."

Chapter Thirteen

Hilary was waiting at the main dock when Shelby got off the boat just after noon the next day. She waved and pointed to her car. Shelby caught up to her and slid into the passenger seat of the red Honda.

"Hi, Hilary. I'm glad you thought to bring your car. It's a bit of a hike."

Hilary laughed. "I thought I might just keep going home after we talk to him. But in that case, I'll give you a ride back after."

"I need the walk, believe me. That will be fine."

Hilary seemed to be in a lighter mood than the night before. Maybe it was the fact that they seemed to be getting somewhere or, at least, now had a direction to move in. She had pulled her hair back in a small ponytail and tied a navy and white scarf around it, which matched the dark tones in her denim jacket.

Shelby directed her to the two-story brown brick building on the road heading out of the village.

"Okay, I did leave a message on his phone this morning saying we'd be stopping by. He didn't call back so I don't know what that means. The parking lot is in the back."

"And I called the police chief and told her about my dad's consulting work."

"Did she say she already knew about it?"

"No, she didn't say either way. All she did was thank me for letting her know."

"Hm."

"There's something else I think I should tell you."

Shelby heard the hesitancy in Hilary's voice and turned to look at her.

"My dad and I weren't really that close. We hadn't been since my mom died. He just sort of buried himself in his work and didn't pay much attention to me, and we never really got it back, even when he remarried. I feel guilty about that now. Like maybe I would have known what was going on in his life if we'd been closer." She sounded on the verge of tears.

"That makes it harder, I'm sure. But you can't beat yourself up about it," Shelby said. She could relate to the dad who paid too much attention to his work, though.

"And although he seemed happy with Giselle, I also think he might have taken on this job here to have some time away from her. She can be kind of high-maintenance."

Shelby didn't know what to say to that. She did feel sorry for Hilary, though. It sounded like she'd had a lonely life.

Hilary pulled in between two larger, newer cars and they both got out, heading to the door. Once inside, Shelby spotted a listing by floor of all the offices and they found the one they wanted on the second floor.

Since there was no reception area, Shelby just knocked on the door, hoping Mr. Sykes was in. After a few minutes, she knocked again and a dejected Hilary said, "I guess we should make a definite appointment next time."

Shelby noticed the open door to the next office and waved Hilary over to it. A young man, looking to be in his early twenties, sat at the desk, staring intently at his computer screen. His wire-rimmed glasses added to his studious appearance, and, from that distance, Shelby could see faint traces of a moustache. His short-sleeved white cotton shirt was buttoned at the throat, and he wore a sedate gray tie.

Shelby knocked on the door marked with a small white sign reading: *James Rooney.* "Excuse me."

He looked up in surprise. "Oh, you startled me. Sorry I didn't hear you."

"That's okay. We're looking for Roman Sykes. Do you happen to know where he is?"

"Yeah, he just ran out to get us some lunch. He should be back any minute. You can wait here, if you like." He pointed to two chairs but before they could sit down, a tall, stocky middle-aged man hurried into the room.

"Had to settle for a ham on rye. Sorry, Rooney." He placed a white paper bag on the desk.

Parker pointed to the two women. "These ladies are waiting to see you."

Sykes's brow furrowed, shifting his black-rimmed glass under his eyebrows. "Oh? Oh, yes that's right. One of you left me a message. Well, come in. I don't have much time but you can tell me what you want."

They followed him into his office, a mirror of the one they'd just left. Shelby and Hilary exchanged a glance as they sat down.

Shelby took the lead. "My name is Shelby Cox. I'm the one who left the message. And this is Hilary Miller, Nathan Miller's daughter. We understand he was working with you on a project."

Sykes looked surprised, then wary, then sad. "I'm sorry about your dad, Miss Miller. I worked with him for well over a year and had a great deal of respect for him." He looked as different from his colleague as possible. No traces of facial hair but his thick black hair brushed the collar of his dress shirt, the sleeves of which he'd pushed up to his elbows.

"Thank you. And I'm sorry to just drop in here but I was hoping you could tell me a bit about the work my father was doing and how often he came to Alexandria Bay."

A look of surprise crossed Roman Sykes's face. "He didn't talk about it?"

"No." Hilary didn't give an explanation.

Shelby stepped in. "How often he had been coming to the village?"

"Oh, he'd usually come every second week, for the day, and then he sometimes stayed overnight when we had a lot to go over. I was mainly providing him with data. His company was hired by the town council to streamline the zoning and planning processes. There was a lot of technological expertise needed and your dad was it."

Hilary nodded, looking proud of her dad.

"Did he ever mention if he had another reason for coming here," she asked.

Sykes looked wary. "No. He never said anything. If he did, what did you have in mind?"

114

"Well, I know he was looking for someone, I'm assuming she was a friend from the past."

Shelby watched Sykes's facial features relax as he gave it some thought. "No, he hadn't mentioned anything or anyone. Now, I'm sorry but I don't think I can help you with anything else, not right now anyway. I have a meeting very shortly. I'm not free to share the details of our work but if you have any other questions, don't hesitate to call. If I can give you some answers, I will." He stood as he talked and held out his hand across the desk.

They both shook it and left, Shelby closing the door behind her. As they walked past James Rooney's office, he was standing at the door.

"I think you should talk to Walt Nevin, he's our manager. He was the one who matched them up, and I know your dad spent a lot of time with him. Here's his card."

Hilary looked at Shelby and grinned. "A lead?"

"Maybe. Let's see if he's available." They retraced their steps to the directory and found his office. They were waylaid by someone sitting at a desk in a small reception area at the opposite end of the building.

"Mr. Nevin isn't in at the moment. I'm Amanda, Mandy. Can I take a message? I'll be sure he gets it." She looked to be in her late teens and eager to help. Her short, brown hair framed a heart-shaped face and when she smiled, the elastics in her braces showed.

Shelby smiled at her. "I'd like to talk to him when he has some free time. It won't take long."

"What is it regarding?"

"It has to do with Nathan Miller."

The girl looked surprised. "Oh, the poor man. I heard what happened. He was so nice. I feel so bad." She shoved a small pad and pen at Shelby. "Here. Just leave me your name and number and I'll make sure he gets back to you."

"Thanks."

"Well, I'm disappointed we didn't get any more information today," Hilary said when they were out in the parking lot. "Do you mind seeing Mr. Nevin on your own? I'd really appreciate it."

"I'll do that. Why don't you send me any questions you might have?"

"Will do. Do you want a ride?"

"No, I'm fine walking. Thanks."

Hilary surprised Shelby again with a quick hug. "Thank you, Shelby. I really appreciate this."

Shelby watched her drive off then started walking back into town, deciding, as she got to the first cross street, to head over to the library. She was certain Nathan Miller had stopped in there; he had been looking for a reader after all. And, she was curious if he might have told them anything else about the mystery woman.

She often enjoyed the walk across town, taking different streets each time and enjoying the variety of residences along the way. She walked past the school, and then, farther along, on the right was the library that shared access with the police and fire departments to their respective parking lots. There was undeveloped land on the left and much the same as the road wound its way out to the main highway. But today she didn't have time to meander.

She found one of the volunteers at the main desk when she entered the library, who told her that the librarian, Judy Carter, was leading a book club in the room set off to the side. She snuck in and took a seat close to the door, trying not to disturb the ten women who were discussing a book they had read. It was the perfect setting, Shelby thought, with three large couches set in a U-formation at the far end of the room, augmented with a variety of chairs, some wooden and hard-back, others upholstered with a well used look, and bookcases as backdrop. When the meeting ended about fifteen minutes later, Judy offered Shelby a cup of coffee in her office and explained about the book club.

"I usually have Nora lead it. She's so well-read you know and is good with leading a discussion. And the women all like her. But she's not too well today so I had to sit in. I used to do it all the time, so it was fun to get back into it. Now, what can I do for you? How are the plans for the murder mystery event coming along?"

"Just great. Nora is a very capable organizer and I've been more in a consulting role than anything. I'm really pleased that Bayside Books is able to be a part of the day-long event."

"I think it's a great partnership for something like this. Edie and I had often talked over the years about doing some joint projects, but we never seemed to get around to it. I'm delighted it's finally going to happen and that Nora's taking the lead on it. She's really been a godsend."

"How long has she been here?"

"Nora? Let's see, I think about five years. Yes, she just stopped in one day, the day before I was going in for a bit of surgery, and asked if we needed any volunteers. She said she'd moved to town a few weeks before and was looking for ways to fill her days, having recently retired. She loved books and just stepped naturally into the role and actually saved the day for Carol, another volunteer who held down the fort that day."

"That was good timing."

"I'll say."

"I was actually hoping to ask you about Nathan Miller," Shelby said, switching to her main reason for being there. "He's the man whose body was found last week. I know he was in Alexandria Bay last fall and again the day he died, both times asking about a woman who supposedly moved here seven years ago. Did you happen to talk to him?"

"I remember him from his visit last week. The time before, in the fall, I was off the day he came in, and I later found out that one of the volunteers spoke to him. Jennifer Turner. She moved away in January, though."

"What did he say to you last week?"

"Much of what you just said. He was looking for someone who was a book lover and so he thought she might have been a library patron. He said he'd talked to Jennifer but she hadn't lived here seven years ago so was unable to help. I couldn't think of anyone off hand, although I have since then. He thanked me and that was the last I saw of him."

"Really? Who have you thought of?"

"Alice Jones, over at the Style Shop. Do you know her?"

"Yes, we've met. Do you know much about her? Where she's from? Why she moved here?"

"Not really. We've spoken when I've shopped there but haven't really gotten into any details. Why do you ask? Do you think she could be that woman?" Judy looked surprised and intrigued at the same time. She reminded Shelby of a teenager with her short blonde hair worn in spikes, and her large purple-framed glasses. Not at all like the librarians Shelby remembered from childhood.

"I have no idea, but that's the right time frame. Is there anyone else you can think of?"

"Not really. I remember Alice because I first met her when I shopped for a dress for my twenty-fifth wedding anniversary and that was seven years ago, next month."

Someone knocked at the door and a woman Shelby didn't recognize opened it. "There's a local author here to talk about the signing this week."

"Oh, right. Thanks, Amanda. I'm sorry, but I need to speak to her," Judy said to Shelby.

"Of course. Thanks for your time, Judy."

"Any time. And I'll see you at the murder mystery event. At least the one that day will have a tidy conclusion."

Since Shelby was already at the library, she decided to pay a visit to Chief Stone at the police station, which was just across the parking lot. Maybe she could find out if she had already known about Hilary's news and if that had any bearing on her investigation. She was pleased to see that the chief was actually in her office rather than on the road. The small detachment of two permanent officers, the chief, and Lieutenant Chuck

Fortune, had already been supplemented to five, in preparation for the busy summer tourist season. However, it didn't mean there was always someone in the office.

"Do you have a minute to talk?" Shelby asked when Stone looked up from her computer screen.

"Sure thing. Would you like some coffee? Not as good as yours, but it's hot." Her voice sounded neutral.

"No thanks," she replied, thinking about the latte she planned to get right after this.

Stone motioned Shelby over to her desk. As Shelby sat in the chair across from her, Stone watched her closely. "What's on your mind?"

"Well, I know that Hilary Miller told you that her dad had been coming to the Bay for some time now, doing consulting work for the town council."

"And just how do you know that?"

"Hilary came by my place last night and it came up in conversation."

Stone looked skeptical. "I see. So, you two are buddies now?"

"We are friends. I met her when she first showed her art at Felicity's gallery."

"And that now makes you her confidant?"

Shelby knew she'd better tread carefully. "I'm not sure what she thinks I am, but she just needed someone to talk things over with. She's trying to find out what happened to her dad. You can understand that."

Stone sighed. "Yes, I can, but I also know that unleashing your curiosity can lead to complications. So, I will tell you I did know about that. His contact here got in touch with me just after Mr. Miller's death."

"Roman Sykes?"

Stone's eyebrows flew up. "No, Walter Nevins. What do you know about this Sykes fellow?"

"Uh, Hilary talked to him."

"Huh. Well, it seems her dad had been visiting frequently but didn't get involved in much else in the village. And, that's all I'm about to tell you."

"Until he started asking about the mystery woman last fall."

"What? Oh, yes, that's right. He did ask around at that point, and also, the day he was murdered. We've established that. Now, why am I not surprised by all these questions?" Stone sounded vexed, but her expression looked pleasant enough. For now. Shelby realized she was probably running out of pleasantries.

"Oh, just one more thing. Do you know how long the body was in the water?"

"Well, from some good old-fashioned detective work, I've determined he went into the water sometime between when you spoke to him and when you found him. How's that?"

Now she was getting testy. The sarcasm was the giveaway, but Shelby decided to chance asking one more question.

"Okay. Can I ask, are you still searching for this mystery woman Nathan was asking about?"

"You can ask." Stone stood and Shelby assumed their talk was over.

"Thanks, Chief," she said, even though she hadn't gotten any information. But she did know when to make an exit.

She wondered if she dared to ask if the chief had questioned Alice Jones, but the look on Stone's face supplied all the answer Shelby needed. She stood quickly. "Okay. Thanks again."

As Shelby reached for the doorknob, Stone said, "I understand your boyfriend is getting a transfer."

Shelby turned abruptly back to her, unsure what to say.

"Look, I know I've had him on my bad books because of all those pranks he pulled as a teen, but I do think he's turned out to be one of the good guys. I hope it all works out for you."

Shelby tried to smile. "Thanks, Chief Stone."

She tried not to dwell on thoughts of Zack as she walked to the Style Shop. She'd been avoiding thinking about all he'd talked about, aside from discussing it with Edie and Erica, and she hadn't come to any conclusions. All of which was made easier since Zack was in Buffalo and probably wouldn't be home for another week or two. She had learned she couldn't count on him being able to come home every weekend. They'd have to deal with it next time though, and she needed to be prepared. But for now, she willed her thoughts back to Nathan Miller and what could possibly have happened to him on Blye Island. And, did Alice Jones fit into that picture at all?

Shelby wondered if she dared talk to Alice again. She fit the time frame for the mystery woman moving to the Bay but that was all she had to go on. How would she know if she didn't ask?

Shelby had to wait several minutes until the two other customers in the store finally left. She'd been admiring a lightweight kimono jacket with geometrical designs in black, brown, and white. This time, she knew better than to look at the price tag.

"Something I can interest you in?" Alice asked as she came up to Shelby. She reached for the jacket and slid it off the hanger while Shelby tried to gauge the tone of her voice. "Try it on. It's very flattering."

"Oh, I'm sure it is." Shelby took her jacket off and slipped the new one over the blouse she was wearing. It felt like silk and, as Alice had said, looked flattering. But even if she could afford it, she knew it wasn't something she'd wear in the store, so where? Good reason not to give in to the temptation. Now, if she lived in Boston . . .

"Thanks, it is tempting, but not in my budget right now, sadly." Shelby handed it back and donned her own jacket again. "It must be hard to work here and not succumb to the temptation to buy everything in sight. I hope you get a good discount."

Alice chuckled. "I do, but I don't really need much from here. I'm pretty casual usually, and I don't go out a lot."

"I get that. If I didn't have to get dressed up a bit for the store, I would probably stay in jeans or workout clothes most of the time. Not that I work out."

Alice laughed out loud this time. That was a good sign.

"So, you haven't really had time to get involved in the social life of the Bay?"

Shelby noticed the sudden rigidity of Alice's spine. "No, I haven't."

"Hm. I know what that's like. I've been here only a year and all I seem to do is work."

Alice seemed to relax.

"And now, with this murder, I'm trying not to get involved, but I do want to find out what happened to Nathan Miller. Had you met him at all? He seemed to be visiting a lot of the shops, trying to find out about a woman he was looking for, someone who had moved here seven years ago."

"Why are you getting involved?" Alice's face gave nothing away except displeasure.

"Well, as I mentioned, I found the body, and his daughter is hoping to get some answers."

"That's what the police are for. I suggest you leave it to them." Alice turned abruptly and walked back behind the counter.

Shelby felt a small shiver slide down her back. No threat there, just a lack of emotion.

"Okay, but just one quick question, please. Did Nathan Miller stop in here a couple of Saturdays ago, the day he died? He did know your name because he apparently asked one of the store owners about you."

Alice blanched. "I can't help you. I have nothing to say, so let's just leave it at that." Alice turned her back on Shelby, suddenly intent on the back countertop.

Well that wasn't what Shelby had hoped would happen. She knew when to make a strategic exit, and this was it.

Chapter Fourteen

As Shelby lay in bed the next morning, trying to convince herself to get up, she found her mind wandering back to that day the previous fall when Nathan Miller had visited the island store. Why was he looking for the mystery woman, obviously not the love of his life as Shelby had originally thought, since he'd remarried after his wife died—to a woman who was obviously not the person he was trying to track down.

And what, if anything, did his work with the town council have to do with it all? And of course, why had he started asking about the mystery woman last fall? What had been the trigger for that?

And why had Alice Jones reacted in such an extreme manner to Shelby's questions? Did it mean anything or was she just super private about her life? It was hard to live in a small town like Alexandria Bay and keep so much of your life hidden away. Shelby had certainly found that out. What was Alice's story and who might be able to give her more answers?

Zack phoned as she was eating her breakfast. She didn't have much of an appetite anyway. Too many things bugging her. She was pleased to hear Zack's voice but at the same time hesitant that he might bring up the topic of her moving.

"What's new with you?" she asked, knowing he probably led a more exciting life than she did these days.

"You know, busy as usual. A lot of stuff I can't really share with you, unfortunately. But I meant to call you last night. I got in too late, though. And I didn't want to take a chance calling when I'd finished work today, in case the same thing happened. How are things in the Bay? Any more news on the body? Or, are you still keeping out of it all?"

She could hear the amusement in his voice. Maybe it was wise not to let him know how much she'd been thinking about it. He did have a tendency to worry about her.

"I don't really know. Chief Stone hasn't opted to include me in her findings and, as you know, I can only do so much."

"Uh-oh. You know that I know that you won't leave this alone."

"You might be wrong this time."

"I doubt it. So, come clean. What have you been doing or, even better, what have you found out?"

He does know me so well.

"Okay, but I'm not really that involved. His daughter found out that he'd been doing consulting work here in town for over a year now, so he hadn't just appeared the two times he came into the store. But what I'm wondering now is why he waited so long to start asking around about this mystery woman? She is at the crux of this, I just know it. So, did he find her, and is she his killer? Or is it someone who knows them both. Why was he looking for her after all?"

"Are you thinking there may be a love triangle going on?"

"It's possible, I suppose, although I would have been surprised. He seemed like such a nice man, sort of tame."

Zack laughed and when he finally had his mirth under control said, "Tame. Interesting description. Okay, so if that's not what it is, any other thoughts?"

"No. I've been trying to find out who the mystery woman might be from the time frame he provided. He said she moved here seven years ago, and I do have someone on my radar, although she's not being very cooperative."

"Which gets your Spidey senses tingling?" he asked, chuckling.

"That's one way of putting it."

"So, who is it? Someone I know?"

"Alice Jones is her name, and unless you do a lot of shopping for dresses at the Style Shop, you might not have run across her." Shelby placed her plate and glass in the sink then looked around for her tote bag. Not spotting it, she thought it must be upstairs.

"Okay, I'll give you that. No, I haven't met her nor do I recognize the name. I'm surprised you haven't found out Chief Stone's thoughts on this theory. You have been known to just get in her face about things and say what's on your mind," he said as she reached the bedroom.

"I probably should."

"No, you probably shouldn't. I wasn't really suggesting that you do that."

"I know, I know, I should stay out of it. And I probably would if it wasn't for his daughter, Hilary. She's really desperate to find out what happened to him. And I can totally understand that."

"So can I, but I'll say it again, it's not your place to find out. But if I were to give any advice, which I don't like doing, I'd say that the reason he was murdered may lie in his home town, not in the Bay. Whatever drove him to search for this woman had more to do with where he came from than where he ended up. I'd think his daughter is better placed to figure that out. Once you know why, you might find it easier to answer the question of who."

"You're brilliant."

"Thank you. You can tell me that as often as you like. But right now, I really have to get going. We'll pick this up later in the week."

Shelby was still smiling as she made her way to the shuttle and still when she unlocked the door to the store. She really enjoyed Zack's early morning calls, rare as they might be, which led to thoughts of waking up with him there in person. Which, of course, was totally unhelpful when it came to making a decision about her future. She knew she'd have to base it on more than fulfilling mornings. She gave her head a shake and tried to focus on the books as she did her usual morning walk around the store. As she did so, she realized that this process was really as much about reinforcing that this was truly her new life as it was about checking that the shelves were tidy and the spaces filled.

Laura arrived on the first boat of the morning, followed by some customers. Shelby watched to see if any of the customers needed help while Laura hung up her jacket in the back. Then when she returned, they had a quick discussion about what still needed straightening.

Shelby then pulled out the wire basket from under the front desk. It's where she'd stuffed all the invoices and other store paperwork that had made it over to the island. Usually it was all handled in the main store but, at times, invoices for special orders were found tucked inside a book. And then there were the lists of the books needing to be pulled from the shelves in order to be returned to the publisher before the deadline. These were books that had been on the shelves for close to nine months with little or no action. If the store wanted credit for them, they had to be pulled and shipped within the week. Shelby dealt with the most critical list and left the others for Laura when she had time.

Later in the afternoon, she was on a break, leaving Laura in charge, and walking toward the door to step outside the castle for some fresh air when she heard some shouting. She turned back inside to see what was happening but was elbowed out of the way by someone wearing a green hoodie. Someone in a real hurry.

"Hey," she shouted as she hit the doorframe before falling to the cement doorstep.

Fast on his heels was one of the two security guards on duty. Shelby struggled to get up but realized she couldn't put any weight on her left hand.

"What's going on?" Laura asked crouching beside Shelby.

"I don't know what happened, but someone's being chased. He ran into me on his way out and here I am. I've done something to my arm, though. Could you help me up?"

She stuck her right hand out and Laura helped pull her to an upright position. "Did you hit your head when you went down?"

"No. I just landed on my arm," Shelby said rubbing it gently.

"You should have that seen to. It might be broken."

Shelby wiggled her fingers. "Not broken, but it's painful, I admit. I broke my other arm when I was a kid and believe me, this isn't that extreme pain."

She looked toward the stairs as Chrissie came down them at a fast pace. Shelby took a step toward her and stopped as a pain shot up her arm. "Ouch."

"What's wrong? What happened? Are you okay?" Chrissie asked, reaching out but pulling her hand back quickly.

"I must have bruised something when I fell on my arm." She held it gingerly across her stomach. "What's happening anyway?"

The pain shot along her arm each time she moved it, but she wanted to know what was going on.

"Our volunteer watching the cameras spotted a guy pocketing something from the antique Eastlake side table in Millicent Blye's sitting room upstairs. She alerted me and, by the time I got there, he was heading down the stairs. I yelled, the security guard took off after him, and he ran. Let me take a look at your arm. I'm the first aider around here."

Chrissie cautiously ran her hand along Shelby's arm. Even the featherlight touch made Shelby jump as the woman touched her elbow.

"I don't think anything's broken, probably just badly bruised. But if it's that tender, I'd go to the hospital and have an X-ray done if I were you."

Shelby nodded.

"I mean now, Shelby. You don't want to leave it too long if it's bad and besides, what can you do around here with only one arm? Laura's here, so you're okay to leave. Isn't that right, Laura?"

"Definitely. I can handle things for the rest of the afternoon and you can let me know tonight if you need to take tomorrow off, too. I'm free all day."

Shelby thought to herself that Laura actually looked pleased at the prospect. Shelby's first thought was what this might mean for Taylor, still out on maternity leave. She shook her head. *Odd time to be thinking that.*

"Okay, you're probably right. I'll just get my jacket and tote bag. What time is it anyway?"

"Why don't we call Terry and see if he can bring his shuttle over?"

"What time is it?

"It's two forty five," Laura answered.

"No, don't bother Terry. I'll grab the boat. It should be here soon."

"You stay here. I'll get your things," Laura said as she disappeared into the store.

"What a downer to find that there's probably more than one thief. I hadn't even given that any thought," Shelby said, trying to keep her mind off the increasing pain.

"I hadn't either. In fact, nothing has shown up on the cameras. I don't see how he hopes to get off the island now. We'll have security at the boat dock."

"What if he brought his own boat?"

"If he did, it would have to be in one of the coves which are hard to access from the island. Or . . ."

"The Grotto," they said in unison.

"There's also the spot that Savannah Page's killer tied up."

"I suppose. How are you feeling? Any dizziness? Can I help you over to a chair?" Chrissie's concern touched Shelby.

"I'm okay. Laura will be back in a minute and there's the boat to catch."

"Well, if you're sure you can manage on your own? I'd like to get out to the dock before the boat arrives and check it out first. Then I'll check the grotto."

"Just be sure you take the other security guard with you," Shelby said, suddenly worried for Chrissie's safety.

"Right. Let me know how you are, okay?" Chrissie said, as she headed for the front door, using her radio to summon the other guard.

Shelby took a deep breath, hoping to ignore the increasing pain. She tried to organize her thoughts. She doubted she could drive herself to the hospital, but she hated to pull Edie away from the store, especially since Shelby was certain it was nothing more than a bruise. A very sore bruise, to be sure. Okay, maybe a sprain. But she hated being fussed over. More like she wasn't used to it. She could always call a cab. Her thoughts flew to Zack. Not that he could help, but it was calming to think of him.

She made it onto the boat with the help of Laura, without making a scene, although the pain had gotten a bit more intense. She was surprised to see Edie waiting at the dock. Laura must have called her.

"Oh, gosh, honey, what a horrible thing to happen. Is it bad?" Edie asked as she looked her over, unsure where to touch Shelby.

"There's some pain but I can move my fingers, so it can't be all that bad. I'm just sorry you had to leave the store."

"Posh. That's not a problem, Trudy's there. I went home and got the car. It's over here."

Shelby gingerly eased into the front passenger seat of Edie's old Chevy Impala and cringed when the car got going with a small jerk.

"I'm sorry about that, honey," Edie said with a sideways glance. "Although I enjoy driving a standard shift, I think I need to get out driving more."

Maybe less, Shelby thought as the car almost stalled at the stop sign. "Maybe you should buy an automatic, Aunt Edie," Shelby said through gritted teeth.

"You're probably right, but I keep putting off buying a new car. This baby's done good by me for almost twenty years now. And I really don't drive enough to put all that money into a brand-new car. Mind you, I could find a used car that's in good condition but much cheaper. Maybe I should go looking on one of my days off. Maybe you could come along with me. I'm sure you'd be more aware of what I should be looking for in a car."

Shelby realized what Edie was doing. She was trying to keep Shelby's mind off the pain. "Sure," Shelby agreed with a sigh of relief as they pulled up at the emergency entrance of the hospital.

Once she'd gotten Shelby safely into the waiting room, Edie parked the car and rejoined her quickly in the waiting room. "You don't have to wait with me," Shelby assured Edie.

"Of course I don't have to, but I want to." Edie patted Shelby's good arm. "Now, should we play a game of I Spy?"

Shelby looked at her quickly, relieved to see the small grin on Edie's face.

Chapter Fifteen

Shelby had a slow start the next morning. She'd slept deeply despite the awkwardness of propping her elbow up on a pillow. She gave the credit for the sleep to the painkillers. She did remember though how upset JT had been with having that pillow in the way.

It had been 2:00 AM when she and Edie had finally left the hospital, Shelby's left arm in a splint to stabilize her elbow. Although not broken, it appeared there was a tiny chip that had come off and was floating around somewhere, but the main problem was a tiny crack and severe bruising. She got up with difficulty and great care, noticing that even JT was now keeping his distance. She made her way directly downstairs to the kitchen, fed him, and then took care of her own needs. As she made an espresso, she wondered about whether to go to work and decided she would do a half-day. When she ran it by Laura, who was already at the store, she was told to stay home. But Shelby had already made up her mind. She could at least help answer questions and tend the cash. What she couldn't do was stay home and feel sorry for herself.

Edie called, also suggesting that Shelby stay home.

"Uh, I seem to recall telling you the same thing a few times last year," Shelby reminded her. "And how did that work out?"

"Okay, I'll admit, you were right, which proves my point."

"Except you were dealing with a knee replacement and later, an injury to that same knee. Much worse than a bruised elbow."

"I don't know why I even try to reason with you. I should realize after all this time that you just do what you want anyway."

Shelby could hear the exasperation in her aunt's voice. "Now you make me sound like a headstrong kid, or worse."

Edie sighed. "I don't mean to. It's just that I worry about you."

"I know, and I do appreciate it. But trust me, going into the store today is just what I need, and it won't be a problem."

After hanging up, Shelby felt a wave of sadness overcome her. That's what she would be missing if she moved away. Having someone, other than a partner, a mother figure, to be there for her. That was family, something she'd been missing for many years and wasn't willing to give up. But she couldn't imagine not having Zack around, either. Sure, maybe they could do a long-distance relationship, but what if it didn't work out? Those long periods of not seeing each other could be an open door to him finding someone else to spend time with. She did trust him, but out of sight, out of mind, right? Oh man, why were things never easy?

When Shelby finally got to the store just after one, Laura took the opportunity to have a short break. It appeared that all the customers were doing the same thing.

Shelby took the opportunity to return a message left by Taylor earlier that morning. She answered on the fourth ring.

"OMG, I was so worried when I heard you were rushed to the hospital," Taylor said, while baby Olivia gurgled in the background.

Shelby chuckled. "I was hardly rushed but, I must admit, it was a horrible evening. But not to worry, it isn't too serious."

"So you say. Are you sure you should be at work? I called your aunt before trying you because I didn't want to disturb you again. She's not too happy you're at the store, you know."

"I do know. We've had this conversation, and it's the same one I had with her last year, if you remember."

"Oh, I do. You're both very stubborn, you know." Taylor said something babyish and muffled to Olivia. "So, how is your arm anyway?"

"There's a tiny crack, but it's mainly bruised so it should be okay in no time at all, if I can just avoid banging into things."

"I know how that is. Your arm now has a target painted on it, right? Well, I'm glad to hear you sounding so cheery and that it's not a major break or dislocation or similar. But you know, if you need help at the store, I can get someone to watch Olivia. Mrs. Carlotti next door has been offering, and since she's a grandmother eight times over, I would feel confident having her sit. I'm happy to come in for a few hours anyway."

"That's so thoughtful of you, Taylor, and I'll keep it in mind. Thank you."

"You're welcome. I'm still thinking of stopping by one day when you're working and introducing Olivia to the world of books."

"I look forward to that."

"So do I, but I gotta run, it's feeding time."

"Thanks again for calling. Bye."

That had cheered her up. Shelby realized how lucky she was to have so many friends, and all so willing to help out when needed. There was no one in Boston she had considered to be a close friend, not even after her many years of living there. That was a sad statement if ever there was one.

The boat ride over had tired her out, she realized, and she plopped down on the chair behind the counter. She wondered if she looked as bedraggled as she felt. She hadn't paid much attention to what she was doing when she'd gotten ready. She looked down at her slightly flared pants, an older pair she'd found at the back of her closet. Not her usual outfit, but she hadn't been able to manage the leggings she usually lived in with only one hand to pull them on. It had been tricky enough trying to get dressed, but determination had won out. Then she wondered what her hair looked like. She hadn't checked it after leaving the boat. She'd also been unable to put it up on a pony-tail so had relied on simply tucking it behind her ears. Maybe she could find a ball cap in the gift shop to cover the curly mess. Maybe the bookstore should order some with their logo on it. They would be perfect to wear in the store on such days. And they could sell the hats to customers. Win, win.

She was sitting there, head resting on her right hand, when Chrissie walked into the store.

"What are you doing here? I thought for sure you'd at least take today off. I just wanted to check with Laura to see how you were doing." Chrissie rushed over and hesitated a moment before touching Shelby's good shoulder.

"Well, as you can see, I'm doing fine. Just a bit tired from the painkillers, but I don't even need them anymore. So, I'm back on duty."

"That's a relief. You had us all really worried. I heard that was a nasty crack you took to your arm. I know though that you'd want the good news." Chrissie folded her arms, looking very pleased with herself. "The guy was caught. He sure was dumb. It seems his plan for escape was to grab the next boat. It seems he didn't know about the surveillance cameras. And of course, when he knocked you over, that sent our security team into high alert. They found him trying to hide until the next boat arrived. He was partway under a shrub, which turned out not to be much cover. At least, it won't be until later in spring."

"Do you think he was part of the earlier thefts?"

"No, it sounds like he was working on his own. A greedy young kid who wanted to make some quick money rather than having to work for it. Anyway, I hope we'll get one thing good out of this." She looked pointedly at Shelby's arm. "I'm hoping for a lot of press and, to that end, I have a local reporter coming to interview me shortly. That may be the best deterrent yet. I'd better get back out there." She turned back at the door. "I'm glad to see you here, Shelby. I was worried. But I hope you don't overdo it. Let me know if I can help out in any way."

"Thanks, Chrissie."

Matthew and Chrissie passed each other at the door. He walked over to where Shelby still sat. "What are you doing back here so soon? Edie said it was a bad break and you wouldn't stay at home."

"Edie may have exaggerated a tad. It's a crack in the elbow and this splint will keep it in place while it heals. So, I can do anything one-handed, and all the "no-handed" chores." Shelby smiled hoping to mask a sharp pain that shot down her arm.

"Well, if you say so, but I want you to let me know the minute you need help with anything bigger or Edie will never forgive me." He had shoved his usual baseball cap back on his head so the brim tilted upward. His tan was now year round—a combination of sun and wind. His lips were flattened in a straight line and his eyes were intense.

Shelby chuckled. "I hear you. I'm glad they caught the guy, though."

"Yeah. Let's hope that's the end of the castle's theft problems. Now, I've got to get back to the garden." He pointed his finger at her. "Remember, call me stat if you need help."

"I will and thanks, Matthew."

He nodded and left. And then the phone rang.

Busy afternoon.

"Shelby? I heard what happened yesterday and I also heard you were right back at work," Chief Stone said without identifying herself.

"Both are true. What can I do for you, Chief?"

"I hope you're doing okay, but you must be if you're working today, right? What time do you finish?"

"I close at five."

"So back in town at five twenty? Good. Wait for me at the dock. There's something we need to take care of."

She hung up without so much as a goodbye or confirmation that Shelby would meet her. Somehow, this neither surprised nor upset Shelby. She did feel her curiosity meter shoot to the top, though.

The rest of the afternoon went quickly, and by the time Shelby stepped off the boat, she was anxiously looking for Stone. She spotted the chief standing next to her SUV in the parking lot.

Stone waved her over and held the passenger door of the SUV open for her.

"Should I be pleased or anxious," Shelby asked as Stone slid behind the wheel.

"A little of both."

She didn't say another word until she pulled up in front of the Style Shop. The *Closed* sign was on the front door, but Stone opened it and waved Shelby inside. Alice was sitting in one of the slipper chairs usually used by waiting husbands. Stone pointed at the other one and Shelby sat in it.

"Now," Stone began, "what we have here is a predicament, Shelby. I understand you've been pestering Alice, asking all sorts of questions, particularly about her background." She held up her hand before Shelby could answer. "I don't want any excuses. I know why you're doing it. You're nosing around in the Miller murder investigation, despite my telling—no, ordering—you not to get involved. Now, you've managed to stir up a bit of a hornet's nest. I just wish you'd asked me about her. You ask about everything else under the sun, and everyone else I might add."

She glanced at Alice who nodded. Shelby wondered who was in charge here.

"What I'm about to tell you is for your ears only, understood? And the only reason I'm telling you any of this is because who knows what consequences there will be if you continue to draw attention to Alice here. The main thing you need to know is that Alice is not the woman Nathan Miller was searching for. But I know that's not enough for you, so I will share this much with you, with Alice's permission. I've known her since she moved here seven years ago. She came to me to fill me in on her background and the fact that she moved, changed her name, changed her appearance and everything else she could think of, to escape an abusive home situation. Now, we don't know if her husband is still searching for her. But we do know that she needs to keep a low profile, so I'll say this once only, and the next time you start this questioning of Alice, I'm throwing you in jail for contempt. Do you understand?"

Shelby was too stunned to answer. She nodded her head instead. She knew she shouldn't keep staring at Alice, but not in her most fanciful dreams had she imagined this was her story. She immediately felt terrible and a bit ashamed for being so persistent.

She tried to apologize but Alice waved it away. "I don't want an apology, Shelby. I just want your word."

"You've got it. I promise."

Shelby looked over at Chief Stone who looked relieved but still serious. "I think I'd like to go home now."

"Right. Goodnight, Alice. Don't worry. Shelby is true to her word except when she's assuring me of something."

That drew a tiny smile from Alice who followed them to the door. Shelby could hear the lock turn after it closed behind them.

It was a silent ride to Shelby's houseboat but as she opened the door of the SUV to step out, Stone said, "Try to keep out of trouble."

Shelby nodded and slowly walked to her door. She didn't look to see if the chief had left. She stepped inside and crumbled into the nearest chair, crying. What a mess she could have made of things.

Chapter Sixteen

S helby had decided she'd go into the store on Saturday for the morning shift. Although her arm had been aching for part of the night, she found there were certain things she could do that didn't bother it at all, like carrying a couple of books. Besides, she thought she'd go stir crazy if she couldn't go in at all that day. JT hadn't proved to be much company as he'd gotten back into the in-and-out routine with the return of the good weather. She knew he'd been spoiled at Edie's when they moved into her house over winter and she'd gotten him the cat flap on the kitchen door. Now he obviously expected one on the houseboat also. No amount of explaining that Shelby didn't own the door and therefore could not deface it, sat well with JT. He just sat there complaining until Shelby opened the door. He'd be back anywhere between two minutes to two hours later, and start his loud caterwauling from the other side of the door. She understood now where that word had come from.

Half a day should do it, and Laura would handle the afternoon. Then Shelby asked Cody to work at the castle on Sunday instead of the main store, since Edie had readily agreed she didn't need him. Shelby realized she hadn't seen much of Cody on his weekends, home from college over the winter, and she missed talking to him. He had such an interesting take on things and was equally inquisitive about the goings-on at Blye Island. In fact, she'd practically had to put him in restraints when they'd been kicking around the idea of some modern-day smuggling taking place at the grotto last spring. He was a smart kid and she knew they'd miss him once he finished college and settled on a permanent job, wherever that might be. She was also sure they'd all, customers included, miss his eclectic collection of bow ties.

She had been at work for a couple of hours when the door opened and she looked up from checking the inventory on the computer to see Zack walk in.

"I didn't expect you this weekend," Shelby said, totally delighted. She knew her face had turned a bright pink and that her breathing had quickened. In fact, she felt her heart pounding so hard she was sure it could be seen through her blouse and resisted looking down to check. She was glad that at the moment there weren't any customers in the store to see their reunion.

"I didn't expect you to end up in a sling. Nor going into work with your arm injured, I might add." He walked over scanning the store, and then kissed her while trying to avoid jostling her arm. "I can't believe you've been in danger, again."

"Well, not really danger and not of my own doing, I might add. I was not trying to capture the thief. I was merely in the way, so it's not my fault. By the way, the guy wasn't even the one who'd been stealing items from the castle all last season.

He was arrested a few weeks earlier. This was some totally new entrepreneur."

"Well, it sounds like you slowed his getaway."

"Not only that. He was observed taking the item by the closed-circuit cameras," she added with a satisfied grin.

"I recall you were the one to first suggest the board install those. You're feeling very pleased with yourself," he stated, teasing her.

"Definitely."

They were interrupted when the door opened and a large family group raised the noise level in the store.

"Are you here on your own?" Zack asked, watching the two adults and five children of varying ages.

"For now. I'm working only a half day, until one."

"Good news. I came over in my own boat, so I'd be happy to take you back to the Bay when you're done." His smile suggested so much more to her, and Shelby felt herself blushing.

"I'd be delighted. So, what will you do until one?"

"Play tourist. I haven't wandered through the castle, just admiring it for some time. I'll be back at one."

He squeezed her good arm and left.

Shelby spent most of the morning thanking castle staff and volunteers who kept dropping into the store to ask how she was. Even the customers took on a solicitous attitude when they saw her sling. She tried not to let it all bother her, but she wasn't used to the intense attention and felt uncomfortable.

Maybe I should *have stayed home.*

When Laura arrived, she tried to get Shelby to sit down in one of the wicker chairs and have a rest. She was in the process of explaining why she thought it wise for Shelby to take Monday off, when Zack walked back through the doorway. Shelby heaved a big sigh of relief as she glanced at the clock. One on the nose. He helped her slip her jacket on, one arm through the sleeve, with the other side draped over her shoulder and arm. Then after she'd introduced Zack to Laura and said goodbye, they left, Zack holding her good hand on the way to his boat.

"One of the perks of being a cop, being able to bring your private boat here," she observed, not for the first time.

Zack smiled but said nothing as he helped her climb into the speedboat.

The noise of the motorboat made it difficult to talk on the way back to Alexandria Bay. Shelby couldn't think of anything she wanted to say, anyway. She was just incredibly happy that Zack had come home, and for her. Once they'd docked back in the Bay, he helped her out of the boat and held tightly to her hand on their way to her houseboat.

She settled herself on the loveseat, as per his instructions, resting her injured arm on a pillow she'd placed on her lap, and waited while he made them both some tea. He kept looking up at her as he did so. When he brought their cups over to where she sat, she spoke before he had a chance to.

"This was absolutely not my fault. None of it. I'd just like to reiterate that fact."

He chuckled. "It sounds like I'm always blaming you for everything bad that happens to you. I don't do that, do I?"

"No, not really. But I do want to point out this has nothing to do with Nathan Miller's murder. I wasn't even doing any investigating."

He leaned toward her and gave her a kiss. "I know. I got the entire story from a still-excited Chrissie Halstead."

"Oh, she is that. I can't decide if she's thrilled to have another thief locked up or if she's feeling guilty he even got that far."

"Probably a bit of both. You had said last fall that she didn't take your advice right away to have cameras installed when there was that rash of thefts going on."

"Hmm. Let's just hope it doesn't happen again."

Zack looked suddenly stern. "This is Shelby Cox we're talking about. As I seem to remember, you've had a few brushes with danger over the past year."

"All past tense. Now, how long are you here and what should we do?"

She was pleased to see the sparkle in his eyes as he looked to be giving it some thought.

"I'm here until tomorrow morning. I have a very early start on Monday and we're having a meeting about it later tomorrow, so I'll have to leave after an early lunch. Does that work for you?"

"Any amount of time you have to be here works for me."

"Excellent. Now tell me more about what's happening with this investigation of yours. Did you suggest to Hilary that the answer may just be closer to her home?"

"No, I haven't. In fact, I haven't heard from her in several days. I just realized that now. I do plan to tell her. I did run into a very uncomfortable situation with Alice Jones, though."

"The woman from the dress store?"

"Yup. I'm embarrassed to tell you about it and, according to Chief Stone, I can't talk about it to anyone. But you are in the law business."

Zack raised his eyebrows and crossed his arms, looking expectantly at her.

Shelby cleared her throat. It really bothered her to talk about what a mess she had almost made of everything, but this was Zack. "She did arrive in town seven years ago, but it seems she's hiding from an abusive husband. The chief has known about it all along. Alice complained to her about my prying, and the chief reamed me out, so here is the newly chastised Shelby Cox." She tried to make light of it but it didn't help that sinking feeling in her stomach.

"Well it sounds like nothing bad came of it, so you got lucky. But you could take that as a warning."

Shelby sighed and nodded.

"So, let me get this straight, your main line of inquiry has been who moved here seven years ago?"

"Yes."

"And that's as far as it's gotten you?"

She nodded, quietly.

"And you didn't think it might be time to leave it alone?"

Shelby was beginning to feel uncomfortable. He had a point, after all. "Well, maybe. I have to admit, I really don't know where to go from here."

"That just underlines the fact that the answer, and the killer, might be closer to this man's hometown and you have no way of checking on that part. In any case, you can bet Chief Stone is doing that."

"Hmm. You may be right, but I wonder about his wife."

Zack threw his hands in the air and then swiveled to grab her in his arms. "No more talk about murder, okay?"

She nodded.

"So, changing the topic here, have you given much thought to my move?"

She wiggled out of his arms, trying to calmly think of what to say. "I have, believe me, and I keep going around in circles about it."

He sat down on the loveseat and patted the spot next to him but she stayed where she was. "I need some distance when we're talking about this," she said.

"Good, so we will talk about it."

"I'd rather not. It will just confuse me more."

"How do you know that? Look, Shelby, I know you're used to being on your own, making your own decisions, the whole thing. But we really do need to talk this out, the two of us. It affects both of our lives and I want to understand just where you're coming from."

She felt her back stiffen ever so slightly. "So that you can try to persuade me?"

Zack's face fell. "So that we can work it out together. That's what this whole future between us will be all about. Sharing, talking, making decisions together. Don't you want that?"

"I do, it's just that a part of me doesn't know how to do that and the other part doesn't even know what I want. So how can I discuss it?" She knew she sounded whiney, but she found she couldn't think straight about this, not with him being so close and sensible sounding.

He sat without saying anything for a few minutes, just watching her. "Okay, I can accept that for now. At least it shows that you *are* seriously thinking about all this, otherwise you could just say no, right?"

She nodded.

He stood. "So, we'll drop the topic for the rest of my time here, but we will have to have that talk soon, Shelby."

She nodded again, certain that if she said anything more, she'd break into tears.

* * *

Their morning got off to an unexpectedly early start with the ringing of Shelby's phone. It was Cody, calling to say he was sick and couldn't cover at the castle that day. Shelby assured him it wasn't a problem and her plans had changed so she would be able to go in. When she finally managed to get her eyes to focus on the clock, she realized she could hear the shower. Zack was already up. She leapt out of bed, not wanting to miss spending any of this time with him before he hit the road. By the time she showered and got dressed, he had a breakfast of scrambled eggs and toast ready. And then, he was gone.

Shelby felt like she was dragging herself along the walkway up to the castle. She knew that was partly from the pain medication but more from the other pain—the one in her heart. When Zack had left, she could tell he was disappointed she hadn't been willing to discuss the move to Boston, and after he'd rushed all the way just to see how she was doing. It was quite sweet that he was so concerned. She wondered if she looked like the ingrate she felt she was.

A couple of tour guides waved to her as she walked in through the open front door and headed to her store. That little bit of cheer made her feel somewhat better, and by the time the first customers appeared a half hour later, she felt like her old self.

Mid-afternoon, she took advantage of a lull in traffic to relax in one of the wicker chairs, sipping a mug of coffee. The slant of the sun made it look like a spotlight was shining on the local authors section, extending to the large potted Maidenhair fern she'd recently purchased. Matthew had been very instructive when it came to making the choice and, just to be sure, she'd googled the plant in order to decide if this was indeed one plant she wouldn't kill. The entire store seemed to be bathed in warmth, and she was smiling when Judy Carter walked in with three people in tow.

Shelby jumped up and regretted the fast action immediately but put on a smile. "It's so nice to see you, Judy. It seems that usually only happens at the library."

Judy chuckled. "It often seems like that's the only life I have. But I've taken the entire weekend off to enjoy a visit from my nephew Brendan," she said as she lightly touched his arm, "his wife, Callie, and their young daughter, Miranda. They're here from Plattsburgh."

Shelby could almost hear the word "finally" in Judy's tone, although she thought that might be fanciful.

"So nice to meet you all."

"Thanks," said Callie. "We've been meaning to take the boat tour of the castles, but this is the first year we thought Miranda might be the right age to get something from it, or at least remember it." She smiled at her daughter who grinned back.

Miranda turned her attention to Shelby. "What happened to your arm? Do you have any kid's books?"

Shelby smiled. Children could be so direct. "Well, I fell and banged up my elbow. And, I certainly do have lots of books for you to look at. Let me show you." She led the way to the small section next to one of the chairs. Brendan had followed and sat down while looking over Miranda's shoulder as she pulled out books to look at.

Callie had wandered over to the new releases section and Judy leaned against the counter watching the others, with a smile on her face.

"It's so nice they're able to visit you," Shelby said as she joined Judy. "Do you get to see them often?"

"Not often enough, but you know how it is. A busy young couple with a growing family."

Shelby thought to herself that she didn't really know how it was, having not been in that position, but she could imagine it. "When do they head home?"

"Unfortunately, as soon as we get back to the Bay. This is the final stop. I'll miss them, but I only worked half a day yesterday, so I have some things to prep at home before going in tomorrow."

Judy was silent a few minutes as she watched her family, then said, "I was thinking while I was going over the minutes from our last library board meeting that it's quite likely that I had actually met Nathan Miller after all. I'm sure he was on the library board in Fulsome Falls. Wasn't that where he was from? I remember meeting him one day. He was with Lynn Innes from our board and she introduced us. They were having coffee at Chocomania. I seem to remember she said they were comparing notes on joint purchasing between boards, or something like that."

"Really? So, he did know someone from around here. I wonder why she hasn't come forward."

"Why would she? Or maybe she has, and Chief Stone just isn't sharing the information." Judy said it so innocently that Shelby knew there'd been no criticism implied.

But Shelby's face flamed. Of course the chief wouldn't tell Shelby anything. That had been a dumb thing to say. Still, she was really curious as to whether Lynn Innes had any relevant information. Did she know who the mystery woman was? Obviously it wasn't her. Shelby realized just how little she'd connected with Chief Stone lately, other than being reprimanded. Not that she expected a free flow of information but, sometimes, if Shelby asked the right questions, she did get enough back to set her on the right track.

So, the question was, who to ask? Chief Stone or Lynn Innes?

Chapter Seventeen

S helby had her hand on the doorknob, shopping list in hand, when her cell phone rang. She fished it out of her purse and was pleased to hear Trudy's voice.

"I wanted to double check with you first thing this morning. I reached all of the book club members and they're keen on coming to my place tonight to make up for the meeting we'd had to cancel last week when I was sick. I thought, knowing how you have some questions once again, if you might be able to join us?"

"Sounds great, Trudy. I'll be there. Usual time?"

"Yes. Seven o'clock and, in case you have a chance to read the book today, it's Victoria Stuartson's latest." She chuckled as they said their goodbyes.

Shelby spent what was left of the morning after her shopping excursion doing what she could to vacuum and dust her home, hoping she would have time later at the store to organize her thoughts for the evening. She needed to make an actual list of questions to ask the Book Club Babes Plus One, who, between them, seemed to know every bit of gossip worth knowing in the town. But it had been a busy afternoon and, on the boat ride back home, she realized she hadn't put anything coherent together and she would just have to wing it. She'd been thinking about where the investigation was going, or not going as was the case for so long now, the questions should come easily.

She finished the smoothie she'd made as soon as she'd arrived home from work, knowing that going to the meeting of the book club on an empty stomach would mean stuffing herself with too many extra yummy foods and desserts. Not that she really had to worry. She'd long ago come to terms with her curves and fluctuating weight. But she didn't want to overload on sugar, and that was a favorite for the gang.

She arrived at Trudy's house at 7 PM on the nose, knowing most of the others would be there and ready to go. Over the past year, and in particular when the previous murders had occurred, Shelby had been a bit leery about talking to the members, even when she was there as a presenter. Their inquiring minds had a way of turning any discussion into one of speculation about the crimes. But tonight, she was relying on that fact to help her get some useful information. Besides, she readily admitted that these meetings were thoroughly enjoyable. They were such an interesting and fun group.

Before she could ring the doorbell, the door was answered by the hostess, who was wearing a bright multicolored caftan tonight, something Shelby would have expected to see on her aunt rather than the usually more conventionally dressed Trudy. But it did look good on her.

She pulled the door wide open. "You're just in time. The Babes are getting a bit rowdy," she explained, eyes twinkling.

Shelby could hear the raucous laughter as she hung up her jacket. She greeted them all with a big smile and noticed the Plus One was missing.

"Hi everyone. Thanks for letting me join in again." She chose the vacant seat next to Trudy.

Her gaze fell on each of them in turn. Dolly and Mimi, the eighty-year-old Noland twins, each waggled their fingers at her; Patricia had adopted a new hair color, a bright copper, something Shelby hadn't seen before; Juliette nodded, and the spiraling orange feather that topped her otherwise unusually plain green fascinator waved wildly; but what was even more unusual was the fact that Leonard Hopkins, the Plus One, wasn't at her side.

"Where's Leonard?"

"Oh, honey," Juliette answered. "He's running late." She leaned towards the center of the room and said in a loud whisper, "To tell the truth, I think he's picking up a birthday present for me. I heard him on the phone earlier." Her smile lit her entire face, making her look at least twenty years younger. Shelby thought he must give some great gifts.

"We heard all about your arm," Mimi said, her voice pitched high with excitement. "You brought down a thief all by yourself?"

Shelby smiled. "Not really. It was the other way around. He brought me down, but they caught him, so it's all good."

"That must be painful though," Patricia chimed in.

"Not so much. The splint is keeping it stable so I'm able to work, which is good."

"I hope it heals real quick, honey," Mimi added.

"Thanks. I appreciate your concern."

Trudy started the two plates of sweets to be passed around the room, one in each direction, while she poured the fruit punch for everyone. When they'd all settled, Trudy took charge.

"Why don't we get started discussing the book, even though Leonard's not here. We don't want it to be too late an evening." She glanced around the room and everyone nodded. "Good. Now, Dolly, why don't you start us off. What did you like best about our book for tonight? If anything?"

Dolly looked at them each before saying with a straight face, "The sex."

They were all still doubled over laughing when Leonard walked into the room a few minutes later. "Did I miss the best part?" he asked, his usual big smile on his face.

Patricia fanned herself with her hand. "I'll say, but we won't have Dolly repeat herself or we'll spend the rest of the evening crossing our legs and wiping our eyes."

"You all know I'm just kidding," Dolly said, this time with a smile. "There was no sex."

Leonard looked surprised but then chuckled as he helped himself to a drink and two of each of the sweets before sitting down between Juliette and Shelby.

"So nice to see you again, Shelby," he said. "We must be getting quite a reputation as a group, aren't we?"

"Somewhat," Shelby agreed, returning his smile. "But I'm enjoying being here, as usual."

"Good. Now, I know I should just keep quiet and listen until I'm caught up but I'm wondering to what do we owe the pleasure of Shelby's company. Isn't everyone else?"

"Oh, yes," said Mimi, clapping her hands.

Juliette nodded again, and Shelby worried the fascinator might take flight. Leonard reached for her hand and gave it a squeeze.

"Okay, you know me too well."

"I'll bet it has to do with the body she found," Patricia said before Shelby could say more. "Am I right?"

Shelby nodded. "I do have a few questions, and you are all so plugged into the community that I thought you might help me sort some things out."

"Oh, yes," Mimi said breathlessly. Her eyes sparkled, but then again, she'd put eye drops in them a few minutes ago.

"I heard the victim was from Fulsome Falls and that he'd been to town on more than one occasion, looking for someone. Am I right?"

"He did have other business here, but he came in the store a couple of time, saying he was looking for a woman who he thought might have moved here seven years ago. So, I was wondering, who might fit that bill? Can you think of anyone who's been living here since then?"

No one answered right off, in fact, Shelby thought the sweets had co-opted their attention. But after he'd finished the cookies on his plate, Leonard answered. "I'm pretty sure that Tamara person at that Bayview Garden Center place moved here around then." He looked at Juliette and explained. "That was the year I built my rockery garden and she gave me a lot of good advice. I know nothing else about her, where she came from or why she moved here, but I'm pretty sure about the year. That would definitely be seven years ago."

"No, Leonard, didn't you put that in the year that I had my gall bladder taken out? Remember, I sat recovering on the lounge chair in your garden, watching while you built it?"

"Are you sure? About the year, I mean. I do remember the surgery and recovery part of it."

"Of course, I'm sure. I remember each one of my surgeries," Juliette said, her middle finger tapping the back of his hand that rested on his leg.

"She does that," Dolly commented and Mimi snickered. Juliette ignored them both but peered around Leonard over to Shelby.

"So, that means she moved here six, not seven years ago, so she can't be your woman. And her name is Tamara Young." She gave Leonard a look then sat back in her chair and ate the brownie on her plate.

"I stand corrected," Leonard said with much decorum. "However, I would like to point out that I may have put the original rockery in six years ago but I totally rebuilt it four years ago."

"Okay, that's a start," Shelby said, trying to hide any look of amusement. "Can anyone think of anyone else who moved here in that time frame?"

Patricia raised her hand. "Alice over at the Style Shop has been in town about that long."

Shelby couldn't think of anything to say, but knew she couldn't leave that suggestion hanging. "You're right," she said, "but I know it wasn't her."

"Well, I was just mentioning her because I remember that she took over Bea's job. Remember Bea Wilson?" She looked around at everyone and they all nodded. "She passed seven years ago. Cancer."

The mood in the room had definitely changed.

"Yes, Bea was such a lovely woman, and I know she's still missed," Trudy said. "Well, I can't think of anyone else, Shelby. Maybe we should get on with the book now, and if anyone thinks of something later, they can give you a call at the store. All right?"

"That would be fine."

Leonard cleared his throat. "Well, I found the book a bit disconcerting. The protagonist was certainly a self-centered, scheming woman with only one thing on her mind."

"Sex." Mimi said it this time, but the laughter wasn't quite as raucous.

Later, as Shelby was getting ready for bed, she thought about the evening and how much she'd enjoyed being with them all. Another thing she might have to give up if she moved back to Boston.

She realized she'd been so busy coming up with a list of "cons", she'd neglected the "pros." The major one being, of course, that she'd be with Zack.

But was that enough?

Chapter Eighteen

Another new lead. Shelby had hoped to find out something useful the night before and the Babes, actually the Plus One, had possibly obliged. Tamara Young. She'd never met the landscaper, but of course, Shelby didn't garden. Even if she lived in a real house surrounded by greenery, she doubted she'd try her hand at it. It seemed that Edie had gotten the entire allotment of the green thumb gene in the Cox family. Her dad hadn't been interested either. Which was fine by Shelby. She did find it odd that Matthew hadn't mentioned Ms. Young, though. The landscaping community in the Bay must be small and known to all involved in the trade. But maybe Matthew dealt with only one company, and not this one. And so, they may not have met. She must stop second-guessing herself. That could lead to embarrassing, or possibly even dangerous, assumptions. What was that old adage about never assuming?

She smiled as she got ready for work. She'd let JT out first thing in the morning and now she wondered if he'd be back from exploring before she had to leave. If not, she'd stash some of his dry food out on the deck and hope he'd be there at the end of the day. Funny, even though he'd been with her for over a year now, she still couldn't help but wonder each time she opened the door if he might move on to newer treats. She'd sure miss him if that was the case. She shook her head. No assumptions. He'd be waiting for her. And If he wasn't?

She supposed she was transferring her unease about her future with Zack to the cat. What would she do if she let him go on his own and the long-distance relationship turned out to be an unhappy one? What if she lost him?

And, what would she do with JT? Could she bring him?

Man, she was really in a state this morning. Time to shake away all of the uneasy thoughts and focus on meeting lots of new people and selling lots of books.

She started the day at the bookstore leaving her sling off, which made it easier to do certain tasks like shelve books. She was able to balance and shove with her bad arm but she then found, after about an hour, that it started to ache. She slipped the sling back on and finished the shelving, in between serving customers.

Just before noon, a group of tourists all wearing identical red baseball caps with the tour company logo on it wandered into the store, practically bursting it at the seams until several decided to leave the space to the book lovers. Shelby breathed a sigh of relief and stopped worrying that some of the stone cats and book-shaped novelties might be shoved off their displays and break on the floor. They'd decided to add the tchotchkes a few weeks earlier, and Shelby was pleased with the sales. In fact, she had been thinking about adding to the variety of items they'd carry and was looking forward to meeting with the specialty sales rep who'd booked an appointment with her in a couple of weeks.

One of the tour group women, a short, slightly stooped woman in her later years, elbowed her way to the desk and set one of the ceramic cats, sitting on an open book, next to the computer.

"I just love cats," she explained to Shelby, her voice a low rasp. "Especially ones with books."

Shelby smiled as she wrapped the feline as best she could and placed it in a bag, making a mental note to order some bubble wrap and tissue paper. "We're getting more of a variety in very soon. Maybe next time you're in the area . . ."

The woman snorted. "I live in Tulsa, dear. I doubt there'll be a next time, but this one will do nicely."

Shelby watched the woman as she continued to elbow her way through her travel mates on her way out of the bookstore. When Shelby turned back to the cash, there was another customer, a male who appeared only slightly younger than the woman, holding a book out to her.

"I'll take this one, unless there's another local history book you'd recommend as being a better read?"

Shelby looked at the title. *A Floating World* by Paul Malo. It was one she'd also read. "I think you'll be pleased with this choice," she said as she placed it in a bag.

As the customers started trickling out of the store, many with purchases gripped in their hands, Chrissie walked in.

"I just wanted to see how you're doing," she told Shelby. She threw a dubious look at the sling. "How much longer will you have to wear that?"

"I actually had it off for a while this morning, so I'll try it for a bit longer each day."

"How are you feeling? Is it still painful? You know, I feel responsible for it happening."

"You do? Why's that? It had nothing to do with you."

"Well, if the security was a bit tighter, maybe that guy wouldn't have knocked you over on his way out the door." Chrissie's gaze wandered around the store. She seemed distinctly uncomfortable, not at all the way she usually came across.

"I can't imagine how tighter security would have changed that, unless you had turnstiles or something at the door, and we know that's not about to happen."

Chrissie shrugged. "You're right about that but still . . ."

Shelby put her good hand on Chrissie's arm. "I'm getting better every day. Don't worry about it. Now, I have a question for you. Do you know Tamara Young who works at Bayview Garden Center?"

"I do. How do you know her?" Her eyes darted to the large bird's nest fern next to the window to the left of the counter. "Did she recommend the fern? It's new isn't it?"

"It is, but I didn't get if from her. I don't know Tamara, not yet anyway. But Leonard Hopkins mentioned at the book club last night that she moved here about seven years ago, which is right about the time the woman who Nathan Miller was looking for moved here." *Of course, he did change that to six years.*

"Oh, I don't think she moved here seven years ago." She shrugged. "Or, maybe it was. I shouldn't say because I didn't meet her until a couple of years ago, but I'd heard she was fairly new to town then."

"Do you know anything about her personal life, like where she came from? Or why she moved here?"

Chrissie looked like she was giving it some serious thought. "I don't think so. At least, we never discussed it. I don't know her personally, only to ask gardening questions. Wouldn't Matthew know? I mean, he dealt with her. Oh, just a sec. I think she did mention at one time, something about a fire I think, but I don't remember any of the details. In fact, she may not have shared anything with me because I don't really know her that well. We had a few chats when she was busy helping Matthew with the gardens."

So, Matthew does know her. I wonder why he didn't mention her? "And you haven't thought of anyone else in town who fits the description?"

"No but I can see you're spending a lot of time thinking about it. Does Chief Stone know that? Well, you know I'm your biggest supporter, so you can bet I won't say anything to her."

Shelby flashed a smile. She didn't realize she actually had supporters.

*   *   *

When Laura came in for the afternoon shift, Shelby was able to take the same boat back to the mainland. She stood at the railing during the trip back to Alexandria Bay. The sun was warm and, although the wind cooled things down, she enjoyed watching the water churning out from the sides of the craft. Her gaze shifted to the shoreline as it became more visible, picking out the two hotels, the houses overlooking the river to the west of town, and then back to the main wharf. She could see there was a long lineup awaiting the next sailing. That could translate into a busy afternoon at the store, she hoped.

Once she'd exited at the dock, she decided to treat herself to a latte before heading to the Bayview Garden Center.

The mid-afternoon coffee lovers were out in full force at Chocomania, she thought as she waited in line to order. When her turn came, Erica first wanted to know how her elbow was doing, then how Shelby was doing in general. Shelby felt like writing out a diagnosis on a card and handing it out to those she met, however, she realized, that was being snippy. Erica was a special person and her concern meant a lot to Shelby. Every now and then though, Shelby found herself slipping back into her old ways, not wanting to share her feelings, and not being used to anyone asking about her or her well-being.

She watched as a mother and two toddlers left a table, then she sat down quickly and enjoyed sipping her latte, trying not to let her mind dwell on anything distressing. She needed this downtime, which quickly changed to chat time as Erica sat down across from her, a coffee cradled in her hands.

"I so need a break. I'm wondering if I should give Rainbow more hours each day."

"It looks like she's good with customers. Did she get the job at Driftwood and Seawinds?" Shelby turned slightly to the left to watch the recent addition to Chocomania. Previously it had just been Erica taking care of the customers, while an elusive, white-gowned chocolate helper stayed in the kitchen. Shelby caught glimpses of that woman every now and then and, although they'd never been introduced, Shelby did know that her name was Sharon and that she helped out a few hours most mornings, starting before the store opened to the public.

"Yes, Rainbow got the job, and I'm pleased for her. She's still talking shifts with them, so I know I've got to make a decision and get my bid in for more hours now, before they decide on days and hours."

Rainbow might have guessed they were discussing her since she looked up at them and smiled. It made her look less severe. It was her hair, Shelby realized, that gave Rainbow a no-nonsense appearance, with it pulled tightly back and the single silver nose ring drawing attention even when Shelby tried not to focus on it.

"I guess I'm just so used to doing it all myself," Erica continued. "I've been doing it so long on my own since my last barista left. It's sort of hard letting go again, even a little bit, you know?"

"Oh, believe me, I do. This splitting shifts with Laura at the bookstore is a good thing but also, driving me a bit bonkers."

"Uh-huh. I hear you. Speaking of which, I was wondering why you have this afternoon off. This isn't the usual day, is it, or have I lost track? Or are you up to something totally mysterious and top secret?"

"No, nothing quite so exciting, and you're right, it's not my usual afternoon off. But this time it was Laura who wanted to switch, and it's worked out for me as well."

"I'll bet you have lots of ideas on how you're going to use this time. Now, any news about anything? Or, anyone?"

"Not about the one you're probably asking about. As for the murder, I was told about Tamara Young. Do you know her? She works at the Bayview Garden Center."

"Uh, we've met but I can't imagine why you and your famous black thumb are asking, except that you wonder if she's the mystery woman?"

"You know me so well. What do you think?"

"Do you know when she moved here? Isn't that the criteria?" Erica stood and grabbed a cloth from behind the counter and wiped down their table, taking her time moving their cups.

"I was hoping you'd know when she moved here."

"No, not that I can think of. It's never come up in conversation from what I can recall. She's mainly a landscaper, but she did give me advice when I was choosing some new plants for the shop."

Shelby followed Erica's gaze around the room. There was a huge fern of some sort in the far corner, maybe four feet wide, hugging the window. And another large fernlike plant in the opposite corner, street side. Plus, a small collection of plants that looked like cactus on one corner of the counter.

"I hadn't really noticed how much live greenery you have in here these days. My eyes always go to the espresso machine first, well that's after looking for you, and the truffles of course, and then to the photos on the wall. I just love the chocolate and the kids." She allowed her eyes to flow over the variety of pictures, both color and black and white, that graced the walls while Erica excused herself to go serve a couple more customers and help ease the lineup that seemed to be forming.

When Shelby finished her latte, she took her mug up to the counter and asked Erica, "Who took that amazing black-and-white photo? It's new, isn't it?" She pointed to an 8 x 10-inch picture hanging on the wall across from the door of a toddler gazing at a plate of truffles. *A younger version of me.*

"That was taken by C. C. Connors. He lives in Watertown but has showings all around the state. I lucked out a few years ago when he came to Clayton. I bought his photo of the hot chocolate being slowly poured into the mug that's been hanging here. I found this new one last week online and decided to switch things up a bit. It's a perfect fit for in here, isn't it?"

"I'll say. I always wanted to try my hand at photography."

"Well, why haven't you?"

Shelby shrugged. "I don't know. Either there were other things to do, or I stalled at the decision-making point, you know, do you start with a course or just dive in?"

Erica chuckled. "Good luck with that. But let me know if you decide to just go with it. I might join you, especially if you take photos outdoors."

"Really? That would be fun. I will give it serious thought and let you know." She glanced at her watch. The afternoon was escaping her. "I'd better get going and see if I can track down Ms. Young. See you later."

She waved at Rainbow behind the counter and left, pausing to enjoy the sun shining on her face before turning right and walking up the street toward the highway. She knew it would be a lengthy walk so she doubled back to grab her car.

The parking lot at the garden center didn't look too full, but when she opened the door to the store, there were a lot of customers to make their way through. Of course, it was a small store stocking mainly tools, ornamental objects for the garden, and water features.

Seeing that there were five customers lined up at the cash register, Shelby took a quick walk around the store, spotting some possible birthday gift ideas for Edie. She had a couple of months to buy something, but there were so many things that looked ideal, she decided she might as well get something now. She gravitated over to the display of stepping stones and chose two, both rectangular, one with a floral design and the other saying welcome. She decided to give the set of solar lights some more thought.

When it was her turn to pay, she stepped up and then asked if Tamara Young was around.

"Tamara? She's probably out back in the shrub area," answered the young girl. She looked to be in her late teens, wearing a khaki-colored shirt with the garden center logo, an embroidered green shrub, sewn above the left-hand pocket. Noticing Shelby's questioning look, she added, "Just go through that door on the right, walk through the potted plants and out the other side. That's where the shrubs are. If she's not there, check in the perennials."

"Thanks."

Shelby picked up her packages and followed the directions, suddenly realizing that such heavy purchases had not been should be taken out to the car first. She spotted a man and a woman at the far end of a row of shrubs and made her way over to them. As she got closer, he walked away.

The woman, as tall as the six-foot shrub she seemed to be working on, had her long brown hair pulled back into a single braid. She looked to be in her late forties but that could have been because her skin looked like it was permanently tanned and weathered. She looked up from the list she'd been checking off and looked over at Shelby.

"Are you Tamara Young?" Shelby asked.

"I am. What can I do for you?"

"I'm Shelby Cox, co-owner of Bayside Books. I know we've never met but we do have a mutual friend, Matthew Kessler."

"Sure, I know him from the castle."

"That's right. I actually run the bookstore location in Blye Castle. I just love the landscaping around there. Matthew says much of it is thanks to you."

"He's being generous, but I do love my work. Are you thinking of doing your yard or something?"

"Not really. I live on a houseboat," Shelby said with a chuckle.

"Yeah, rather hard I guess although you could probably handle some hanging baskets and planters, I'd think."

"You're right. Any suggestions?"

"Follow me."

Tamara led the way into the covered greenhouse and went directly to the annuals section, picking up two hanging baskets bursting with color. "What about these? You do have someplace you could hang them, right?"

"I guess, sure. One at least by the door, either one. I think pots would be more practical though." She looked around and her face lit up. "I like that tall red one. It would look great on the upper deck. And maybe one more." What was she doing? She wasn't a plant person and she certainly hadn't planned on buying anything.

Tamara walked over to the door and came back with a metal trolley, placing the bright red one on it. She then got a second, shorter pot in lime green and held it up. Shelby nodded.

"How about flowers to go in them. You could buy hanging planters and just place them inside the pots."

Oh, well. "Sure. What would you suggest?"

Tamara disappeared a minute then came back with two planters, filled with multicolored plants. As she paid for them, Shelby felt pleased, knowing they'd add a cheery touch to her home. Tamara helped her load the car.

"I think you'll be pleased with your purchases," she said.

"I'm sure I will. Say, before I go, do you mind if I ask you something?"

Tamara looked curious. "About plant care?"

"No. You see, I'm the person who found the dead body last week, in case you heard about that. I'm just trying to get some perspective on his death."

"How could I possibly help with that?"

"I know it seems strange. But does the name Nathan Miller mean anything to you?"

"No, should it?"

"That's the name of the man who died. He's from Fulsome Falls—a couple of hours from here. But he came to Alexandria Bay looking for a specific woman. He said she'd moved here about seven years ago."

"I get it. And you think since I'm a relative newcomer that it could be me?"

Shelby shrugged. "Just wondering. I'm really curious who she is." She wondered what Tamara was thinking.

"Well, I'm not the person. Not only do I not know this man, I moved here six years ago." She sighed and pulled her gloves off to tuck a stray strand of hair behind her ear. "I'd left Albany a couple of years before that and moved to Watertown but decided it wasn't for me. So, here I am."

She shrugged and put the gloves back on. "Now, I don't see how I can be of any help so if there's nothing else, we've got to check this inventory before tonight."

"No, there's nothing else. Thanks very much, though."

"Uh-huh. If you have any more questions, though, about the plants I mean, don't hesitate to get in touch." Tamara had already dismissed Shelby, turning back to her colleague and checking tags once again.

As Shelby drove home, she thought over what she'd achieved, aside from the unexpected purchases. Six years didn't seem far off seven. But there didn't seem to be any surprises with Tamara, nothing being covered up. At least, she didn't think so.

However, Shelby reminded herself, she'd been wrong before.

Chapter Nineteen

Shelby woke up on Wednesday morning, and realized, from the soreness of her left arm, what a mistake yesterday's decision had been to carry all her garden center purchases from the car to the houseboat. She decided to take her mind off it she would revisit what Tamara had said. She'd first moved to Watertown but then came to Alexandria Bay. What if the mystery woman had done the same? What if, seven years ago she had moved to town A and then, at another point, moved to Alex Bay? Or, moved to the Bay but now was no longer here? Maybe he'd been on a wild-goose chase, but something must have tweaked his interest recently. Otherwise, he would have asked around about his mystery woman much sooner, right? After all, he'd been in and out of the village for over a year. There seemed to be two possibilities. Either someone had mentioned her or he must have seen her.

Shelby perked up. Maybe he saw her, followed her to the island, confronted her, and she killed him. But if that were the case why had the mystery woman come to Blye Island? And how would they ever find her? Was she someone local or a tourist Nathan saw in the lineup for the cruise?

Or maybe he had a meeting with someone who turned out to be his killer or was he followed to the island? Maybe he'd even been followed to the Bay. Was it the mystery woman who killed him or was his death not related to her at all? And, they were no closer to finding out anything about the mysterious deposits nor Nathan's trips out of town. And what, if anything, did the eagle feather have to do with it? He did have it in his pocket. Again, it could mean nothing.

Give it up. She was driving herself crazy and she had a busy day ahead.

Partway through the morning, Shelby received a call from Walter Nevins's office saying he would see her at 1:30 that day. She thought about phoning Hilary but decided she should wait until she'd talked to him. Hopefully, she'd have something useful to share.

By the time Laura arrived at the store, Shelby was ready to leave but waited until the next boat in order to help out with a sudden influx of shoppers. Back on the mainland, Shelby had time to stop in at Chocomania and order a liquid lunch.

"This should keep me going," she told Erica, sipping the hot latte. "I have an appointment shortly at the council offices, so I'm gonna grab my car and be off."

"How about we get together later this week for dinner or something?" Erica suggested.

"Love to. Can we nail down a day when I come in tomorrow?"

Erica nodded, already moving onto the next customer. "See you then."

Shelby nodded and took another, longer sip before heading to her car.

She reached Walt Nevins's office with ten minutes to spare. The same young woman sat at the reception desk and smiled at her when Shelby walked in.

"Thanks for helping arrange this appointment," Shelby said, not really sure if that's what had happened but at least Mr. Nevins had gotten her message.

"No problem. He's really got a busy schedule, not like some of the guys around here who like to pretend they're busy." She smiled and Shelby noticed her braces were gone. *I'll bet that feels so much better.*

Shelby chuckled. "Have you worked here long?"

"Around six months. I was sort of unsure what I wanted to do after high school and a friend had gotten a job here and said I should apply. So here I am."

"Great. Do you like the job?"

Mandy shrugged. "Sometimes. Some of it. Mr. Nevins is a good guy but some of the others. . . " She let the thought trail off and punctuated it with another shrug.

Roman Sykes appeared at his office door at that moment and gave Shelby a surprised look. He didn't bother to say anything, though, and turned to go back inside his office.

"Like that guy," Mandy said in a low voice. "Not nice unless it gets him somewhere."

The door to Nevins's office opened at that moment and he welcomed Shelby inside.

"I want to thank you for meeting me," Shelby started.

He held up his hand. "It's not a problem, but I should let you know, I don't have much time." He looked like he was smoothing his hair back over his head but he was bald. Perhaps recently so, Shelby thought. His squint also led her to believe he needed glasses. He wore a blue sports shirt with the sleeves rolled up to his elbows, and no tie.

"Now," he continued, an encouraging smile on his face. "What's this all about? You mentioned Nathan Miller?"

"Yes. I was in here the other day with his daughter, but she had to go back home to Fulsome Falls. She just was curious about what her dad was doing here. We know his consulting firm has a contract with the town and that you're his contact person."

"That's correct. He's been working with us for about a year and a half now. It was such a shock to hear about what had happened to him. And here, in Alexandria Bay. I can't quite believe it all."

"Did he mention any other reason he might have for coming to town? Or anyone?"

Nevins seemed to give it some thought. "Not that I can recall him mentioning. Why do you ask?"

"Well, he had stopped into some stores, mine included, asking about a woman he thought had moved here."

"No, he never mentioned it to me. Look, even though he was a friendly guy, we never really got around to discussing anything personal. And we didn't socialize. He was good at what he did and always met the deadlines, so that was all that I really cared about." He glanced at his watch. "Look, I'm sorry, but I have a meeting to prepare for." He stood and offered his hand. "I'm sorry I couldn't be of more help."

Shelby shook his hand. "Thanks for seeing me. I appreciate it." Shelby thanked Mandy again, as she walked past her desk.

"No problem." Mandy gave her a wide smile.

Shelby walked back to her car slowly. It seemed a bit odd to her that Nevins wouldn't have had a meal with his out-of-town colleague or something. She glanced up at the fourth-floor windows and noticed someone at a window, watching her or maybe just looking at the parking lot.

She was certain it was Roman Sykes.

* * *

Shelby's next stop was the main bookstore, where she hoped to pick up a supply of bags. They'd recently ordered some paper bags with small handles that were good for the environment, as an experiment. So far, the feedback had been good. And she needed more. She'd suggest they place another order, fast.

When she walked through the door, she could hear Edie over in the far corner, speaking loudly to a customer, someone Shelby didn't recognize, from the back anyway. Shelby hadn't heard Edie use that angry tone before and couldn't imagine what would set her aunt off like that. The woman appeared to be well-dressed, in a tailored navy suit, the sunlight beaming through the front window highlighting auburn highlights in the curly dark hair that caressed her shoulders. And, she wasn't backing away. Shelby couldn't tell how old she was.

Shelby decided she'd just duck out rather than interrupt whatever was happening. It wasn't like Edie to treat a customer that way, so whatever was going on, it must be personal. But, from the back, the woman didn't look like any of Edie's friends, either. Not that she'd known Edie to argue with anyone. She'd be sure to ask about it later but for now, she decided to discreetly leave.

Edie glanced her way, which caused the customer to do the same. Nobody said anything for several seconds and then the stranger spoke first. "Are you Shelby? Of course, you are. I'd know you anywhere." Her smile had softened, and she'd extended her right hand as she moved towards Shelby.

Interesting. "Yes, I am." Shelby felt an odd tingling at the back of her neck and stayed where she was.

"No, don't you dare do it," Edie said, her voice tight, as she reached out and grabbed the woman's left arm.

Shelby saw the fury in the woman's face before she turned back to Edie and pushed her hand off. "That's not for you to say, Edie."

Edie sidestepped the woman and got in front of her, blocking the way to where Shelby stood, her mouth hanging open. She couldn't believe what was going on. It was totally surreal. This wasn't her calm, friendly aunt. Shelby's mind whirled.

"We'll let Shelby decide," said the woman. "She's a grown woman."

Edie and this woman stood, trying to stare each other down. Shelby felt frozen in time until the stranger finally said, her voice softer, "I know you care, Edie. I get that and it's wonderful. You've been amazing all these years. But I care, too, even if it hasn't seemed that way."

"You have a funny way of showing that."

"Yes, well I don't claim to have done the smart or right thing. Please, just let me try to make things right."

"You're doing this for yourself, for your conscience."

"I'm doing it for Shelby, too."

Shelby took a couple of steps backward, suddenly chilled with a feeling of dread in the pit of her stomach. She knew what was coming, although at the same time, she felt like she didn't. She felt like running away but, instead, she waited, holding her breath.

She saw Edie's shoulders sag and knew the battle had been lost and won. Edie stepped aside and plunked down on the arm of a chair, watching Shelby, a hopeless look on her face. The woman took several steps forward, then stopped.

"Oh, your arm. What happened? I hope it's not too bad." She looked and sounded flustered. "I guess I didn't have this well thought out, but we're all here, so it's best just to say it straight out. Shelby, I'm Merrily, your mother."

Shelby felt hot and cold, sick to her stomach and joyous, scared, and happy, all at once. Words wouldn't or couldn't make their way to her mouth. But both women were watching her, waiting for her reaction

"I'm sorry, but I can't deal with this right now," Shelby said and ran out the door.

She heard her mother calling after her, but she kept walking fast, all the way to the houseboat. Once inside, she locked the door and sat down on the loveseat. JT came charging down the stairs and leapt onto her lap, stretching his front legs up and pushing his head under her chin. She patted him without saying anything, staying that way for a long time until he curled up in her lap and started his grooming routine. She couldn't process what had just happened. Her mind was in shutdown mode.

She wasn't sure how long she sat like that before she heard a knock on her door and Edie calling out to her, "Please let me in, honey. I want to help."

She'd wanted to be alone but suddenly she wanted to have Edie with her. She placed JT on the spot she'd been sitting and unlocked the door. Edie swept in, took a close look at Shelby, and walked her over to the loveseat.

"Sit here while I get you something."

Shelby heard her rummaging through the cupboards and then she came back with a glass of red wine.

"I couldn't find anything stronger, which is what you need after such a shock, but this will help." She sat down beside Shelby. "Drink."

Shelby took several sips and then finally asked, "How dare she, after all this time? She has some nerve. What is she doing here?"

Edie took hold of Shelby's free hand and gave it a small squeeze. "She just waltzed in out of the blue a few hours ago and said she was here to make amends. She wanted to see you. She said something about asking for your forgiveness."

Shelby could tell from Edie's voice that she didn't think much of that.

"But why now, after all this time?" she repeated. She hadn't realized she was shaking until Edie reached out and squeezed her am.

"It seems that her husband died last year, and I guess that really hit home. You know, the death of a loved one can have you re-evaluating your life, especially in your later years."

Shelby took another sip and turned to face Edie. "Do you believe her? I mean about her reason for being here?"

"I guess I do. I mean, why else would she come here? I'd imagine it's a very hard thing for her to do. But that doesn't mean I agree with what she's doing. I know how hard it was for you to accept the fact that she'd run off in the first, and I'm betting you still have some bad times about it. So, for her to suddenly appear? Uh-uh. I wasn't going to let her put you through that. I was trying to send her on her way when you showed up unexpectedly."

She paused and, after a few moments added, her voice weary, "Which may have been the wrong thing to do."

Shelby just stared. She wasn't sure herself what the right thing would have been.

Chapter Twenty

Sleepless in Alex Bay. That would make a good movie title, Shelby thought, as the phrase kept returning throughout a restless night. She knew if she didn't get some sleep, she'd be a wreck at work the next day but it was hard getting to that point. She tried thinking about Zack and was happy he hadn't called that night. She wouldn't have known what to say to him about Merrily, and she knew he'd realize she was upset about something. She needed to wrap her head around what this meant before she could share it with anyone else. Then she tried switching her focus to the murder, but she still wasn't able to get past the basic facts. Mainly because there weren't too many other ones, aside from the fact that he had a bank account that surprised his daughter and had a consulting job in Alex Bay, also unknown to his family. And then there was that woman no one seemed to know about.

Shelby even skipped getting her usual latte on the way to the island the next morning, knowing Erica would immediately know something was up and not wanting to mention yet that her mom was back in town. So, bleary-eyed even after two cups of coffee at home, Shelby stayed out on the deck during the short ride, hoping the chilly wind and occasional spray of water would do the trick and perk her up or, at least, give her a burst of energy.

The phone rang at almost the same second Shelby was unlocking the door to the store. It was Edie.

"I'm just checking to see how you're doing today. Did you manage to get any sleep?"

"Not much, I have to admit. And I'm not really sure how I'm doing. It's still just too weird, you know? I keep hoping to be hit by this bolt of awareness or maturity, something that will tell me what to do next."

"Well, you could tell her you don't want to see her. Or, you could go out for a coffee with her and hear what she has to say. So, two choices, really." Edie sounded so calm and reasoned, compared to her reaction in the store.

Deep down inside, Shelby knew that she had just been skirting the issue. "Thanks, Edie. Right, as usual."

"Look, honey, if you'd like the day off to sort things out, I'd be happy to send Trudy over. I can manage here on my own."

"No, I'll be okay." She looked around the store and immediately had second thoughts. "Actually, that might be a good idea. I do think I need some alone time to first wrap my head around this and figure out how I feel. You sure you don't mind working solo? Laura might be available."

Edie chuckled. "I can do this with eyes shut and my feet up, so don't you worry about that. I've been doing it for over thirty years, after all. I'll send Trudy on the next boat as soon as she gets in. Give me a call if you want to talk, okay?"

"I will. And thanks, Aunt Edie."

Shelby quickly got the coffee going and did some quick tidying, all the while trying to remember if she'd planned anything special at the store for that day. She knew she had to give Nora a call sometime today, but she could do that later from home. When Trudy arrived on the first boat of the morning, Shelby was ready to hop onto it as it swung back for a return trip to the Bay. She didn't know how much Edie had told Trudy but, fortunately, she asked no questions. Shelby was grateful for that. She thanked Trudy and made her escape.

Once on board, she found a seat by the window and spent the trip staring at the world passing by, trying not to think about anything. She'd been a practitioner of mindfulness when she'd lived in Boston, but hadn't done much of it lately. Time to make more regular use of that skill, obviously.

The thought did manage to creep in that, despite what she'd said earlier, what she really needed was to give her brain a rest from trying to puzzle out what to do about Merrily. She did have one task she'd been meaning to do, so this seemed as good a time as ever to tackle that and then get back to making decisions, hopefully with a clearer mind.

When she left the boat, Shelby pulled out her cellphone and checked the address for Lynn Innes that she'd googled the day before. She'd wanted to pay her a visit ever since hearing her name from Judy Carter, but she hadn't gotten around to it. It looked to be another easy walk. That was one of the many appealing perks of living in Alexandria Bay. She seldom needed to use her car though it was nice to have it for occasional weekend excursions or longer errands.

In no time at all, she found herself in front of Lynn's house, a two-story Cape Cod style with white siding. She guessed it to be a bit on the pricey side and also noted the accompanying Lexus parked in the driveway. She realized she should have put her walking time to better use and come up with an idea of how to approach Lynn. Sometimes the straightforward one didn't work best. She guessed all she could do was play it by ear and took a deep breath as she walked up to the front door to push the doorbell.

After a brief wait, the door was opened by a woman who had at least two-inches on Shelby in the height department, and about thirty years in age.

"Yes?"

"Are you Lynn Innes?"

"I am. And who are you?" Her expression was one of curiosity. Shelby wondered how long it would take to turn it to one more closed or worse yet, threatening.

"I'm Shelby Cox, from Bayside Books. I was wondering if you had a couple of minutes? I'd like to ask you a couple of questions. It won't take long."

The look of curiosity held on Lynn's face. "I'm intrigued. Fine, come in."

After Shelby had placed her jacket on the parson's bench in the entry, she followed Lynn into the formal living room just off to the left.

"This is a lovely room." Shelby let her gaze wander over the large selection of sizes and styles of artwork that decorated the walls. "What an amazing collection."

They were the backdrop to a room done in a variety of shades of pink. Nothing too glaring and all of it matching. Shelby would have bet this was a professional job because even though she wasn't too fond of pink, she found herself admiring the room.

Lynn smiled. "Yes, my husband Charlie and I are collectors. We like to help new artists along in their journey, but also we can't resist our favorites from some of the more established ones."

Shelby watched Lynn as she looked around her room with satisfaction beaming on her face. Her short, dark hair sported a wide swath of silver that framed her face, which looked fully made up, even on a weekday. Of course, Shelby's version of make-up consisted mainly of eyeshadow and lipstick, with maybe something a bit more dramatic around the eyes for a date. In fact, the black pencil skirt and lavender sweater set, obviously cashmere, seemed a bit much for a weekday, too. Maybe she was just about to head out somewhere, in which case, Shelby thought she'd better get on with the questions.

"Won't you have a seat? Now what can I do for you?" Lynn asked.

Shelby sat across from her and steeled herself. "I heard you were a friend of Nathan Miller. My condolences on the loss of your friend."

Lynn gasped and Shelby could see she was truly rattled. Was it his death or her mentioning the friendship, or both?

"I'm not quite sure where you got that impression. I do know that's the name of the body that was found in the Bay recently. It was the talk of the town for days. Now, I don't think I can be of any help, and I was just on my way out."

Lynn stood up but Shelby remained seated. She couldn't believe how rude she had become and how quickly. No, maybe that was too harsh, more like pushy, in the extreme.

"I was hoping you'd know who it was he came to town looking for. I don't mean to cause you any trouble or embarrassment, but I'm sure that information could be related to his murder."

Lynn sat back down. "And why is his death so important to you?"

"I found his body, and it's stayed with me. And also, his daughter is a friend. I know the police are good at their job, but I just have these questions that won't go away." There, she'd said it. Hopefully, they were the right words.

Lynn looked to be in thought but then she asked, "How are his family taking it?"

That surprised Shelby. Was that an admission that she knew him after all?

"As well as can be expected, I guess. I know only his daughter who, as you can imagine is quite anxious to get some answers, too. I know how it feels. When I lost my own dad, I tried desperately to get all the details. I needed to know in order to get closure, although I'm still not sure if I've managed to achieve that."

Lynn shook her head. "Hilary, isn't it?" She didn't wait for an answer but, rather, took a deep breath and intertwined her fingers then stood again, walking over to the dark carved mantle above the fireplace. She looked at a display of four framed photos for a few minutes. Shelby couldn't see the actual pictures but, from the sag of Lynn's shoulder, she knew they were meaningful.

When Lynn turned back to face Shelby, her expression was one of determination. "I can't believe I'm about to tell you all this, but I do feel badly about his death. And I'd like to help his daughter if I can. I know she was important to him. However, this is to be kept in strictest confidence. Do I have your word on that?"

Shelby nodded but didn't respond.

"I have known Nathan for many years. He was on the library board in Fulsome Falls, and I have the same role here, but I'm sure you already know that. We seemed to have a lot in common and became very close friends, meeting for coffee or lunch whenever he was in town. He was doing some consulting work here, you know."

"So, you saw quite a bit of him?"

"Well, uh, you could say that."

Shelby had the impression that despite Lynn's demeanor, she was uncomfortable talking about this. "Did he happen to mention that he was looking for a woman who'd moved here about seven years ago?"

"He did, actually, the last time I saw him."

"When was that?"

"A few weeks before he died." Her voice broke and she tried to cover it with a cough.

"Did he happen to say why he wanted to find her?"

"No, but he said he thought he'd seen her in the village one day. He described her but it could have been anyone. I was really curious, though, I mean, he was a married man."

"He was." Shelby gave some thought to what she was about to say. She could be way off base but she felt she wasn't. She just wasn't sure what Lynn's reaction would be. Probably not a good one.

"I shouldn't ask this but, as I said, I'm trying to find out why he died, so I'm hoping you'll excuse me. But, was there a bit more than friendship between you and Nathan?"

The shock showed on Lynn's face and then her expression hardened. "That's hardly any of your business. I said we were friends. That's all you need to know. I don't know anything else about any of this." She stood as she added, "I think you should go."

Shelby asked as she walked toward the door. "Did your husband know Nathan?"

Lynn's hand flew to her mouth. "Charlie? He has nothing to do with this. And I hope you won't speak to him about any of this."

Shelby knew deep down that she had no business nosing into the Lynn's private life. But what if she had been having an affair and what if her husband knew about it? And what if he was the killer?

"I won't talk to your husband, but I do want to know if Chief Stone has talked to you about Nathan Miller?"

Lynn looked startled. "The police chief? No, why would she?"

"Because she needs to know everything about Nathan's goings-on in Alexandra Bay." Shelby's gaze didn't waver as she watched the emotions passing over Lynn's face.

"All right. I can understand that. I'll give her a call in the morning."

"That's good. Thank you for talking to me."

Lynn nodded and Shelby left. She let out the breath she'd been holding as she closed the door behind herself.

Maybe she was way off base but she doubted it. There had been something going on between Lynn Innes and Nathan Miller, and she was sure it wasn't just friendship. But had it led to his death?

Chapter
Twenty-One

S helby leaned over the railing of the shuttle the next morning, feeling mesmerized by the roiling water being thrown aside as they headed to the island. She felt a kinship with the churning water, her mind also swirling with too much to think about. Why did all this have to be happening at the same time and right now? Just when she had finally started to feel like Alex Bay was her home, Zack hit her with the news of his move, and now Merrily shows up, wanting back into her life. And, of course, there was the murder. When had life gotten so complicated?

She didn't find an answer in the deep, dark waters, so turned her gaze to Heart Island and it's magnificent Boldt Castle, as they passed. There was so much history and grandeur in the Thousand Islands. And to think it was all right there for the touching. Who wouldn't want to call it home?

She tried to focus on her own piece of this wonderland as she made her way up the path to Blye Castle. She was pleased she'd taken the previous day off, even though she hadn't reached any conclusions about either of her personal dilemmas. At least she felt more in control of her emotions. Hopefully, Lynn would be true to her word and talk to the chief today. That was the best thing Shelby could do for the case at this point.

Chrissie rushed into the store just as Shelby had gotten the coffee going.

"I just wanted to see how you are," she said, pointing to Shelby's elbow. "I haven't seen you in a couple of days and I worry about you, you know. We're all family here."

"No pain anymore, and I'm only mildly incapacitated for a couple of more weeks, it seems. Thanks for asking, Chrissie."

"No problem. Just let me know if I can do anything, okay? Gotta run. I have a seniors' tour coming in on the first boat. You might want to steel yourself." She grinned and disappeared out the door.

Shelby heard the boat horn, signaling that the fun was about to begin. She realized she did feel good, physically at least. Maybe she should have changed the working schedule for the day to do the entire day rather than split it with Laura again. It would at least help keep her mind off things. On the other hand, she thought Laura needed the money that the extra hours would bring in. Besides, way deep down, Shelby acknowledged that she was looking forward to spending a few hours on her own deck, with JT on her lap, reading and sipping some iced tea. And maybe making some decisions.

Shelby could tell the seniors were approaching from the amount of laughter coming down the hallway. In fact, the first group to shop in the store kept up a constant chatter punctuated with a lot of laughing. Shelby couldn't help but feel good in their presence and actually missed them when they'd left.

Just before noon, she looked up to see Hilary and another woman entering the store. *Her stepmother, maybe?*

"This is my stepmom, Giselle, and this is Shelby," she said with a puzzled frown. "What's wrong with your arm?"

"It's a long story, but the upshot is my elbow is splintered and splinted. It should heal in a few weeks." She gazed at Giselle. "It's very nice to meet you, but I'm so sorry about your loss."

Giselle gave a small smile and brushed her hand across her shoulder-length blonde hair. The silver highlights twinkled as the sun streaming through the window behind Shelby fell on them. She wore bright red lipstick, in stark contrast to her pale skin tone. She looked very stylish in a navy suit with a short rain jacket over her arm. But she looked sad.

"Thank you, Shelby. It's been a major shock, but Hilary and I are trying to get through it." She grabbed Hilary's hand and held it for a few seconds. "I'm sorry about your injury."

"Thanks. Can I get you both some coffee?" She was dying to know what was up but didn't want to be the one to get things started.

Hilary shook her head and looked at Giselle who said, "Not for me, thanks. I've already had my quota for the day. You have a very nice store here."

She started wandering slowly around, looking at the shelves. She moved with confidence, like she was used to being watched, and turned back to them briefly, smiled, and went back to scanning the shelves. Hilary watched her for a couple of minutes longer, looking impatient, then focused on Shelby.

"Giselle, too, wanted to see where it happened. And she wanted to ask you some questions, if you don't mind."

Giselle moved back over to them then. "Yes, I wondered if you could tell me something about the woman Nathan was asking about."

Shelby hesitated, wondering what Giselle could be getting at, but before she could say anything, Giselle explained.

"I was wondering if it was my old friend Lucy Todd he was looking for. I'd lost touch with her just before we got married, and I guess I've been talking about trying to track her down for so long now that Nathan took it in his head to do the leg-work. He was such a dear like that. I really have been missing her. We've been friends since childhood, and she just sort of dropped off the face of the earth. I'm hoping nothing bad has happened to her."

That didn't sound too good. "I'm sorry, I can't tell you much. As far as I can remember, he talked only in vague terms but did stress that she liked to read."

Giselle's expectant look turned to one of disappointment so Shelby added, "Trudy Bryant who helps out in our main store in town, and Felicity Foxworth who owns the art gallery right next door, also talked to him. You might want to check with them."

Giselle brightened. "Thanks, I'll do that." She turned to look around the store again. "Can you recommend a book that might help take my mind off everything?"

"What do you like to read?"

Giselle shrugged. "Oh, mainly women's fiction, you know, Elizabeth Berg, Jodi Picoult." She paused, walked over to the nearest shelf, and pulled out a book. "A focus on friendship. That kind of thing."

Shelby noticed Hilary grimace and wondered what she preferred to read.

"That one is fairly new. I'll show you a couple of other recent arrivals you may not be aware of and you can see if any of them are of interest." She led the way to the new arrivals shelf and pulled out three books. Giselle took them over to one of the two wicker chairs next to the side window and settled in to thumb through them.

"Thanks, Shelby. She really doesn't seem herself," Hilary said when Shelby had rejoined her.

"I'm glad you're here. I've been meaning to give you a call." She didn't add *but my mother turned up.* "I spoke to Walt Nevins the other day."

"You did? That's good. Did he mention anything useful?"

"He liked your dad but they weren't really friendly, just colleagues."

"Oh, that's too bad." Hilary's shoulders sagged.

Shelby thought back to her visit to Lynn but decided this wasn't the time to mention it. Besides, what could she really say? It was mainly speculation at this point.

"Have you checked with Chief Stone?" Shelby asked. "Maybe she has some new information."

"I called, but she said there was nothing new. Do you think she's stonewalling me?" Hilary's large eyes looked even wider and lost now.

"I don't think she'd do that." *Only if she wanted to keep you out of the investigation.*

"I know it must be hard for you both, but I also know that the chief is a smart cop and she's working hard on this."

"Oh, I don't doubt that, but I feel like I need to be doing something more. Do you have any other leads to follow?"

"Not really. But I'll keep asking questions."

Hilary smiled and seemed to relax a bit.

Giselle rejoined them and passed one book over to Shelby. "I'll take this one—thanks."

Shelby pointed to the other two in Giselle's hand. "If you just leave those on the counter, I'll put them back on the shelves later."

She rang up the purchase and was surprised when both women gave her quick hugs as they left.

Hilary paused at the door. "If you think of anything, call me, please."

"I will."

Laura came rushing into the store just after they'd left. "I didn't think I'd get here in time. Megan wasn't very cooperative this morning."

"Teenagers, eh? Well, you made it. I hope you didn't rush too much. I wouldn't have minded staying."

"If you get a move on, you can probably catch the same boat."

Shelby didn't need to be told twice. She grabbed her belongings and hurried down to the dock, the last person to board.

Back in town, she went straight to the houseboat and lay down for a short nap. JT was happy to join her and when the alarm went off twenty minutes later, Shelby felt much more refreshed. She thought about that slow afternoon she'd envisioned but then decided to walk over to Scenic View Park. She always did her best thinking when on the move. As she reached the street in front of Zack's house, she stopped and stood staring at it. Another decision to be made. She really had them piling on these days. She missed him, and that only seemed to be getting worse. What was she going to do? Think about it another time and hope he didn't ask again when he called later? For the moment she didn't have any better plan.

As she stood by the pavilion overlooking the river, she heard someone calling her name. She cringed, worried it might be Merrily. She hadn't yet thought of what to say to her mother. Well, actually, right now, she didn't really want to see anyone. She wanted to be alone, but nevertheless she turned, a smile on her face.

She was surprised to see Izzy Crocker walking purposefully towards her. She hadn't talked to Izzy since they had first met the previous fall. That was the only time they'd met, even though the woman had been Merrily's best friend for years. At the time, Shelby had been struck by how well-dressed and dignified the older woman had seemed in her equally dignified house. Now, here was this woman in her mid-seventies, white hair escaping its bun, wearing dark green cargo pants and jacket.

Izzy was out of breath when she reached Shelby. "I'm sorry to chase after you, but I saw you walking over here and I wanted to talk to you about Merrily. I understand you know she's back in town?"

"Yes, I saw her briefly yesterday. She was at the main bookstore, and I walked in on a bit of an argument between her and Aunt Edie."

Izzy reached out and touched Shelby's arm. "I know what a surprise that must have been, my dear, and I hope you don't mind my intruding. But Merrily came over to see me last night. She was in quite a state and was very surprised when I told her you and I had met. We talked for quite a while and when she left she asked if I would talk to you. I did tell her I wouldn't try to influence you at all, but then I started worrying and thought I'd like to see how you are for myself."

Shelby relaxed. "Thank you, Izzy. Like you said, I was surprised, shocked even, and I still am. But I'll be okay. I just have to figure out what's next. What I'm going to say to her."

Izzy linked her arm through Shelby's. "Let's walk, shall we?"

They headed down toward the river and waited until they'd crossed the short footbridge onto Casino Island before Izzy spoke again.

"You know, I love your Aunt Edie. She's one of the most level-headed women I know, except when it comes to fashion," she added with a chuckle. "I admire her. She's running a successful business. However, and please don't tell her I said this, she has too much emotion invested in all this to be giving you unbiased advice. She loves you dearly and wants you to be happy. And she was also betrayed by Merrily's actions. These two factors have got to be influencing her, I'm certain about that."

She looked over at Shelby who nodded.

"Good. Now, remember what I said last fall when we first met: your mama was a fish out of water up here and, unfortunately, she and your papa got married too fast. They were too young and they hadn't had any time to really get to know each other or what they wanted out of life. When an out presented itself, in the form of the wealthy, intriguing Gerald Steiger—not a wise thing, of course—Merrily took it and never looked back. I thought then and I know now, after talking to her, that leaving you was her biggest regret. But she wasn't cut out to be a mama at that point in her life anyway, and not with that affair of hers going on. I truly believe she thought you'd be better off with your papa and Edie. She respected Edie and hoped she would be a good surrogate mama for you. She had no idea that your papa would behave like he did and also run away, taking you with him and away from Edie."

She sighed. "As we get older, we often look back with some regret at paths not taken."

Izzy paused and pointed to one of the benches looking out toward Boldt Castle. They sat and watched as a freighter made its way at a good speed up the river.

"What are you thinking, Shelby?"

"I'm not really sure. I guess deep down inside, I know everything you're saying is true but I still have this visceral emotional reaction to it all." She realized her hands were tightly gripping each other and she slowly unclenched them.

"And that's totally understandable." Izzy patted Shelby's hands. "It just shows how important all this is to you. In fact, you did tell me part of the reason you'd come back to the Bay was to find out about your mama. Well, this is your opportunity. She's here for a few more days, staying at the Skyliner, Room 624, in case you want to make contact with her. But I'd say, for your own peace of mind, you need to have that talk with her. And I think you first have to decide where you're coming from on it. I hope you'll excuse my intrusion into your private life, but I felt I had to say something. Now I'll let you sit and think. I should be getting home and starting dinner anyway."

She patted Shelby's arm and started to walk away. "You call me anytime you want, you hear?"

Shelby nodded. "Thanks, Izzy."

She sat for about another twenty minutes and then headed home feeling surprisingly calm for the first time since seeing Merrily. She realized they did need to talk before Merrily left town. Shelby picked up the phone and called the hotel. She left a message saying she wanted to meet Merrily for coffee and a talk. Then she tried to put it out of her mind while she searched the fridge for ingredients that would make a passable dinner.

Zack's call came at 9:15 PM, just as she was walking upstairs to the bedroom. It had been a quiet evening with no call from Merrily, which had given Shelby a lot of time to think. Unfortunately, it wasn't about Zack. As she heard his voice, she hoped he wouldn't ask about the possibility of her moving.

"What have I been up to this week?" She repeated Zack's question before answering it, stalling, wondering if she should share the news about Merrily on the phone or in person. But she valued his opinion and now was the time to get it.

"For starters, I met my mom." He knew the story behind Shelby's mom up and leaving so many years ago.

She heard his intake of breath. "Your mom? How? Where?"

"She's here, in Alexandria Bay, and she came to meet me. I walked in on her and Edie arguing in the store and she identified herself, much to Edie's chagrin."

"Hell of a way to meet. Did you get a chance to talk?"

"No, I sort of ran because I was just so shocked and I couldn't think of what to say. But I bumped into Izzy Crocker today, you remember her, and we had a long talk. So, when I got home earlier today, I called the hotel where Merrily is staying and left a message about meeting for coffee. I haven't heard back from her, though."

"How are you doing? How do you feel about all this?" She could hear the concern in his voice.

"I'm not sure. My head's still reeling, and I keep checking myself for a reaction. I guess it's a mixture of anger, bewilderment, anticipation, and some joy. After all, she is my mom. And you know, I'm just thankful that I heard the story about what happened between her and my dad before she just appeared in town. I've had several months to let it sink in, although I have to admit, I don't think I've really resolved all my feelings about that yet. I may still be a bit in shock, too."

"I wish I was there, Shelby. I don't know what I could do, but at least I'd be there for you."

"Thanks, I know that and it means a lot. But this is something I have to figure out on my own. Actually, Merrily and I have to figure it out. I'm not sure what she's hoping for in the future, and I don't know what I want so we'll just have to wait and see." Shelby paused, suddenly all talked out.

"Be careful what you wish for, I guess," she added, with an attempt at lightheartedness.

"How's your arm?"

"It's feeling pretty good as long as I don't bang it against anything, thanks. So, what's happening at your end?"

"It's been busy. We caught the bad guys who have been on our radar for months now, so they won't be doing any more damage. But there's still plenty of them left out there, especially now that the good weather's here. That's why I'm calling tonight. I have a lead to follow up on tomorrow night so I'll be tied up once it gets dark and they get on the move."

"More smugglers?" she asked, feeling like he was so far away from what was happening in Alexandria Bay.

He chuckled. "No comment. I'm so sorry, but I have to cut this call short. We're doing surveillance tonight and it's just about my turn to relieve but I'm pretty sure I'll be home next weekend. Okay?"

"Better than okay. I look forward to it."

"Yeah, me too. Sweet dreams, Shelby." His voice had dropped to that sexy level that sent shivers running up her spine.

Now that brought a big smile to her face.

Chapter
Twenty-Two

Saturday mornings were usually quite busy, no matter what time in the season, and this one proved to be just the same. Shelby was surprised to see Giselle Miller walk through the door just as a young couple with three lively toddlers was leaving.

"Good morning, Giselle. It's nice to see you, although I hadn't expected to quite so soon. Is Hilary with you?" Giselle looked more casually dressed than when Shelby had first met her, but even in casual pants, jacket, and a scarf that looked like a watercolor of a pond, she looked polished.

"No, she's away for the weekend, visiting her former college roommate in Syracuse. It will probably do her a world of good. I hope it takes her mind off everything. Which is why I'm here." She paused and looked around the store, dropping her voice and moving over to the counter when she noticed an older woman sitting in one of the wicker chairs, reading.

The customer had been there for about half an hour, but Shelby didn't mind. It gave the store a cozy look.

"Oh. Is there something I can do for you?"

"Well, yes. I know you've been a big help to Hilary, visiting the offices where Nathan was working. A comfort, even. But I'm hoping in the future you'll try and deflect her seeming need to do all this. I think the investigation is better left to the police."

"It's not that I don't agree with you, but I think Hilary needs to feel she's doing something to help. It can be a long wait otherwise."

"You don't need to tell me about that." Giselle sounded sharp, and Shelby was immediately sorry she hadn't thought first before speaking. "I'm sorry, I didn't mean to snap. It's gotten to us all. But I worry especially about Hilary. She and Nathan were so close, and while I've never tried to replace her mother—she is a grown woman after all—I still feel I should watch out for her, especially now that he's gone."

She lowered her eyes and sniffed. Shelby wondered if Giselle really believed what she'd just said. That wasn't how Hilary had referred to her home life.

"Do you understand what I'm saying?" Giselle asked, raising her face to look directly at Shelby. "I think she's on a wild-goose chase and just getting more stressed out by it all."

"I guess I can understand that, but I'm not quite sure what I can do about it."

Giselle's smile didn't quite stretch to her eyes when she continued, "Well, like I said, I think the best thing you could do when you hear from her next time is not get into a discussion about any of this with her. I know she's been sharing some personal details about Nathan's banking in particular. That's really none of your business, if you don't mind my saying so. And you're the only one who can convince Hilary of that." The smile remained on Giselle's face, but Shelby felt a sudden chill in the room. *None of my business. She's right.*

"I'll do my best, Giselle." *Which may not have anything to do with deflecting Hilary.*

"Thank you. I do appreciate that. It's for Hilary's own good, you know." She turned and took a step toward the door. "Oh, and if you happen to come up with anything more about the woman Nathan was trying to track down, or if that friend of yours who owns the gallery does, I'd really appreciate it if you'd let me know." She pulled a piece of paper out of her purse and walked back to the counter, handing it to Shelby. "I'm still wondering if it's my old friend."

Shelby guessed Giselle must have anticipated the outcome of their little talk. Neatly printed in black ink was her name and phone number.

Shelby didn't realize how intense the encounter had been until Giselle had left. She shrugged her shoulders a few times to loosen the tightness that had settled there. As she did so, the woman in the chair stood up and paid for the book she'd been reading. Shelby watched her leave and stood staring at the closed door for a few minutes, her mind running over what Giselle had said.

She couldn't quite get a take on Giselle. She had seemed a bit aloof and removed the first time they'd met but, of course, that was probably due to the circumstances. Today she'd come across as all warm and confiding before turning a bit intense. Did she really have Hilary's best interests at heart?

Why am I even wondering about this? It had nothing to do with her, she admitted. None of it. Sure, she'd talked to Nathan, briefly, and sure, his body had been found next to her house-boat. But other than that, she should just take Chief Stone's advice on this one and back away. Let others sort it out. Yes, that was good advice. Giselle was right; Chief Stone was right.

She gave her head a shake to clear the cobwebs and phoned the main store to check on the arrival of some back orders, hoping they'd finally come in. The call took longer than expected as Trudy went on to describe the latest antics of one of their favorite customers. Shelby knew the woman well as she often visited the castle location on days she was bored. She'd given up driving her car when she turned ninety but managed to get around on foot extremely well. And her favorite pastime was reading, so she used a lot of those steps walking to the library or the bookstore. And, on days she wanted a change of scene, she hopped the cruise boat to the castle, using her season pass.

Shelby knew she'd been daydreaming again when she realized Trudy had stopped talking. Was she waiting for an answer? Shelby desperately searched for any clue as to what Trudy had been describing and almost laughed with relief when Trudy suddenly said, "Sorry about that. Someone in for a special order. Oh, well, I'll tell you more about Henrietta another time. Have a busy day."

"You too." Shelby hung up and marched straight to the back room, filling a coffee mug with some hot brew, hoping that might do the trick and bring some alertness back to her brain.

As she sipped her coffee, she considered what her next move should be. Obviously, nothing to do with Hilary.

She realized that at the back of her mind was also the realization that she hadn't heard back from Merrily. What did that mean? Had she had second thoughts about getting to know her daughter better? Had Shelby's reaction chased her away? That thought scared her. She reached for the phone, calling the hotel once again and spoke to the front desk only to discover that Merrily had checked out for the weekend but had a reservation for Monday. That sounded strange. Shelby wondered where she'd gone and why. Monday she'd call the hotel again and hopefully get some answers.

The next hour filled out with several customers each buying several books. Shelby had to admit to herself that her arm had reached its limit for the day. She just hoped the final hour would be quieter

As she was getting ready to close, she realized she'd been thinking about Nathan's murder for the past few minutes. And then there was Giselle's request that she stay out of it all. She finished counting the cash, wondering what her next actions should be. She did have to admit that the best thing would be to not get involved any further in the murder investigation, and she resolved to stick with it.

Until Hilary called.

"Hi, it's Hilary. I saw on Find My Friends that Giselle was at the castle earlier today. Did she talk to you?"

"Um, yes she did."

"Can I ask about what?"

Shelby thought quickly. Giselle hadn't said anything about not telling Hilary, although it would be a strange thing to tell her. But Giselle hadn't specified.

"Um, she was hoping that I wouldn't get involved with your dad's personal life any more. She's worried about you, Hilary, and thinks that if I help out, you'll just get even more involved. She thinks it's a dead end that will leave you even more upset." *Or something along those lines.*

There was a long silence before Hilary spoke again. "She said that, did she?"

Shelby knew it was a rhetorical question and didn't answer. She'd let Hilary drive this conversation.

"So, what did you tell her? Did you agree? I guess you had to, but that may actually be a good thing. If she thinks you're out of the picture, you can still help me on the sly."

"I fudged it and said I'd do what I could. You know, though, I think I can understand why she doesn't want a stranger knowing so much of all this personal stuff about your family. However, I didn't totally agree nor did I say I would help you. I don't think she noticed." *She was so wrapped up in what she was saying.* Shelby thought it best not to add that last bit. It sounded sort of snide, even if it was true.

"Hah, that sounds like Giselle. Okay then, I've gotta go. I've been visiting a friend in Syracuse but we'll talk tomorrow, okay?"

"Sure."

She heard the boat whistle as she was closing the shop and skipped hanging around to talk to a couple of volunteers near the front entrance. Even so, she barely made it before the boat pulled away. She took a seat inside the cabin next to the window and let her eyes enjoy the view while her mind played around with thoughts of Merrily, Nathan, and Zack of course. She tried to focus on the shoreline that was getting closer at a fast rate. She needed to calm down and take charge of what was going on in her life. Maybe she should sign up for the course on Mindfulness being offered at the recreation center. Or maybe she should just attempt to deal with one issue at a time.

She'd convinced herself this was this best course of action by the time she reached her houseboat. She was looking forward to a quiet evening at home, maybe grilling a fillet of salmon that tempted her from the fridge, and hope for at a least a phone call from Zack.

She didn't notice the small white envelope wedged in between the door and frame until she started to stick her key in the lock. She pulled it out, but there were no clues as to who had left it, in fact, her name wasn't even on it. It felt like a USB stick, though. That was intriguing.

She let herself in and held the door open while JT rushed out. She watched him race along the dock to the narrow piece of rocky shoreline and make his way to the mishmash of shrubs and bushes to the right. She could only imagine what temptations awaited him there. Once again, she said a silent prayer that he'd come back.

The envelope was next and she carefully ripped it open, trying not to destroy any note that might be tucked inside. There wasn't one, only a USB stick, which wasn't labeled.

She quickly made herself an espresso and then flicked her laptop on, inserting the stick once it was up and running. She then settled in and clicked on the first item listed as *Email*. It turned out to be an email from Walt Nevins to Nathan Miller. In it, he asked Nathan to let him know if irregularities on Roman Sykes's part appeared when it came to the awarding of contracts. Apparently, Nevins was concerned about rumors of bribery and kickbacks. It was dated in January. The other item, labeled *Reply*, was an email from Nathan to Nevins stating that he was onto something and would have the needed proof by the end of the week. It was dated the Wednesday before he died.

Shelby sat back and reread the two emails, wondering what it all meant. It appeared that Nathan had agreed to Walt Nevins's request. But, had he been able to gather the proof before he died? Was that why he'd been murdered? Had Roman Sykes found out what was going on and was now a possible suspect? And just as importantly, who had left this for her? And why?

She wondered if Hilary might know about this, maybe some follow-up notes in Nathan's files at home, but surely she would have shared that information with Shelby if she had it. She tried giving her a call but got voicemail instead. Maybe Hilary wasn't back from Syracuse yet. She left a message then printed out the two emails before shutting off her computer.

Did Chief Stone know? Surely she had found out about Nathan's consulting job by now and she'd also have investigated it thoroughly, finding out about all of this. But what if she hadn't?

Before Shelby had a chance to follow that thought through to some action, a ping alerted her to a text message from Erica asking if she wanted to come over to her house for a light meal. Shelby replied that she'd be over shortly and went to quickly change and pull a bottle of red wine out of the cupboard.

She enjoyed these spur-of-the-moment meals with Erica, which seemed to happen at the end of a busy day at Chocomania, when Erica was still wound up, and when her new boyfriend, Adam, was on call with the fire department.

Of course, the final ingredient was Zack being out of town.

Zack. Well, she wasn't going to dwell on that topic tonight. But maybe Erica would be a good sounding board for just where the murder investigation was headed, what with this latest development.

Of course, the person she really needed to talk to was Roman Sykes.

Chapter
Twenty-Three

Erica answered the door of her narrow two-story white clapboard house before Shelby even had a chance to knock.

"Good timing. I just glanced out. Welcome to my humble abode." Erica grinned.

The thought "house proud" flashed through Shelby's mind. Erica had good reason to be pleased with her fairly new infill house. There weren't many of them in the Bay area, but it totally suited her needs. She had painted the open plan main floor in a buttery shade which added a feeling of space to the small area. Shelby knew that the two bedrooms upstairs were both a pale mossy green, more conducive for a good night's sleep, Erica had said.

Shelby handed her friend the bottle of wine she'd brought and followed her toward the back where the kitchen overlooked the small yard that sported more patio stones than grass.

"I'm glad you hadn't already eaten," Erica said. "I know it was last minute but full disclosure, Adam and I had planned dinner out but he got called out to a fire just outside of town.

I'm learning that time is not your friend if you're waiting for dinner so we'll try again tomorrow night. Maybe."

"Well worth the wait, though, I'll bet."

Erica smiled. "You bet. Now, I have this deconstructed Niçoise salad I thought we'd put out on the table and just sit and eat and drink. How does that sound?"

"Deconstructed. Niçoise. Sounds like you're channeling your brother."

Erica gave a fake shudder. "Oh, I hope not. Have a seat and tell me about your day." She poured their wine and then sat across from Shelby at the small wooden table. The after-work hours Erica always looked totally different from the business Erica, hurrying around behind the counter with her short hair either totally covered with a small scarf or pulled back from her heart-shaped face by a headband.

"My day. Let me see, fairly busy at the store and one memorable customer."

"How so?"

"I need to backtrack to yesterday when Hilary Miller came in with her stepmom, Giselle. We talked and they left. Then today, Giselle came back on her own and basically asked me to lay off the investigation. She said she was worried about Hilary getting so involved in it."

Erica sipped her wine and looked thoughtful. "So, what did you say?"

"Well, she also basically told me it was none of my business, at least the personal aspects of Nathan's life weren't, and I guess I couldn't disagree with that. I agreed with her and then she left."

"But did you say you'd back off?"

"Not outright."

Erica snorted. "Hah, you are good." She shoved the large serving plate toward Shelby. "Here, help yourself. So, what now?"

"Well, Hilary is supposed to call tomorrow, and I guess we'll have to figure out what's next. But that's not the most interesting thing that happened. When I got home there was an envelope with a USB stick shoved between my door and the frame."

Erica paused in reaching for the salad dish after Shelby had finished with it. "You read it, of course?"

Shelby nodded. "Well, Hilary found out Nathan was doing some consulting work for the local town council and we both talked to his contacts here. So, on the USB was a letter from the department manager, asking Nathan to report any irregularities he might come across."

"What do you mean, irregularities?"

"Evidence of bribery or kickback. And it named one employee in particular."

"Do you know if he agreed to do it?"

"He did because there was also an email from Nathan saying he'd have proof by the end of the week, and it was dated the week he died. I'll talk it over with Hilary tomorrow and see if she can find something more, now that we have a specific concern to track. This is really good, by the way." Shelby took another mouthful of the salad.

"I'm glad you think so. Of course, it took me hours to prepare." Erica chuckled as she scooped another spoonful of tuna onto her plate. They continued eating in silence.

"So, let me take a wild stab here," Erica finally said. "You're thinking this named employee might have something to do with the murder?"

Shelby shrugged. "It's not that far-fetched. I'm just not sure how we go about proving it."

"A good way would be to take that USB to Chief Stone."

"Oh, I will, eventually. I just want to take a stab at seeing where this leads first. Besides, what's to say she doesn't already know? She's good at her job, and I'd be the last person she'd tell about this."

"Okay, agreed. I can see how you'd like to do that, but it could be dangerous."

"It's more likely it won't be happening. I know nothing about projects and contracts so how can I figure it out?"

"I wonder who slipped you the USB? Maybe whoever it was could get you more information."

"Exactly my thoughts. I plan to go back to their office on Monday morning, but I can't think of who I spoke to that would have been likely to share that letter. I mean they were all very business-like. Unless . . ."

"Unless, what? You know who it is?"

"I can't be sure, but there was a guy who suggested I talk to the manager. I wonder if it was him? Or even the receptionist, but why would she do that? And, how would she have access to the files?"

"You won't do anything foolish though, right?"

"Absolutely not. Now, why don't you tell me more about how things are progressing with Adam?"

"Oh, Adam. I really like him, you know?"

"Do I hear a 'but' there?"

"No but, just a lot of caution. I don't want to get my hopes up too high and I don't want to make any assumptions."

"Nice and easy?"

"Exactly. And just how you should be approaching this investigation of yours."

Chapter
Twenty-Four

S helby woke to a beautiful sunny morning and a sore arm.
She must have been sleeping on it and immediately regretted having abandoned the pillow armrest so soon. She guessed
she'd be wearing the sling again, for at least one more day
anyway.

The nice weather brought out the tourists, but most seemed
to want to spend their time on the island outdoors, wandering
around the majestic lawns and gardens. She couldn't really
blame them, standing on the wraparound verandah before
going into the castle. Shelby took extra time before going into
her store, to take in the view and noticed a long lineup at
the Sugar Shack down near the river. There were also several
people sitting on the bench that hugged the wall of the large
gazebo over to the left and at the bottom lawn where it met
the pathway. She'd bet some of those people were enjoying an
ice cream cone. She knew she could probably just stand there
all day with the sun warming her, watching the delightful
view, but she did have work to be done and after that, she was
expected at Edie's.

Later in the morning, when things had quieted in the store, Shelby tried calling Hilary to fill her in on finding the USB stick. She also wanted Hilary to check if Nathan had made any mention of the contents, particularly his email to Nevins, on his computer. She had to be satisfied with leaving a message, wondering if Hilary had decided to stay longer in Syracuse. Hopefully, she might have some information, if it could be found.

Shelby sat staring at the door, thoughts still on Hilary, when Chief Stone walked in.

"Were you hoping I'd walk in?" Stone asked with a raising of an eyebrow.

Shelby took a second to process that Stone was kidding. "This is how I get most of my customers to appear. I sit and stare."

Stone chuckled. "Well, since you're ready for someone, anyone, I just wanted to check on you."

Uh-oh.

She reached the counter and leaned against it. "No more dropping in all around town asking women when they moved here?"

Shelby couldn't tell if this was still part of the lightheartedness. She decided to take it at face value. "No, I haven't."

"Is there anything else you want to tell me about?"

What did she know? Hilary had mentioned their visit to Nevins, although Shelby had never talked to Stone about any of it. And, she sure wasn't about to mention the USB stick, not until she'd talked it over with Hilary. Had Lynn gotten in touch with her?

"Well, I did have a talk with Lynn Innes, not asking if she was the woman, but wondering if Nathan Miller had mentioned anything to her. Lynn said she was going to contact you."

"About what?" Stone's eyes narrowed. "Just what did you ask her?"

"She's a friend of Nathan Miller's so I suggested she let you know that, just in case you hadn't heard, because I thought you'd want to be sure you'd talked to everyone here he knew."

Stone continued looking at Shelby, her expression not changing, and then finally said, "Okay, well thanks for that. I'll be sure to give her a call."

* * *

Shelby slowly walked over to Edie's for supper, after first making a stop at home to feed JT as soon as she got off the boat. She then had to slide out the door before he had a chance to follow. Now that the better weather was back, the cat seemed to be trying to recapture his wandering tendencies. Shelby knew she shouldn't try to hold him back but rather, be pleased when he did return. Or, maybe she should. She'd have to find another cat owner and talk it over. Should she be trying to train JT to be an indoor cat?

She didn't have an answer as she reached Edie's. As she opened the gate, she could see Matthew walk in front of the living room window. She'd been wondering if he'd be there. He was, more times than not, but Shelby never knew until she arrived. She felt a bit relieved. At least that meant two hot topics would not be discussed—Merrily and Zack.

Shelby knocked on the door and walked in as Matthew disappeared into the kitchen. She dropped her jacket over the stairway railing and followed him, sniffing the enticing aroma wafting through the doorway.

"Oh, man. That smells like ginger carrot soup. Am I right?"

Edie turned away from the stove and smiled at Shelby. "You are right. I needed to use up some carrots, so, my favorite fall soup makes an appearance in spring."

"I sure don't mind. It's one of my favorites, too, and I could eat it any season. How about you, Matthew?"

"I like any soup that Edie creates. Actually, make that any meal."

"Tactful."

Matthew grinned. "So, how was your day at the store?"

"Pretty busy but that's not a surprise. This sunny weather lures the early bird tourists, that's for sure."

"I always find that time to be so interesting," Edie said, pointing to Matthew and making a drinking motion.

"Oh, right. What can I get you Shelby?"

"I'll start with just plain water, thanks. I'm so thirsty, I'd probably drink a glass of wine all in one gulp."

She watched them both at work, Matthew mixing drinks for the two of them then pouring some water for Shelby, and Edie, once again, facing the stove and stirring her soup. Now, if they weren't a great couple, she didn't know who was.

When Matthew looked up at her, she wondered if he could read her thoughts, his smile was so instant and a bit conspiratorial. She noticed he was a bit more dressed up this evening and it looked like his hair had been recently trimmed, although the natural unruliness lingered. But he had abandoned his usual plaid flannel shirt and worn jeans, and instead sported a short-sleeved navy plaid cotton shirt and what looked like fairly new dark gray chinos. The crease was still crisp. *Interesting*, she thought. What did it mean? Shelby had to remind herself to stop being so fanciful when it came to those two.

"Let's all take a break and enjoy our drinks in the living room," he said, nodding his head in Edie's direction.

Shelby took the cue. "Come on, Aunt Edie. I'm sure the soup is at its resting stage."

Edie laughed, wiping her hands on a towel, and followed them both. "You're right, a watched pot and all that." She smoothed her swishing floor-length patchwork skirt under her as she sat and accepted a drink from Matthew.

After they'd all had a sip, Edie asked Shelby, "Now tell me, how is your arm?"

"Fine. Really fine," Shelby answered, a bit too quickly. She tried not to think about it, preferring to just carry on with what she was doing, although with caution. She didn't dare mention this morning nor that she'd been wearing her sling again, which she'd deliberately left at home.

Edie stared at her, saying nothing, but Shelby knew that look.

"Okay, maybe it's sore at times, but that's to be expected. It's probably reacting to the changes in weather or something," she finally added.

"Or something," Edie agreed. "Something in this case being working too hard. I'll bet you are leaning books against your arm as you shelve them. I'll bet you're carrying piles of books from the back room to the selling floor. I'll bet you carry a bag filled with something in one hand, and a loaded down purse in the other, when you're on the move."

"Maybe. But it really is healing and feels eighty percent better. Honestly."

"What was it you told me about people using the word *honestly*, Matthew?" Edie turned her head towards him.

"Ah, I'm sure I said to never trust someone who used the word *honestly* in a phrase. It probably means the opposite." He grinned and looked at Shelby. "It's a known fact in police interrogations."

"Seriously?" Shelby asked, a bit annoyed. She knew she used the word a lot. Was she truly not being honest?

Edie laughed. "Oh, don't get all tied up in that, Shelby. We mean it in good humor. Now, I know I shouldn't ask this but, what have you found out about that mystery woman Mr. Miller was searching for?"

This was more like it. "I thought I had two good possibilities, but it turns out, I was wrong. But there is something else of interest that was happening in his life, and it might be an even better lead although I'm not quite sure."

A timer went off in the kitchen and Edie sprang to her feet. "We'll have to continue this around the table. Supper is officially ready. Everyone to their stations."

Shelby smiled, following Edie into the kitchen. She was certainly in a good mood. And that was so good to see. At least she hadn't brought up the two topics Shelby was determined to avoid. *Still. Avoid.* Maybe she could keep the talk centered around the murder, especially if she could draw the two of them in by asking them for their opinions and even, maybe helping her figure it out.

They were just finishing the main course when Edie asked, "And what about Tekla Stone? You haven't mentioned her bothering you lately."

"That's right," Shelby said. "I actually hadn't seen her until earlier today. She stopped by but didn't offer anything about what stage she's at in her investigation. And I thought it wise not to ask although I did have a tip for her. I'm dying to know how the investigation is going, though."

"And what about the daughter, Hilary?"

Shelby nodded, chewing her final piece of roast beef. When she finished, she sipped her water and then answered. "I've heard from her several times. In fact, she and I did a little fact-finding mission a few days ago."

"And just what facts did you find?"

"Well, Hilary had found out that her dad was actually doing some consulting for the town and he's been making weekly trips, sometimes even more often, to the Bay over the last year."

"So, he probably didn't specifically make those two trips here to ask about this mystery woman," Matthew ventured.

"I was thinking the same thing. But why did he wait a few months before trying to find her?"

"Maybe he'd been asking all along, only at different locations," Edie suggested.

Shelby gave that some thought as Edie collected the dishes from the table. She jumped up to help. "No way, missy. You just sit there and rest your arm."

Shelby felt a bit useless but did as she was told. "I guess that's possible, but in that case, he must have narrowed it down to finding her someplace connected to books."

"Or art. Remember Felicity's art gallery."

"Absolutely. So, what made him visit us all when he did, and not once but twice?" She did get up to help Edie serve their slices of pecan pie. "This investigating business can be confusing and tricky."

"I guess that's telling you something," Matthew suggested.

"What?"

"When the train isn't getting anywhere, it's time to jump off."

"I know there's a deep message there," Shelby answered with a chuckle.

Edie started laughing. "He's saying, it just might be time to butt out."

Chapter
Twenty-Five

Shelby had felt guilty all evening not telling Edie that she planned to call Merrily the next day. She told herself it was partly because Edie hadn't asked and partly because she hadn't wanted to bring up the topic while Matthew was there. But she knew it was really because she was worried about Edie's reaction even though it was her suggestion. She did appreciate the fact that Edie also had concerns about any pain that might result from such a meeting. But it was Shelby's life, her decision, and something she knew she had to do.

She'd found it hard to fall asleep, going over and over in her mind what she planned to say. She would be measured and totally in control, not letting any of the anger or hurt take over the conversation. She had some questions and deserved answers. But she had no goal in mind. This woman was a stranger to her, and there had been too much hurt when she'd found out that Merrily had abandoned her. How could they ever get beyond that?

She had phoned Merrily first thing in the morning and found her in her hotel room. Shelby got right to the point, suggesting they meet in the hotel's restaurant for coffee at 10:30 AM. She was relieved she'd called Laura the day before and asked her to work all day. Shelby hadn't been sure what state of mind she'd be in after seeing Merrily. She might need even more alone time to try to figure things out.

She took great care in getting ready, choosing to wear a black top with small white polka dots and three-quarter length sleeves. She paired it with a pair of black leggings, which she struggled into, and zebra-striped booties. It had been her go-to outfit for meetings in her previous working life, whenever she'd needed a boost of confidence. *And I sure need a shot of that right now.*

* * *

She arrived at the hotel with moments to spare and paused outside to take a deep breath, trying to slow her racing heart. The restaurant opened onto the lobby, opposite the outside door. *It's now or never.*

Merrily was sitting at a table for four, partway across the room, next to the window overlooking the bay. She had obviously been watching the door and waved when Shelby entered.

Shelby gave a hesitant wave back and slipped out of her jacket as she made her way over. She sat across from Merrily, and a server appeared immediately with a cup of coffee.

"I took you at your word," Merrily said with a hesitant smile. "You did mean coffee, didn't you? It wasn't just a saying?"

Shelby gave a small laugh, feeling a slight easing of the tension she'd been feeling all morning. "Yes, I really meant coffee. It's my go-to in the morning."

"Hmm, I'm a tea person myself. I'm not sure where that came from. Oh, silly me, of course I do. My mama was a tea drinker, never coffee." Merrily sipped the tea that was already in front of her. "I had to rush home unexpectedly on the weekend, but I wanted to get right back, hoping we could connect. I'm so glad you called this morning. Now, I'm rambling. I have to tell you, Shelby, I'm really nervous about this meeting."

"You are?" That gave Shelby a feeling of control.

"Yes. I don't want to blow it."

"I guess I'm feeling the same way," she admitted, enjoying the Southern lilt of Merrily's accent.

She took a long sip of her coffee, using the time to study Merrily over the brim of her cup. She was looking for a similarity between the two of them, the one that Izzy had mentioned the first time they spoke. She couldn't really see it, although she had to admit, she didn't spend much time analyzing her own looks. For starters, their hair was a different color. While Shelby's was dark, like her dad's, Merrily was a blonde and it looked natural. Well, maybe there were touch-ups at her age, but with her skin tone, she was definitely in the blonde category. And she kept it very fashionably in a sleek bob that skimmed her shoulders while Shelby's hair would never be sleek.

She thought there might be some similarities in their features, the narrow nose and definitely the eyes. They both had hazel eyes. This pleased Shelby, though she wasn't quite sure why. She'd have to give that some thought.

Merrily was also a much more stylish dresser, wearing a long-sleeved linen top in a variety of greens and blues, looking more like a watercolor than a piece of clothing. Pearl studs were her only jewelry except for a large diamond and gold band on her left hand.

Merrily smiled as if she knew she was being sized up. "Well, that's a good starting point. I've been playing this scene over and over in my head, wondering what to say and what you would say. I know you're upset and angry, and you have every right to be. But I think it's best if I just say outright, I'm so sorry that I hurt you so deeply. I was young and lonely and foolish. I guess, I was basically self-centered. I just wanted to get away from Alexandria Bay and back to my old life. I was very careless and you paid for it. I know also that your dad paid for it, too. I wish I'd had the opportunity to apologize to him, but I'm sure, it wouldn't have made any difference anyway."

Shelby hadn't realized how tightly her hands were gripping her cup until Merrily stopped talking and looked expectantly at her. *My turn, I guess.*

"I don't know what you want me to say. I don't even know what I want to say. I don't even know how I really feel. I guess, I'm still dazed by all this. I hadn't been told about any of this growing up. I thought you were dead, but since I found out just last year that you had walked out, I've tried really hard to come to grips with it all. I knew I had to work it out in my mind, but I guess I've been avoiding it because I still don't know what I feel." She noticed Merrily wince as she was speaking. But it was all true. She had walked out on them.

"You're right, though. I am deeply hurt and angry. Nothing prepared me for the news that you'd abandoned me and my dad."

Merrily sighed. "I guess that's perfectly understandable." She sat staring out at the water for a few moments before going on. "You know, Edie was right. I shouldn't have just shown up like this. I should have eased into it, in some way. It's too big a shock, and it puts you in a very unsettling position."

She looked at Shelby. "Is there anything you want to ask me? I promise I'll try to answer honestly, and as best I can."

Shelby's mind went blank. Merrily had already talked about why she'd left, or rather, her state of mind at that point. Izzy had filled in a lot of the details already. What did that matter, anyway? She knew the real question.

"Why did you never try to get in touch with me all these years? Didn't you ever wonder about me?"

Merrily looked stricken. "I did wonder, believe me, even though I tried very hard not to dwell on it all. I told myself you were in good hands. Your father loved you, as did Edie. I thought the two of them would be good influences and raise you well. In fact, I can see your dad did that. But I hadn't realized that he had also basically run away, taking you with him, shortly after I left. I did try to contact you, a couple of times. I phoned, but Ralph wouldn't let me talk to you. He told me he had cut me out of your lives. And when you were older, I wrote a letter to you, but I'm guessing now that you might not have gotten it."

Merrily looked like she was moments away from tears. She took a deep breath before continuing. "I'm sorry you didn't have a mother or a mother figure in your life. I had assumed Edie would step in to help out until he remarried. Who could have known he'd react in that way?" She looked surprised. "I didn't really mean it to sound like it's his fault. It was totally mine."

Shelby didn't say anything because she couldn't think of a thing to say.

Merrily sat searching her face and finally said, "I was hoping we can make our way to something, friendship maybe."

Shelby let that sink in but wasn't sure what she thought of it, then asked a question that had been on her mind since she'd learned the truth. "Do you have any other children?"

"Yes, a son and a daughter. They know nothing about you. I guess, because I didn't want them to know how badly I'd treated you, and Gerald, my husband, wasn't about to share with them that we'd run off together. Gerald passed last year. And, I want you to know, as soon as I get home, I'm going to tell my kids all about you. That is, if you want to have contact with them."

Shelby hadn't thought that far ahead. She had a brother and a sister. Something else she had no idea how to feel about. Although, she did acknowledge to herself that it was probably an exciting prospect. Maybe, just a tiny bit.

Shelby shrugged, not quite willing to put any words to the test.

"Look, Shelby, I made a mess of it all. I admit it. But I would like another chance. I know you need to think this all through. You have your life here, and you've done very well without me. But I'm hoping, after I leave here this afternoon, you will think seriously about it and get in touch with me." She slid a piece of paper across the table.

Shelby looked at Merrily's name, address, home phone and cell numbers. It felt like a promise of sorts, or maybe she was reading too much into it. She stared at it for several moments and then tucked the paper into her bag.

"I will think about it."

She didn't want to be there any longer. It had all been said by now, and she felt her emotions very close to the surface. She needed to think; she needed not to be here with Merrily. She stood and grabbed her jacket. "I have to go now. But I will do as you ask. I just need some time."

Merrily nodded. "I totally understand. And, thanks for meeting with me. That means so much to me. I really want this to work, Shelby. Please call me."

Shelby hoped Merrily wouldn't want to hug her. She gave a quick nod and walked out of the restaurant without looking back.

Two thoughts kept running through her mind all the way back to the houseboat: *That was the woman who abandoned me. That was my mother.*

* * *

Early afternoon, she started getting antsy, wishing she hadn't taken the afternoon off from work. It had seemed smart at the time since she really had no idea what her frame of mind would be after meeting with Merrily. But now she found the worst thing was trying to do mundane tasks at home, which gave her brain far too much time to keep revisiting the coffee meeting and wishing she'd said more or, in some cases, different things.

Her phone rang and she grabbed it, happy for the distraction.

"Hi, Shelby. It's Hilary. I got your message."

"I'm glad you got back to me. Do you have a few minutes to talk?"

"Sure thing. What's up?"

"Something very peculiar happened on Saturday. An envelope was left for me at the houseboat and it contained a USB drive, nothing else."

"Did you open it?"

"Yes, and there were two emails, one from Walt Nevins to your dad, dated in January, asking him to try to find Some emails about some illegal things happening in the office, particularly involving Roman Sykes. The other was from your dad to Nevins stating he'd found something and would share it once he got the proof. It was dated a few days before he died."

Hilary sucked in her breath and slowly let it out. "Oh, wow. That is so freaky. Do you think that's what got Dad killed? Was it Roman Sykes?"

"I have no idea, but it's worth following up. I'd like you to check your dad's computer again and any other files he might have from this job. Maybe he has notes about what he found out."

"I've gone over everything already, though."

"But we didn't know then what to look for. This might be the break we need."

"You're right. I'll get right on it and let you know if I find anything. And Shelby," she paused, "thanks for everything you're doing. I don't know what I'd do without you. But please, be careful."

"I will. Talk to you later."

She let JT back inside, one more time, and then decided to put the rest of the afternoon to good use. She needed to go back to the town council offices and talk to James Rooney and Mandy again. If she wasn't mistaken, one of them had to be the person who had slipped her the USB stick. Who else could it have been?

The first thing she noticed when she reached the fourth floor was the reception desk was empty. Totally empty. No sweater draped on the back of the chair. No pads of paper. No tissue box wedged between the baffle and the light fixture. She wondered where Mandy was. Maybe she'd gotten a promotion and moved elsewhere. She'd have to ask if she planned on talking to her.

The doors to Walt Nevins's and Roman Sykes's offices were closed, but she was happy to see James Rooney's door open and him sitting behind his desk. She knocked on the doorframe.

"Hi, I'm Shelby Cox, remember? Do you have a minute?"

He looked almost pleased to see her. "Sure, come on in. A pretty face beats reading reports any time."

Shelby inwardly cringed. She walked in but stayed a distance from his desk.

"I just wanted to thank you for leaving the envelope at my place the other day."

"The what?" Rooney looked confused.

"I found an envelope at my door the other day and it came from these offices. I assumed it was you who had left it." She decided not to mention the fact it held a USB drive nor the contents.

"I don't know why you'd think that." He looked and sounded puzzled.

"Well, when my friend and I were in the other day talking about Nathan Miller, you were the one who steered us to

Mr. Nevins. I just thought. . ." She let it dangle, now totally unsure if she should be telling him anything. "Oh well, I guess I shouldn't have assumed." She gave a small, self-deprecating laugh. "I'm really sorry to have bothered you." She turned and headed to the door.

He stood and met up with her as she left his office.

"Is this anything I should know about? It sounds highly irregular."

"No, I'm sure it's all okay. Just some information about Mr. Miller being in town and his daughter can handle it from here. Oh, there is something else. Is Mandy around?"

"Mandy? No, she's not with us any longer."

"Oh, do you know where I can find her?"

"Sorry, I don't have a clue."

"Okay. Thanks, again."

She walked quickly to the elevator, not wanting to answer any more questions. On the ride down, she was mentally kicking herself for just jumping in. She should have thought it out more carefully.

But if it wasn't James Rooney that left it, then who? Mandy? And if so, how could she find her?

Chapter
Twenty-Six

"So, what do you think? Does it make sense?" Shelby asked Erica, after explaining her newest theory when she stopped by Chocomania on her way to the store Tuesday morning.

Shelby had made a list before going to bed the night before, hoping that seeing it all written down would help her make sense of it all. She still leaned heavily toward the killer being someone related to Nathan's consulting job, be it Roman Sykes or someone else he hadn't named. And how would she find Mandy without even knowing her last name? However, she also now questioned whether Nathan's time frame about his mystery woman was reliable. He had been asking about her the day he died, so she was still very much on his mind.

She briefly went over her visit to the town council offices but realized she didn't have time to really get into everything at the moment.

She also wanted to talk about her visit with Merrily, but a quick look at the clock indicated that the discussion would be best left for a leisurely evening spent with a bottle of wine.

"Hey, are you busy tonight?" Shelby asked on the spur of the moment as Erica slid Shelby's latte across the counter to her. "A hot date with Adam by any chance?"

"Nope. Why do you ask?"

"Do you feel like coming over and sharing some wine with me after supper?"

Erica gave her a hard look. "Something other than the murder is bothering you, isn't it?"

"Major league."

"Zack?"

"Of course, but that's not for tonight. I could use a sounding board again about the murder, and I haven't told you the latest about Merrily."

"You do juggle a lot of emotional stuff, don't you?"

"Yes, far too much drama. So, seven?"

*   *   *

Nora flagged Shelby down on her way to the shuttle.

"I'm so glad I ran into you."

"What are you doing down here this early?" Shelby asked, taken by surprise. She'd been in dreamland thinking about the night before and her long phone call with Zack. She couldn't decide if it had been disheartening or cheering. He'd asked all the right things about her, about her arm, what was new, what happened with her mom. But it was what he'd left unsaid that worried her a bit. No talk about his promotion. Of course, she didn't want to talk about it either, so she should be pleased. But, didn't he want to know if she'd reached a decision? She realized she was being totally irrational and welcomed the interruption.

"I was just at the Black Fox Bistro finalizing the food for the mystery evening. You know, they like to handle any catering requests before they start getting ready for their lunch opening. I think it's pretty well set, and their price is within our budget, so I'm really excited about it all. But I also want to double check some things with you. Is it all right if I tag along on your commute?" She pointed to the shuttle and Shelby agreed, thinking that since they were having a business meeting, she could stretch the "employees only" rule of the shuttle. She was also impressed that Nora would volunteer her weekend to work on the event.

The allure of the sun kept them on deck, standing at the railing, which didn't allow for much talking. By silent agreement, they waited until Shelby had unlocked the store and put the coffee on. Then, both armed with steaming mugs, they stood at the counter while Nora laid out some spreadsheets and pointed out what she'd recently added.

"So," Nora began, "what do you think? Should we comp the businesses we're working with and give them a pair of tickets each?"

Shelby read all the new notations, giving each serious consideration. It did make good sense from a PR standpoint, and surely those free tickets wouldn't make or break the mystery event in any way. Shelby was now even more impressed.

Finally, she answered. "How about if we extend those free tickets to the library volunteers and Judy also? Surely we're not expecting the librarian to contribute to the library fundraiser?"

Nora beamed. "I agree. I'm not sure why I didn't think of that myself. And, of course, I'm expecting the rest of the volunteers who aren't on shift at the library to be helping out, so they shouldn't pay."

"You didn't think of it because you wanted to let me feel like I'm actually making a contribution to the planning."

"Oh, I know you're busy running the store." She took another sip of her coffee then set the empty mug down. "And, I also hear you're investigating that murder."

"Where did you hear that?"

"It *is* a small town, you know."

"So I'm continuously told." Shelby gave it a moment's thought before answering. She didn't want those rumors getting back to the chief, although they probably had already. "I'm not really investigating the murder, I'm just asking some questions on behalf of his daughter, Hilary."

"By the way," Shelby said, trying to changing the topic, "have you heard back from that final author yet?"

"Trisha Dupont? Oh yes. Didn't I show that in the spreadsheet?" She pulled it closer. "No, I didn't. My bad. I will bring that up to date."

"Not to worry. In fact, I'm super impressed with how organized you are. The spreadsheet blows my mind. Have you done all of this before?"

Nora started folding up the spreadsheets and stuffing them away before she answered. "You think so? I love planning events but using the spreadsheet is beginner's luck, believe me. I'm no computer whiz. And to come up with the content, I just tried to put myself in the place of a reader attending the event and wondered what would make it perfect. The rest is all due to some of the wonderful business owners in town who are going out of their way to help make it a successful day."

"You have a way with them, I'd say. So, I guess we've covered all the bases?"

"Unless something else comes up, like an author cancels at the last minute, I think we're in great shape. But I do have something else to discuss with you." She looked suddenly serious. "I'm afraid I won't actually be able to attend the event itself."

"What do you mean?" Shelby was shocked. She hoped she hadn't done anything to offend Nora.

"I'm moving out of town. It's come up very suddenly and I've been trying to get all the loose ends taken care of for the event including getting Katie Moore, another volunteer at the library, to take over for me—I don't know if you know her?"

Shelby shook her head, although the name sounded a bit familiar.

"Well, she's great and has agreed to step in. Anyway, I've gone over most things with her and she's on board. I hope you don't mind my coopting her like that without discussing it with you."

"Of course not. She's representing the library in your place. Where are you going? I'm sorry, that's really intrusive. We'll be sorry to see you go."

Nora laughed. "That's okay. I have an aunt in Albany who is getting old, but she wants to stay in her house. It's hard for her and she's asked if I'd move in with her. I spent a lot of time and years taking care of my mom and, when she passed, I felt really lost. What I inherited permitted me to not have to look for a job so that's when I got involved with volunteer work. But I can continue to do that anywhere. And, I've been giving it a lot of consideration. I just didn't want to say anything until everything fell into place." Her smile was tentative. "You're my inspiration, you know."

"I am?"

"Yes. Why, you uprooted your life and moved here to help your aunt. I figure, if you can do it and be happy, so can I."

Shelby didn't know what to say. "That's, uh, I really don't know what to say."

Nora smiled. "That's okay. I just wanted you to know."

"It was a big decision for me to move back here, but it was coming back home for me, so that played a big role in it," Shelby admitted. "I'd lived in Lenox for only a couple of years and, before that, I hadn't even changed houses since we moved to Boston when I was a little kid."

"Well, I've been here long enough to start feeling comfortable but not put down roots. So, when my aunt asked, I thought it was as good a time as any to leave. Now, I'd better head to the dock so that I can catch the next boat back to the mainland. Do you have any questions for me before I go?"

"Not that I can think of."

"Okay. I'll keep in touch. And I will see you before I leave. Thanks again, Shelby."

"No problem." Nora's announcement had come as a surprise, but Shelby wasn't worried. The details had been taken care of and if an author did cancel, Katie would be able to handle it. All good, although it would be sort of sad to see Nora go.

They'd had a good working relationship and she'd hoped there would be a lot of joint ventures with the library.

Shelby had been involved with Judy at the library earlier in the year in planning some joint programs, but not on such a large scale as the murder mystery. She was really impressed with the many programs they offered to those struggling with literacy and wanted the store to be able to help as much as possible. She was pleased they'd come up with the idea to donate the proceeds to Read, Learn, Grow, the local literacy non-profit group. She was already planning to have the bookstore order another selection of books for people struggling to learn to read. She felt it was the least Bayside Books could do and, fortunately, Edie felt the same way.

Her first customers in the door were a book club from Gananoque, right across the river on the Canadian side of the border. They packed themselves into the small space of the bookstore. Shelby counted fifteen readers. *So much larger than the Book Club Babes,* she thought to herself. *How would you even get a word in edgewise at a meeting?*

Her question was answered by a middle-aged woman, her jet-black hair held back from her face with a bright red headband, and wearing an equally visible and matching raincoat, even though it wasn't raining. Shelby did admire the black polka dots spotting the coat, though.

"My name is Jackie," she said by way of introduction to Shelby, "and I'm the organizer of this gang. We call ourselves the Fiction, Food, and Fun Friends and all of those get equal play in our meetings." Her smile widened, showing off her bright red lipstick even more.

Shelby laughed, enjoying her enthusiasm. "It sounds like a busy group. Tell me, do you all read the same book and how does everyone get a say at your meetings?"

Suzy leaned one arm on the counter and partially turned so that she could watch her friends as she spoke. "No, to the first part. We read whatever we want, but it has to be fiction. And then we go around the table or the room, and everyone does a short talk about their choice and why they recommend it. Meanwhile, the rest of us are taking notes, if it sounds of interest. And, of course, the food is set out in front of us so we don't have to take a break for it."

"And you started this up by yourself?"

"Me and Piper, the redhead over there."

Shelby followed her gaze and saw the bright red hair and the black outfit. The reverse of her friend, Jackie. Shelby tried to suppress a chuckle but not too successfully. Jackie glanced at her then started laughing.

"We do it so they can keep track of us on days like today. Well, even at meetings." She obviously knew where Shelby's thoughts had been.

"It's effective. Do you often take day trips like this?"

"We like to do one a season and explore the area, hopefully tying it in to some reading. One of our members has been here before, and he suggested it. I'm hoping to find a novel that's set in the area. Any suggestions?"

Shelby nodded and led the way to the mystery section. "Take a look at this," she said, pulling a copy of *Back to the Bay* by Erin Lively. "It's about a woman who moves back home trying to find herself and find romance with bit of a mystery." *Just like me.* She didn't have time to continue her usual spiel about it because Piper appeared.

"Can you give me a suggestion, too?" she asked. "In fact, I think the more the better. Most of us have the same thing on our minds."

Shelby looked around the room and, indeed, most of the members were standing there, looking at her.

Shelby took a few steps backward and pointed to the shelf at her right. "This is the local author section, but you'll find most are non-fiction books. As for novels set in the area, there is one set during Prohibition and takes place along the river. I'll just go and look it up."

Shelby was checking the inventory on the computer when another person said loudly, "It can also be set anywhere in Upper New York state."

Shelby nodded, thinking how she wished Laura were there to help out. She heard Chrissie Halstead's voice rise above the din as she introduced herself.

"I see everyone's eager for a book. If you have any questions about the castle while you're waiting, I'd be happy to answer them."

She made her way to the counter and slipped behind it, standing next to Shelby. "Want me to bag?"

Shelby nodded, and finding the title she'd been looking for, led Piper to it. Then she scurried back to the counter where several book club members had already found what they wanted and were waiting to pay.

About twenty minutes later, the store was empty of customers but Chrissie had stayed behind.

"Thanks for your, help," Shelby said rubbing her sore arm. She hadn't given any thought to using it as little as possible and was now feeling the ache.

"Not a problem. I saw them all march in here, on a mission it looked like, and I knew Laura wasn't here. I had some time and I always enjoy being in here. Now, how's that arm?" She looked pointedly at Shelby who continued massaging.

"It's really much better, thanks. I forget sometimes and use it a bit too much."

"Understandable. Or so I've heard although I don't know anyone who has a splintered bone floating around in her arm. Can you feel it?" Her eyes scrunched closed as if she were trying to feel it, too.

Shelby shook her head. "No and it's not likely I will at any point, according to the doctor. Thanks, again for your help." Shelby was anxious to get off the topic of her arm.

"Any time," Chrissie said, heading to the door. She stopped and swung around to face Shelby again. "Any more happening on the hunt for Mr. Miller's killer?"

"I haven't heard a word from Chief Stone lately." Thankfully, she thought, remembering their last talk.

"I was wondering more about what you'd been up to. I can't imagine you letting this go. Especially since I've seen his daughter around again. I'll bet she's still keen to have this solved." Chrissie's eyebrows rose in a questioning look.

"She is, but there's not much she can do about it. She was asking some questions about that mystery woman, but she didn't get any new answers."

Chrissie took a couple of steps toward Shelby and asked in a lowered voice, "But do you have any clues as to who she is? I've been wracking my brain, but I guess I just don't get out enough to meet new people."

Shelby thought that odd since she'd always considered Chrissie to be a bit of a social butterfly.

"Not since breaking up with Carter, that is," Chrissie added. Then she smiled. "Of course, not while we were together either, I suppose. We tended to spend most of our time together, alone. Oh well, enough of that. You know, Shelby, I think I'm ready to start dating again. Maybe Zack has some single buddies he could introduce me to. I always did love a guy in a uniform."

Shelby laughed, trying to ignore the pang she'd felt at the mention of Zack's name. She was glad Chrissie was open to dating again. And Erica had a new guy, too. It seemed that romance was in full bloom in Alex Bay this spring. While Shelby still had a decision to make.

Shelby had just finished reshelving books when the door opened and she looked over to see Lynn Innes entering. That surprised Shelby because it was the first time Lynn had been in the store at least when Shelby had been working.

That wasn't a surprise in itself. Few locals visited, preferring to shop at the main store. But there were some who loved the boat trip and wandering through all the castles on the run and would buy season passes that covered both the boat fare and the castle entry fees.

Lynn paused just inside the door and looked around the store. Seeing that it was empty of other customers, she marched over to where Shelby was straightening books. She projected an air of being all business, from the navy pant suit and large scarf draped around her shoulders, to the determined look on her face.

"You told Chief Stone about me, even though you gave me your word."

Shelby could hear the barely controlled fury in Lynn's voice. It threw her and it took her a few moments to think of a reply. Her hands were shaking, which she hoped didn't show.

"I didn't tell her anything except to ask if she'd heard from you. You do remember you promised you'd speak to her after we spoke? And, when she hadn't, I suggested she talk to you. I didn't tell her why or give her any details. But it was important she know about any of Nathan Miller's connections in town."

She held her breath, waiting for a response be it verbal or physical. Of course, Lynn Innes wouldn't hit anyone, would she? Shelby could see the anger disappearing from Lynn's face and her shoulders sag before she took a deep breath and spoke.

"You're right. I'm sorry to have berated you like that. I have to admit, I was really reluctant to tell her about it, and I guess I tried to push it out of my mind. I was just so mortified when she stopped by." She looked around the store, a bit more slowly this time. "It's very relaxing here, isn't it?"

Shelby also relaxed her shoulders and got her breathing back to normal. "It is. I enjoy spending my hours here."

She watched as Lynn wandered slowly around the room, ending up back beside Shelby.

"I apologize and I'll leave now." She reached the door and turned back. "You must think so badly of me."

"I'm not the one to be judging," Shelby said. "No one really knows what someone else is going through."

Lynn nodded and then left. Shelby walked over to one of the wicker chairs and sank into it. She couldn't believe what had just happened. This whole murder investigation was getting her into so much hot water. Maybe it was time to bow out. Of course, she'd had that thought before. But she didn't have any time at the moment to continue that line of thinking because two young children burst into the bookstore followed by their parents. And behind them, two more couples. Shelby gave her head a quick shake and stood to welcome them.

When Shelby glanced at the clock later, she realized that she'd been so wrapped up in the steady flow of customers she'd lost total track of time. She barely made the boat after rushing through the closing sequence. But she wasn't complaining. It had been a good day both in terms of schmoozing and sales, she thought as she leaned on the railing, watching the wake made by the heavy boat. She was looking forward to a relaxing evening with Erica, just gossiping and no talk of murder.

Chapter Twenty-Seven

E rica arrived while Shelby was still on the phone with Hilary. Shelby made motions for Erica to make herself comfortable. She had one last question for Hilary.

"So, there's nothing you can find that tells us what your dad was up to?" Shelby asked Hilary.

"Nothing, which is totally strange, don't you think? It's almost like he didn't want anyone to find out."

Just what Shelby had been thinking.

"But look, I'll keep looking around. How weird is that, though? And does that make Roman Sykes a suspect? Have you told the police?"

"Not yet but I will. And I'll also scan these and send them to you. We'll talk later, okay?"

"Yeah, okay. And thanks," Hilary said as she hung up.

Shelby turned to Erica. "Sorry about that."

"Not a problem," Erica answered as she took off her jacket and then pulled a bottle of red wine out of her large blue and yellow tote, one that matched the scarf she'd worn earlier in the day, Shelby couldn't help but notice.

"That's thoughtful," Shelby said. "But I had fully intended to supply the wine. My whining, so to speak, so my wine."

"I'll bet mine's more tempting. Take a look at the label." Her eyes sparkled, and she had a mischievous look on her face.

Shelby checked it. "Wow, I'm thinking pricey or what? I'm impressed."

"My dear brother, being in a good mood for a change, stopped by with a case for me. No occasion, just wanting to be something other than a pest, for a change."

"I could have told you he had a generous side," Shelby nodded in appreciation.

"Really? Well, I know I can share this with you because you have said you're not romantically interested in him, right?"

Shelby held her hands out, palms up. "Not at all."

"Good. Well, his off-again, on-again thing with his maybe/maybe not girlfriend, Serena, is in off mode at the moment and, I have to admit, my shoulder was not a good one to cry on last week. I already had a lot on my mind."

"You did? I'm sorry. Was there anything I could have helped with?" Shelby realized with a feeling of guilt that she'd been so wrapped up in her own problems all week, she hadn't left room for the concerns of others.

Erica shook her head. "No, it was all store related. But Drew is so entitled sometimes. It just comes to a head on the rare occasion. That's a build-up of over twenty-eight years, you know." She grinned. "So, let's just enjoy, okay?"

"Sounds good to me."

Erica twisted off the cap and poured, using the glasses Shelby had set out on the counter. She took a sip and smiled. "Well done, baby brother."

Shelby led the way over to the comfy chairs. She sat and then sipped her own wine. "Um, that is really good. Maybe you should keep this in mind for future reference. Just don't hold back; tell him what's on your mind. It's obviously the right thing to do."

Erica chortled and almost choked on the sip she'd just taken.

"Would you like some cheese and crackers? I should have thought of it sooner."

"Uh-uh, I'm good. Okay, so spill. What's on your mind?"

Shelby took a longer sip and tried to relax her shoulders. "I had coffee with my mom yesterday morning. That still feels so strange to say. I had coffee with Merrily."

"You did? Good for you. How did it go? Or, is that why we're having wine?"

Shelby took a minute before answering. "I don't know. I just don't know how I'm supposed to feel. What she told me about her reason for leaving was much what Izzy Crocker had already said, so it wasn't a real shock. But I kept thinking, this is my mom. She did choose to abandon me, although according to her, she did try to get in touch with me. Which would mean if it's true, my dad wouldn't allow it. How am I supposed to feel about all that? I don't know how to react. I mean, I don't even know what to call her."

Erica put her glass down on the side table and reached over to touch Shelby's arm. "I can't imagine what you're going through, and I can't tell you anything you need to hear, because

I don't know what that would be. I do think it will probably take a while to work through all this and that you shouldn't be too hard on yourself. After all, there's no deadline, is there? You can take all the time you want to sort this through. At least you talked to her, you know how to stay in touch, I imagine. That is, if you want to."

"Yes, in fact, that's pretty much what she said, to take my time figuring it out." She looked up at Erica. "Erica, I have siblings. A sister and a brother."

"Wow, that's great, isn't it? Or, if you take what I say about Drew to heart, you may not think it's so great," she added with a chuckle.

Shelby laughed, relieved for an easing of her stress. "They don't know about me, but she said she would tell them when she got back home."

"So, they're a question mark for you, at this point anyway." Erica sat back and picked up her glass, taking a longer sip. "How do you feel about that part?"

"I'm a bit excited? I think? I used to wonder what it would be like to have a sister or brother but I knew I'd never have one. I guess it all depends on if they want to get to know me. And on just what kind of relationship my mom and I work out."

"So, it sounds like that's the direction you want to go in. You seem to have made a decision already."

"Hm, maybe I have."

"Have you told Edie about all this?"

"Not about the coffee date. I probably should have, but I felt I should sort it through a bit more. Now I'm not so sure because I'm getting nowhere."

"Talk it over with Edie. She's a remarkable woman, according to my mom. And she should know, they've been friends since elementary school and also working together in the bookstore for so long. I'm sure she'll know what to say and, at the very least, she'll be there to support you."

Shelby sat quite still for a moment, looking at her dear friend. "How did you get to be so smart?"

Chapter
Twenty-Eight

S helby's phone rang as the morning shuttle approached the
island dock. When she looked at her phone, she saw it was
Taylor. Shelby realized she hadn't talked to her in a few days,
and she eagerly answered, her hand covering one ear so that she
could hear better.

"Shelby, I'm so glad I caught you. We haven't talked for a
few days."

"That's on me, I'm afraid," Shelby admitted, feeling instantly
chastised.

"Uh, you're not the one with baby business completely filling your waking hours, so no, not on you at all. Although, I'm
betting you've been a bit preoccupied with some extra-curricular
sleuthing. Am I right?"

"You may be somewhat right. I've tried to stay out of it,
really I have, but I feel like I keep getting dragged into things."
Shelby sighed.

"Well, I'm anxious to hear some of the details and also to
hear about your arm. I can tell you're on the shuttle so I won't

255

keep you. I was thinking I might stop by for a visit with Olivia this afternoon for a bit. Would that be okay? Are you going to be there all day?

"I am, and that would be great. Is it Olivia's first boat ride?"

"It will be, and I'm hoping she won't get seasick." Shelby could hear a momentary panic in Taylor's voice.

"I hadn't even thought about babies getting seasick."

"Neither had I until I decided to visit you." Taylor gave a small laugh. "Anyway, she naps around two every day, if I'm lucky, so I'll try to make it over before then, okay?"

"Sounds great. Can't wait to see you both."

Shelby went in search of Chrissie and Mae-Beth as soon as she arrived at the castle, to tell them about Taylor's upcoming visit. Both said they'd be sure to stop by and see the baby. She wondered if Matthew would be interested but then decided it probably wasn't high on his to-do list.

Chrissie was actually the first person through the store door when Shelby got back from her wanderings. "I should have given you this when you stopped by earlier, but my brain wasn't in gear yet." She handed Shelby a stack of flyers. "They're for the big island event, Blye Days. What do you think of the name? Better than Victorian Days, don't you think?"

Shelby nodded but didn't get a chance to get a word in edgewise.

"I thought you might use them as bag stuffers. I'm having the posters done professionally so I'll get you some as soon as they arrive." She glanced around the bookstore. "Actually, I guess you probably only need one, to stick on the door. Okay, two, one for each side. But your walls are already covered with bookcases and I'm sure you don't want anything in the windows."

"You're right about that. I'm more than happy to use the bag stuffers, though." Shelby picked one up and looked it over. "It looks great. Who did the artwork?"

"Laura did. You didn't know she's a closet artist?"

"No, really? I'll have to ask her about that."

Just then an elderly couple walked in. Chrissie gave Shelby a little wave and left.

"May I help you?" Shelby asked them.

"I've heard you have a good selection of books by local writers. Just point me in the right direction, please," answered the man while the woman had already wandered off to look at the display of books on the wicker table on the other side of the room. Shelby showed the man what he was looking for and then started checking the phone messages. By the time the couple left, each with a couple of books, the store was beginning to fill up. Shelby had little time to think about anything but answering questions until she looked over at the door a little after noon and saw Taylor walk in, baby Olivia tucked into a carrier.

Shelby excused herself from the customer she'd been trying to help, with little success so far, and hurried over to Taylor. Her pixie haircut had spikes of blonde hair sticking out all over the place and her cheeks were glowing, signs of her recent boat ride.

"I'm so glad you made it. Let me see your sweet baby." Shelby smiled and put out her hands.

Taylor maneuvered Olivia out of the pouch and handed her to Shelby, then tried smoothing her hair. "You asked. Just give me a moment while I get out of all this."

257

The customer noticed the commotion and walked over, asking for a peek at the baby. By the time Taylor returned from the back room, several customers had gathered around Shelby, all entranced by the smiling Olivia. She looked as intrigued by the goings-on as a seven-month old could be. Her blue eyes were wide open, and a smile teased her lips. Wisps of dark hair stuck out from under the pink knitted hat.

Taylor laughed. "She loves attention," she said as she removed the hat and undid the matching knitted jacket. She then collected Olivia in her arms. The baby gurgled happily.

The customers wandered back to the shelves, and Shelby beckoned Taylor over to the counter.

"Can I get you a cup of coffee?"

"If you can believe it, I'm off coffee while I'm still breastfeeding her. I don't want any extra caffeine making its way into her system. She's already hyper enough, especially at bedtime."

"She's always been so calm whenever I've seen her." She couldn't take her eyes off the baby. Funny, because she'd never considered herself to be maternal. Actually, she hadn't given it much thought at all.

"Saving it up for the witching hour. How's business?" she asked, lowering her voice.

"Fairly steady. I'm anticipating another successful summer, though, and just trying to get ahead of things this year."

Taylor nodded. "I remember how everything was so new for you last year and look at you now, still standing," she said with a laugh.

"Yeah, imagine that. It was thanks to you and everyone else at the store. I miss having you here," Shelby admitted.

"Not half as much as I miss being here, I'll bet. Not that I'm anxious to leave Olivia, but a few hours of book talk with adults would be heaven. Is Laura still working out okay?"

Shelby looked sharply at Taylor. She wasn't worried about not getting her job back, was she? "She's doing just fine, learning the systems quickly. I've coopted her more than she signed on for, with my elbow and everything. She says it's all good, but she's also said she's looking forward to when it's just a few hours a week."

Taylor's shoulders relaxed and Shelby realized her supposition had been correct. "You be sure to let me know when you want to ease back into the schedule." She peered over at Olivia who appeared to have fallen asleep. Shelby raised her eyebrows in an unspoken question.

Taylor grinned. "She was restless last night, so I'm not surprised she's nodded off early."

A customer tiptoed over and tapped Shelby on the shoulder. "I'm sorry to bother you but I need some help," she explained in a soft voice.

Shelby nodded and followed her back to the mystery section. "What can I do for you?"

"I'm looking for *Mission Impawsible* by Krista Davis. Do you have it? I can't seem to find it here."

"That's not the latest one, is it? I think it came out a few years ago, right?"

"Yes. I'm reading them in order. I'm absolutely firm on that. Since we were here touring the castle, I just thought I'd pop in and see if you have it. I know it's a longshot but I also wanted to see your beautiful store. I've heard so much about it."

That pleased Shelby.

"No, I'm sorry we don't have it here. Unfortunately, we don't have enough space to carry many older titles. I could check the inventory and see if our main store has it. If they do, they could put it aside and you could stop there when you get back to Alexandria Bay, if that's where you boarded the boat."

"That would work out well." The woman nodded with enthusiasm and a thick strand of dark hair worked its way from behind her ear. Shelby walked softly over to the computer and pulled up the inventory then grabbed the phone and walked back to the customer.

"They do have it. I'll just give them a call. And, your name?"

"Diane. Diane Forrest. That's great. Thanks for your help."

Shelby nodded and went back to where Taylor was gently rocking the baby in her arms.

"I almost jumped up to help the customer," Taylor said with a chuckle.

"I'm glad you were able to restrain yourself, for Olivia's sake," she said in a whisper.

"Oh, you don't need to whisper. We've kept noise levels regular so that she will sleep through anything, and she usually does. So, how's the murder investigation coming along?"

"I'd expect you'd hear more about that from your husband, being the law and all."

"He's getting more tight-lipped as he gets older. Or maybe it's that he leaves the office totally behind him when he comes home to us, which is actually how I prefer it."

"I get that. Well, my *investigation* isn't going much of anywhere. As you know, I've been checking around to see who might have moved to the Bay seven years ago and although I've had three possibilities, they're all definitely out of the running." She hesitated to mention the fact that she was also looking into Nathan's consulting role and just what his extra task for the manager involved. After all, she didn't want that getting back to the chief. Not that Taylor was likely to spill the beans to her husband, but she couldn't say what she didn't know.

"I didn't know you had so many possibilities."

"Well, that's not a lot, not when there's that criteria to fit into. But I'm wondering if anyone is really being candid with me, for whatever reason." Shelby shrugged. "It's getting very complicated. Say, do you happen to know a guy named Charlie or Charles Innes?"

Taylor gave it some thought. "Not personally, but isn't he an accountant or something? I think Chuck had him do our taxes last year. I never met the guy, but I'm sure that's the name of his business. Why?"

"Great. Thanks for the info. I'd rather not say why right now, if you don't mind." She looked over at the door as Chrissie walked in and gave a little squeak. "Here comes the fan club."

Chrissie rushed over and gave Taylor a hug, avoiding crushing the baby. "Oh, let me see her. The first time she's visited the castle." She peered closer as Taylor repositioned her arm to give Chrissie a better look. "She is so adorable. What's it like being a mom?"

Shelby noticed another customer looking quizzical so left the two talking and went to help the man. By the time she'd helped find him a suitable gift for his mother's birthday, Chrissie had left only to be replaced by Mae-Beth Warren. The word had gotten out about Taylor and Olivia's arrival, and various volunteers and staff spent the next little while whipping into the store to see them. By the time it was 1:00 PM, Olivia was awake and Taylor moved into the back room to feed her. When she'd finished, she looked around the almost empty store and suggested to Shelby, "If you'd like to take a lunch break, I can man the store."

Shelby looked a bit dubious.

"See, I'll just put Olivia back in her pouch and she's happy just to be upright and moving around. Now, go. I'm really happy to do this."

Shelby could see that, so she agreed and grabbed her sandwich, heading to a picnic table positioned in the sunlight. She was happy she had wrapped her scarf around her neck, under her jacket. Though the day was sunny it was still a bit on the cool side.

She had just finished when she noticed Merrily stepping off the boat that had just pulled in at the dock. She quickly stuffed the sandwich container in her bag and sprinted back to the store. She'd just told Taylor that her mom was heading that way when Merrily walked into the store. She stood in the doorway and looked from one side of the room to the other, smiling when she saw Shelby.

Awkward, Shelby thought, since she wasn't prepared this time. She thought Merrily had already left town and said as much.

"I'm leaving tomorrow morning. I just wanted to spend some more time visiting Izzy and then I thought I'd take a look at this store. I haven't been in the castle before."

"This is Taylor Fortune," Shelby introduced her, "and her daughter, Olivia. Taylor works part-time for us, except for right now while she's on maternity leave."

Merrily's smile was warm. "Very nice to meet you, Taylor, and your little one. I guess Shelby's filled you in on who I am."

"Well, I do know you're her mom," Taylor ventured to say, after a quick glance at Shelby. "Nice to meet you, too."

"Thank you. I won't interrupt you two. I wanted to take a look through the castle and I'll pop in just before I leave, Shelby." She disappeared through the door before Shelby could comment.

"And there you have her," Shelby said at last.

"Are you okay?"

"Probably. I just hadn't expected to see her here today." Shelby unclenched her hands, not realizing she'd done it in the first place. "We had coffee the other day and talked through a few things." She turned to look at Taylor. "There's still so much that needs to be settled, but it will take time."

Taylor nodded. "I can understand that." She reached out to touch Shelby's arm and smiled. "I guess we'd better be heading back. I have some shopping to do and Chuck thought he might be able to come home early."

"I'm so happy you came by and, as you can see, most of the castle was also."

"That was fun." She pulled her jacket on, the same one she'd worn when she was pregnant, Shelby realized, with a full cut that allowed her to enfold Olivia, still in her carrier, inside it.

"I'll see you real soon," Shelby said, giving her a loose hug.

"Drop in anytime. I look forward to adult company," Taylor said and, after taking another glance around the store, left.

By 3:00 PM, Shelby was starting to get a bit antsy. The afternoon had slowed down after Taylor left. Merrily had stopped in for a quick goodbye, but it had been busy at that point. Now Shelby could feel her lack of a full night's sleep playing havoc with her ability to focus on what she was doing. She'd offered to take on the task of keeping the website up-to-date, adding events and lists of new arrivals. They were even listing titles that were available for preorder. It was a lot of extra work, but it was something Shelby could do from the island location.

She was pleased when Nora appeared, complete with her trusty briefcase.

"Sorry to just pop in unexpectedly but I wanted to check with Chrissie Halstead about the plans for Blye Days here on the island."

"Are you involved in that, too?"

"Well, Chrissie lives down the street from me and we were talking out in the front yard one day, and she mentioned the event. I tossed around a few suggestions, and she's asked for my input a few times. I told her I'd keep working on it until I leave but I think she's got most of it well in hand. She's very competent, you know."

"She is. It's a big job doing the PR for the castle, but she's a hard worker. I'm sure she'll miss your help, though. When do you leave?"

"Here's your hat, what's your hurry?" Nora said with a loud laugh.

"Oops, not very tactful." Shelby smiled, though feeling embarrassed. "I did mean when is your big move?"

"It's coming up way too quickly which is why I wanted to take care of this last detail before handing things over to Katie. I should have brought it with me yesterday. Now, take a look at this final draft for the flyer," Nora said, without answering the new question also. "Let me know if you have any more changes."

Shelby put it on the counter and studied it carefully, but realized part of her brain was wondering about Nora.

"Is it okay?" Nora asked.

"Yeah, it looks great. You've done a really super job."

Nora looked pleased. "Thank you, Shelby. I had a lot of fun doing it." She tucked it back in the folder, which she replaced in her briefcase. She paused as if trying to decide what to do next, then asked, "By the way, have you heard anything more about that death or figured out where the mystery woman is?"

"Not really. I'm sure the police are making headway, though." It sounded good anyway.

"I still can't believe there was another murder in town. I guess none of us can. I wish them luck. You know, maybe it doesn't have anything to do with the woman. I mean, maybe he was involved with something else in town."

That just might be true. Had Nora heard anything about Nathan's consulting job? Was the word out in town? Not that there was anything to hide about the job itself, but she knew Walt Nevins didn't want any news getting out concerning his employee problem.

After Nora left, Shelby thought over everything she knew about her. She hadn't yet crossed her off the list, just in case the time frame was wrong or Nora had lived somewhere else before coming to the Bay, as Tamara had done. She found it hard to think of her in the role of the murderer, though. What would be her motive? And how could she act so calmly when talking about his death? No, Nora was not at the top of the list. That spot belonged to Roman Sykes.

* * *

Shelby stepped off the boat after work and stopped in at the Mango Lagoon to pick up the dinner for two she'd ordered. The colorful artwork depicting tropical settings, and, even more so, the exotic aromas of an unusual menu put her in a good mood.

By the time she'd reached Edie's, she had what she'd say set in her mind. Edie greeted her at the door.

As Shelby was emptying the food cartons into serving dishes, Edie said, "This is such a pleasant surprise. I was pleased when you phoned to suggest it." She finished setting the table, put her hands flat on it and leaned on them. "Although, I get the impression there's something you want to talk about."

Edie's lime green top clashed with the green in her multi-colored long skirt. She either didn't know or didn't care and Shelby realized, that was one of the things that was so great about Edie.

"Huh. Missing the subtleness?" Shelby paused, looking over at Edie.

"A little. Is it about Zack?"

"Well, partially. Is it that obvious?"

"Only if you take into consideration that you don't seem quite as ecstatic about his calling you on a Sunday evening or even his coming home on a weekend lately. Which tells me you haven't settled this in your mind yet."

"You're quite observant, aren't you?" Shelby said with a small smile.

"When it comes to you, yes. Also, let's just say, I'm enjoying living vicariously through your romance."

"What about your own?" *Oops. That just slipped out.*

Edie's demeanor changed and she was suddenly serious. "It's nice, no better than nice. It's pretty exciting that at my age and stage there's someone like Matthew in my life. But I don't kid myself. This is the most it will ever be, and that's okay. He still has so many ghosts in his life about his wife's death and all that happened after, I don't think he'll ever set them right. So, he'll never be able to entirely commit to someone else."

"Wow. I didn't realize. And, you're definitely okay with that?"

"Shelby, I've known it from the start and I've kept reminding myself so that I keep it all in perspective and am honest with myself, unlike you about Zack."

"Whoa, that's a bit brutal." Shelby hadn't expected that comment. It felt like a reprimand. Maybe it was.

"I'm sorry if you think that. It's not meant to be. But I've watched you fall head over heels in love with the guy, even if you won't totally admit it to yourself. Look, I know how guarded you are about your feelings and I think this has taken you totally by surprise."

Shelby nodded but didn't answer. She had no idea Edie had been so tuned into what was going on in Shelby's brain. She set the dishes on the table.

"I am starving. Let's eat and enjoy," Edie suggested, passing one of the cartons to Shelby and opening the second one.

"Good idea," Shelby agreed as she passed the Pad Thai Edie had requested and spooned out some Pra Goong, her go-to dish, for herself. They switched dishes and passed around the final two and then ate in silence for several minutes.

"This is delicious," Edie finally said. "And to think, I'd never even thought to eat there until you moved here. In fact, there's a lot of things I never did until you arrived on the scene." Edie smiled. "Speaking of which, and no pressure meant, but what have your thoughts been about what Zack has asked?"

Shelby found it hard to swallow.

"I haven't really come to a decision, but I can't get it off my mind. And I'm not ready to tell him what he wants to hear. I readily admit I do know what worries me about a long-distance relationship, though."

Edie said nothing but raised her eyebrows.

"Look how long Dad and I lived in Boston and how few times we got together with you. Boston, that's where Zack would be moving. The distance hasn't changed any. It's just too easy to grow apart when you're living apart.

Edie took a sip of water before answering. "Oh, honey. You can't use that as a basis for any decision. It is a six-hour drive, but that's not such a big deal these days, if you don't want it to be. Like I've said, with you and your dad, he was reluctant to come back here, you know that. And, I guess it was some stubbornness on my part, but I didn't make many attempts to visit you. I was mad at him. And I regret it, deeply. I should have been the better, more reasonable person and put aside my hurt feelings to be able to spend time with you. In hindsight. It's a pain."

Shelby wasn't sure what to say. She felt on shaky ground here. "But, even now, Zack doesn't come home very often and he's that much closer." She closed her eyes for a moment and took a deep breath.

"It's because of his work, I know that. And he's often secretive, working long hours, who knows where. But it's important to him and he enjoys it. I would never say or do anything to interfere with that."

"Then there's the flip side, right?" Edie asked, concerned.

"Yes. He'll be so busy, consumed with his job and I would be back in Boston where I don't really know many people. I didn't have many close friends growing up and I certainly haven't kept in touch with any of them. And you know what a difficult time I have making new friends. And I won't have a job right away. Anyway, what could I do? I was an editor and then worked in a bookstore."

"Well, I'd say that's your answer, try to get a job in a bookstore. You'll come highly recommended," she added with a big smile. "And as for friends, look how many you've made here. That was your doing, so don't give me any of that malarkey about having a hard time doing it. Although that may have been so in the past, you went ahead and did it and now have some very close friendships, I'd say."

"Well, you know as well as I do that being a part of the bookstore was responsible for that. It was fairly easy to fit into the community and of course, everyone knows my Aunt Edie." She sighed. "I guess I'm just wallowing in self-pity, right?"

"Now you are being silly."

Shelby glanced quickly at Edie. She wasn't sure about that tone of voice but she saw the smile on Edie's face and felt the tension start to leave her shoulders.

"You know I truly believe that you and Zack will find a solution," Edie continued. "You two are in love and you want to spend time together. However, I can't help you make that decision and also, I know you know that I should not figure into it either. Like I've said, I'd miss you terribly if you move but it won't be like before. Now we are truly a family and that means we'll keep seeing a lot of each other. No matter where you are. Especially since you're a business partner, we'll have to confer even more often. So, you base your decision entirely on you and Zack. Is this what you want for your future? Is he who you want?"

"That's certainly to the point."

"Of course it is, and that is exactly the point." Edie crossed her arms on the table and leaned forward.

Shelby closed her eyes for a moment and took a deep breath. "I guess what's also bothering me is that I'm not used to feeling special to someone. I don't know what he sees in me and I'm afraid if it's just us off somewhere, he'll begin to question that too."

Edie shook her head. "Well that's just ridiculous. You are special and you have to believe that. From what I've seen, he's so smitten, the discovery part will be more like a great adventure. I'm pretty certain about that, from my great wisdom gained over the years," she gave a small laugh, "that he would have realized by now you're not the one, if that's how he felt. Give yourself a break, honey. He asked you to move with him. Doesn't that prove something?"

"How can I tell if he's the one?"

"Hmm, personally, I've always thought that if you can't live without someone, that's a pretty good indicator."

And there it was. She knew they wouldn't get any further talking about this. It was between Zack and her now, as it really always had been. She also knew she had to share with Edie what she'd said to Merrily. She wasn't looking forward to this conversation either.

"I have something else to talk over with you."

Edie's eyebrows rose in inquiry but she didn't say anything. Shelby thought that was because Edie already had an inkling of what was coming. They hadn't discussed Merrily again but she knew that Edie must be waiting to hear something more about her.

"It's about Merrily. I still find it odd to call her Mom. Do you think that's unusual?"

Edie smiled even though her eyes didn't. "I think that's the most normal thing of everything that's been happening. I'm assuming you've talked to her."

Shelby thought she sounded wistful. "Yes, yesterday morning. We had coffee and she tried to explain why she'd done what she had and why she was back now. We decided I should take time to think about what, if any, relationship I wanted to have with her. And now she's gone back to her home."

"That sounds wise," Edie answered and Shelby realized she had probably been holding her breath.

"I know how hard you took it when you found out she was still alive so this couldn't have been easy. And, I applaud Merrily for backing off after saying her bit. You do need time to think, and that's why I won't jump in there with my two cents. This is another instance when you have to figure out what's best for you and do it."

She let out a deep sigh. "Thanks, Edie. I appreciate that."

"So," Edie said after a few minutes, her tone of voice changing into a livelier one, "would you like any dessert?"

"Always," Shelby answered, feeling relieved they'd discussed everything. She could tell Edie was trying hard to keep her tone light when talking about Merrily, which in itself was very telling. Another decision. There seemed to be a lot of those these days.

Chapter
Twenty-Nine

S helby had been disappointed when she'd arrived home after her dinner with Edie to find she had missed a call from Zack. However, he had left her a message saying he'd be home on Friday night and was looking forward to catching up. She knew what that meant. She thought about that on the shuttle ride over to Blye Island the next morning, wondering, if she were to think it through at different locations, if it might make the decision easier. Like, how would it feel not taking the shuttle most mornings? What would it be like not working in the castle? Not shelving books in the store? Not planning book events? What would she do with her life in Boston?

What also came to mind was something Nora had said about not getting too settled in one place. Would that be her fate, also? Her thoughts wandered to what had been happening in Alexandria Bay lately. There seemed to be a lot of women on the move these days. She knew Alice's reason, of course. She'd really had no choice. Nora had also been running away, it sounded like, leaving the pain of her mother's death. But Shelby knew her reasons were different. She'd been running *to* a new life with Edie and, if she left, it would be going forward to a new one with Zack.

What about Tamara Young? Shelby thought back to what they'd discussed. No, she had readily admitted that seven years ago she'd lived in Albany and then, after three years, moved to the Bay. She hadn't given a reason for the moves, but what did it matter? Someone had mentioned something about a fire but then again, what did it matter? The timeline was all wrong.

She'd managed to put it all completely out of her mind by the time Felicity called just before Shelby was switching off for the day with Laura at 1:00 PM.

"It's nice to hear from you, Felicity. What can I do for you?"

"I just remembered something else Nathan Miller said to me that Saturday. I remember the name of the mystery woman." Her voice ended on a higher pitch, and Shelby could hear the excitement in her voice.

"What is it?" Her own curiosity ramping up.

"Margo Parker. That's what he said. I can't believe it's just come to me, but that's what happens every now and then. You'll find out when you reach my age, not that I'm that old," she hastened to add. "I like to think of it as having amassed so much information over the years that sometimes new bits just get pushed into the corners. But Margo Parker is definitely the name of the mystery woman."

Margo. "And do you remember if he said anything more about her?"

"Not that time, but my new part-timer, Kathleen, who filled in for me on that last Saturday when I was out of town, said Nathan Miller saw the poster for your murder mystery event at the library and wondered if his mystery woman, well, that's not what he called her, but if she had been involved in planning it. Apparently, she'd helped put together a lot of events when he knew her. Isn't that interesting? I don't know why I'd forgotten that except when I was moving your poster, to a better place you understand, where it will get a lot more attention, it reminded me."

Shelby smiled at Felicity's reason for moving the poster. But as to what Nathan had said, she didn't have a ready answer. Nor did she come up with a reason for never having asked who had tended the gallery while Felicity was away. That should have been an obvious question.

"That's certainly interesting," she said after a moment's thought. "Are you going to call Chief Stone and tell her? Or, did she already talk to Kathleen?"

"I'm sure she has, I mean, I told the chief at the time but Kathleen wasn't working the day she came in to talk to me."

"Did Nathan by any chance mention talking to anyone else in town?"

"You mean besides you, Trudy, and someone at the library? Those are the only ones I've heard about, and he wasn't the one who mentioned them. You were the one who told me, I think. Anyway, I just wanted to let you know about the name. Have you had any luck figuring out who this woman is? I know for sure that no one by that name lives around here."

"She might have changed her name if she didn't want to be found." Of course, she had, so knowing the name wasn't that critical after all. "Did you mention this to anyone else?"

"No, it just came to me and I thought it might help your investigation."

"Thanks, I appreciate that."

She'd just hung up the phone when it rang again.

"Is this Shelby Cox?"

"It is. What can I do for you?" She couldn't place the male voice so probably not a regular customer.

"This is Roman Sykes, if you'll recall we spoke when you came into our offices to talk about Nathan Miller."

She almost dropped the phone she was so surprised. She gathered her thoughts and her voice. "Yes, I do."

"Good. James Rooney was telling me about some documents you'd gotten. I may be able to help you with those. I'll be at a building site close to where you live later this afternoon. I could come by your place if you're home around four or you could meet me at the site. It shouldn't take long."

No way did she want him at her place; and how did he know where she lived anyway? But she did wonder what he had to say. He certainly wouldn't be the person who'd dropped them off for her but then again, he might assume the emails were about something else and have some interesting information for her.

"Sure, I'll meet you at the site. At four."

"That sounds good. It's about a five-minute walk along Bay Road. Turn left at the T-bone at the end of Mack Street. See you later."

Indeed.

* * *

Shelby found the building site easily. It looked like a two-story office building might be going in, although since it was at the framing stage, she had no real idea. Roman stood outside the fence that surrounded the build site. The gate was closed and had a lock on it. Roman took off the hardhat he had been wearing and greeted her.

"What will this be?" Shelby was curious. It looked like prime real estate, overlooking the water, but she couldn't remember hearing about it in any public meetings.

"Retail on the ground level and a floor of offices above. The crew has stopped for the day, which is a good thing or we'd never hear each other. Would you like to see the back and the view?"

She hesitated and he pointed over to a temporary wood walkway that ran along the right side of the fence, toward the back.

"It's quite safe, no rough spots and since the work for the day is over, no dust."

He led the way and she followed. When they reached the back, she stood for a few minutes looking at the view. "This is quite a view. I'm surprised something commercial was allowed to build here." She remembered the villagers' protest when another resort was being considered. Even though it would have brought in more tourists, and therefore more revenue, they didn't want the precious shoreline eaten away with large buildings. She wondered if this was part of what Nathan had discovered.

Sykes looked surprised. "It's a good location and will be good for the economy." He turned to face her. "Now, what I really want to talk about is those emails you told Rooney about. He didn't say what they were about."

"No, because I didn't tell him." She left it at that.

"I was hoping they were about the project we were working on. I can't find the notes Miller was planning to send me and wonder if that's what those are?"

"I couldn't say."

He took a step closer. "Couldn't or wouldn't?"

"Well, how do I know if they're the notes you want unless you tell me what they are?" She could see his face turning red, and stepped backward.

"I need them and they should not be in your possession, whatever they are. They belong to the office, so maybe you should just hand them over to me and stop nosing around in our business."

His facial expression hadn't changed although he was close enough that she could see a darkness in his eyes.

"You're right. I will do just that. I'll take them to Mr. Nevins first thing tomorrow morning."

He blanched and she noticed him flex his hand open and shut.

He spun around and walked toward the water. She wondered if she should take advantage of his distance and get out of there but he turned back around to face her before she could act.

"I need to know what they're about so why don't you just tell me. I know you read them." He took a step forward.

"I didn't really pay that much attention to them."

"I find that hard to believe since you came to the office and were asking questions. Well, I'll save you the trouble of going back there. You can just give them to me now. I'll see that Nevins gets them." He stuck his hand out.

"I don't have them with me. It's not something I just carry around."

"I'll walk back to your place with you in that case."

"Not right now, I'm on my way to meet someone for dinner."

"Now you're making me angry, Miss Cox. I don't believe you, and now you're playing games. None of this concerns you and if you don't hand the files over and stop asking questions and butt out, you will definitely regret it. You don't want to push me too far."

A chill spread through her body. Why had she agreed to meet him here? Because she hadn't realized no one else would be around. She did the only thing she could think of. *Bluff it out.*

"Anyway, I've already turned them over to the police." *Which is what I should have done right away.*

He grimaced. "I don't believe you."

She started backing away, careful to keep on the walkway. "Look, I don't know the significance of the emails and I don't have them. So, I'm just going to leave, and you are not going to follow me." She whipped her phone out of her pocket. "Or I promise, I will call the police."

Sykes stepped toward her then stopped. Shelby didn't wait any longer. She turned and ran to the road and the short way to the village. She didn't look back, but she was sure thankful she was wearing sneakers.

She didn't slow down until she reached her dock and then looked behind her. No Sykes. Once inside the houseboat, she doubled over and took several deep breaths.

She knew she had to do what she'd told him she'd already done. She called the police.

Chapter Thirty

C hief Stone arrived within ten minutes of getting Shelby's call. She stomped on the dock which got Shelby's attention. She had the door open and was waiting by the time Stone got there.

"Okay, tell me what this is all about," she said as she removed her cap but stood standing just inside the door.

Shelby took a breath. "How much do you know about Nathan Miller's consulting job with the town?"

Stone looked annoyed. "I don't know why it surprises me that you've found out about that. So, tell me what you know and why you called" She looked over at the loveseat and sat there.

Shelby sat across from her. "Hilary came across his contract with the consulting firm so we thought we'd talk to someone there about the work he was doing."

"This was Hilary's idea?"

"Uh, it was a joint one."

Stone snorted. "And did you not think to call me and make sure I had this information?"

"You didn't know?"

"I didn't say that." She shook her head. "Just tell me what happened from there."

"We went to the office and found out how often Nathan Miller had been coming to town but that was about all. As we were leaving, one of the guys suggested I talk to Walt Nevins, the manager."

"And did you?" Stone's voice made Shelby think carefully about how she would tell the rest of the story.

"Yes, but he didn't know much either. A few days later, someone stuck an envelope with a USB drive in my door and on it were two emails." She paused to look at Stone's face before continuing. "One was from Nevins asking Nathan to check to see if one of the employees was involved in taking bribes and the other was from Nathan saying he would have the proof by the end of the week. That was sent the week he died."

She watched Stone's face for any sign of surprise. There was no reaction. A poker face.

"Did you know about what Nevins had asked him to do?"

"I'm not going to tell you, Shelby. That's far more information than a civilian should have. I will take the USB drive though." She stood and held out her hand.

Shelby had anticipated that and handed it over. "There is one more thing."

"Go on."

"I thought it might have come from James Rooney, the guy who'd suggested I talk to his boss, Nevins, so I went back to thank him and maybe find out if there was more."

Stone took a deep breath and shook her head again. "And was he?"

"That's just it, he wasn't. And then I got a phone call from another employee, Roman Sykes."

She noticed a spark of interest this time. "He said he could probably help me and asked me to meet him at a building site this afternoon, which I did. Then he demanded I give him the emails and stay out of it."

Stone snorted.

"He actually threatened me and then I told him I've already given them to you." Shelby tried to look contrite. "I told him I'd call the police if he followed me, which he didn't do."

Stone paced slowly from the front door to the kitchen counter and back.

"That could have been a dangerous situation, but I'm sure I don't have to tell you that. Why didn't you bring it to me right away?"

Shelby didn't have an answer that Stone would like. "I know—it was dumb."

"Yes it was, just like you continuing to nose around in all this after I told you not to. Now, I'll take care of this . . ." she held up the USB ". . . and Roman Sykes."

She let herself out without another word.

Chapter
Thirty-One

S helby called Hilary as soon as Stone left and filled her in on what had happened,

"That must have been frightening for you. Do you think he's the murderer? Is she going to arrest him?"

"She didn't say anything to me about that. You might give her a call tomorrow, though, after she's had a chance to get over my withholding evidence." Shelby grimaced as she thought of the anger on Stone's face as she had taken the USB drive. She hadn't said much, which had made it so much more uncomfortable for Shelby.

"That sucks, you won't get in trouble, will you?" Hilary sounded genuinely worried.

"I think not. We've been down this road before, but I did tell her we both visited the office initially so be prepared."

"Well, I am his daughter. She didn't think I'd just sit around and do nothing, did she?"

"That's clearly what she was hoping. Anyway, we'll keep each other posted."

The next morning, it all seemed like a dream. How could she have gone over to meet the guy who was being investigated by Nathan Miller, and alone? She'd felt fairly safe since she hadn't told Rooney about the contents of the emails. But she hadn't counted on Sykes already having been alerted to it all. She was so tempted to call the chief and see if he'd been arrested for murder.

At least then Shelby wouldn't have to worry about Sykes prowling around. If he was the killer, then that let the mystery woman off the hook, but Shelby still wondered who it could be. And until she heard differently, the woman still could be the murderer.

That thought stuck at the back of Shelby's mind at work that day and later in the day when the foot traffic had been slow for some time, she decided to list what she knew about the woman. Not much, she realized. Only that Nathan thought she'd been here for seven years, that she was a reader, and also, there was his comment to Felicity about the woman being involved in the planning of a lot of events. Not much, but it did point to one person, Nora. She didn't fit the seven-year mark but, like Tamara Young, she could have lived somewhere else before moving to the Bay. She certainly liked books enough to volunteer at the library. And, she had dynamite skills when it came to organizing the mystery event.

The phone rang, interrupting her concentration. She didn't recognize the number but the caller identified herself as Mandy.

"Do you remember me, from Mr. Nevins's office?"

"Of course. How are you? I've been wondering how to get in touch with you. I missed seeing you last time I was there."

"That's because I was fired." Shelby could hear the anger in her voice.

"Oh, I'm sorry. That must have come as a shock."

"It did. I didn't deserve it, but poor Mr. Nevins didn't know everything that was going on. That Roman Sykes is a real scumbag and told Mr. Nevins that I stole something. I didn't, I swear, but it was his word against mine and I was gone. At least they didn't call the cops." Now she sounded almost in tears.

"Why would he have you fired?"

"Because I know things. I know about his little schemes but again, who would believe me? He wanted me out of there, but I wasn't going without taking a little something. He accused me of stealing, so guess what, I stole that USB drive."

That explains a lot. "How did you get hold of the emails?"

"I have access to all of Mr. Nevins's files and I just happened to come across the email from Mr. Miller when he'd left his laptop open one day. He'd had to go to Mr. Sykes's office and I'd brought a coffee and just happened to read it. So, I sent it to myself."

"Why give it to me?"

"Because you're trying to find out who killed Mr. Miller and I think that's proof that Sykes did it. I want you to nail the guy."

"You took quite a chance, Mandy, but I have turned it over to the police."

"I understand and I'm glad about that. I guess if they track it back to me, I'll have to face what happens, but I'm not sorry I did it. And if it helps nail that creep, then it's worth it."

After Mandy hung up, Shelby thought about what Mandy had said and implied. She did agree, it looked like a strong motive but what happened now was up to the police. If they asked, she would tell them about Mandy. That was all she could do at this point.

Shelby turned her attention back to her list. Nora? It did make sense. Shelby needed to have a talk with Nora as soon as she reached the mainland. She pulled out her phone and called her at home.

"Hi, I hope I'm not interrupting anything. I just wondered if you had a few moments to talk."

"About the event? Look, I'm in the middle of packing but why don't you come over? I can talk while I'm working."

"Actually, I'm still at the store but just about to close. Would 5:30 be okay?"

"That's fine. Should I see if Katie can join us?"

"That's not necessary. I'm sure you can answer my questions."

Shelby took down her address and started the closing routine.

When the boat docked, she decided not to go home first but head straight to Nora's. She reached the house with the red door a few minutes later. The same color as Zack's front door. *Zack*. Not a good time to be thinking about him. It seemed to Shelby that there were no safe topics to dwell on these days. Not murder, not Merrily, certainly not Zack.

She knocked and the door was opened almost immediately by a breathless Nora.

"Come in, but please excuse the mess. I hadn't realized how much I'd accumulated over the years. It's almost all boxed and ready to ship."

Nora had her hair pulled back with a sports headband holding it in place. She wore a T-shirt that was stretched out of shape and jogging pants, certainly the most casually dressed Shelby had ever seen her.

Shelby followed her into the living room and saw what Nora meant. She did have a lot of boxes there. "It looks like you're almost ready to go. You must have been at this a while." Maybe it wasn't such a spur-of-the-moment decision.

"Well, I leave on Tuesday, which I can't believe is coming so soon. So, what's this about the event? Something new come up?"

Shelby paused a moment. What should she say? She should have thought it out more carefully. She didn't have any solid proof, just a bunch of random facts that Shelby thought, when viewed together, might point the finger at Nora.

Of course, this was all based on the premise that Sykes didn't commit the murder. He might have. Shelby would have to be tactful.

"I just wanted to run some things by you. It's more like thinking out loud."

Nora glanced at her but continued her packing. "I'm listening."

"I was just wondering where you'd lived before coming here."

"Before here?" Nora gave her a quick look before kneeling and busying herself with wrapping objects in a roll of newsprint sitting in the middle of the floor. "I lived in Syracuse but it was too busy for me, so I moved here."

"And how long did you live there? It sounds like you moved there from a town similar in size to the Bay."

"Why are you asking? I don't see how that's important. It was a long time ago."

"Seven years?"

Nora stood abruptly and placed the wrapped object in a box. She didn't look at Shelby nor did she answer her.

Shelby took a deep breath. "You've obviously had experience doing these events before, haven't you? I mean you're so competent."

Nora looked a bit relieved by the new question.

"Well, yes, I have. I love doing them in fact, I had at one time thought about a job as an event coordinator but it didn't happen." She shrugged.

"Apparently Nathan Miller's mystery woman was someone who had put on several of these over the years. And I know you love books and reading, that's obvious because you're volunteering in a library. So, I'm sort of jumping all over here, but I'm talking to all the women who fit the profile. For instance, my friend Taylor told me she moved here seven years ago. I hadn't known that but it was a help to get that information. It made me think about the need to take a closer look at assumptions, for starters."

Nora blanched. "I'm not sure what you're getting at." Nora began worrying the roll of packing tape she held in her hands.

"Well, I started thinking that just because you moved here five years ago doesn't mean you're not the person who moved away from Fulsome Falls or wherever it was, seven years ago. You could have gone to Syracuse first. And that's what you did, right?"

Nora gave a small uncomfortable laugh. "Really, Shelby. I do wonder why you'd even think it was me. I'm sure the police have a lot more information and know who it is." She looked around at the boxes. "I'm sorry, I can't help you anymore, and I do have a lot of packing to finish."

Shelby could see Nora's hands holding the roll of tape were shaking. Nora picked up a green and blue glass vase for wrapping and it slipped through her hands, breaking into large pieces on the floor.

"Oh no," Nora cried out and knelt down, cutting her hand on a shard of glass as she tried to brush them into a pile. She let out a small moan and looked around. "I need a tissue."

Shelby pulled one out of her pocket and hurried to her. "Make sure there isn't any glass embedded and then apply pressure with this."

Nora did as she was told, tears forming in her eyes. She plopped down onto the floor and just stared at the mess. After a few moments, the tears started flowing.

"I've made such a mess of it all." She added in a softer voice, "It was an accident."

Shelby wondered if she meant the broken vase or something more sinister. She thought it best to let Nora get it out of her system before saying anything.

Finally, Nora stood up and hurried down the hall. Shelby wondered if she was hiding or trying to get out the back door but after a few moments, Nora returned with some tissues in her hand. She wiped her eyes and blew her nose.

"I wish I was dead," she finally said. "I'm just so, so sorry and feeling so guilty. I don't think I can go on living with the guilt. It was me. I am the mystery woman."

She shook her head and kept shaking it as she whispered, "I killed Nathan Miller. I didn't mean to, but I killed him."

Shelby felt her jaw drop. She hadn't been sure what she'd expected when she entered the house but she did know that deep down inside, this wasn't it.

"I should have confessed right after it happened, but I was scared. I didn't want to go to jail. But I know I should have told the police. I didn't mean to kill him, you see. I really didn't. I was just so frustrated and angry."

"What happened? How did you know him?"

Nora blew her nose again and went back to where she'd been sitting.

"I knew Nathan when I was living in the Fulsome Falls area. I was a volunteer in the local library, and we were on its board together. Well, I took over as treasurer, a job which I did for several years. And then I left. I needed to move away after my mom died, so I went to Syracuse for a few years before coming here. But it was too big. I really didn't enjoy being there."

"But why was Nathan so intent on finding you?" *Were you lovers?* "And, why did you change your name? To avoid him tracking you down?"

Nora sighed and nodded. "My real name is Margo Parker. I changed more than my name. I've had a nose job, a new hairstyle and color, and these glasses are just props. I did it all not because of him originally, but because for some time before I left Fulsome Falls I'd been transferring small amounts of money from the board account into my own bank account. It built up over time." She looked at Shelby, her eyes brimming with a fresh onslaught of tears. "Nathan found out just before I left, and he started blackmailing me."

The monthly deposit to Nathan's account.

Shelby didn't want to interrupt even though she had a lot of questions. It took Nora a few minutes to continue. She looked lost in the past; her gaze unfocused.

"How did he know where you were?" Shelby finally asked.

"I'm not sure. He told me he'd seen me walking down the street one day and thought it was me. I mean, I sort of tilt to the left when I walk. You may not have noticed but it's because of an old injury. It totally threw me when I saw him leaving the castle, and I knew why he was there. I was running out of money so I'd stopped paying him last August. When I heard about someone asking questions in town, I knew it was Nathan. So, I decided it was best to confront him, meet him head-on and plead my case. That's all I wanted. That's all I'd planned to do." Her voice was pleading. "I just couldn't keep on paying him."

Shelby decided not to be taken in by Nora's emotion but press on with her questions. "Why did you do it in the first place?"

"I needed the money. Originally, I used it to help pay my mom's medical bills and then when she passed, I just left town, taking the money. I've had a few paying jobs but nothing that gave me a good salary, so I was relying on the money. But I knew that might soon change. I didn't try investing the money or anything like that, so that I wouldn't leave a trail. But I guess I did after all."

"Didn't you feel any guilt?"

She nodded. "I did at first but I just tried to push it out of my mind. By then, I was enjoying the lifestyle, being able to buy things I couldn't before. But finally, when I realized I was running out of money, I just stopped paying Nathan. I'm sure that's when he started trying to track me down. I still don't know how he did it but I heard from Jennifer that he'd been in the library asking about someone. Me."

"Did you decide then to kill him?"

"No, I would never choose to do that. I'm not a bad person. I'm not a murderer. It just happened. I had hoped never to see him again, but there he was, on the island, and I knew we had to talk. He'd never stop looking for me and I couldn't run forever. I saw him coming out of the castle, quite by accident, and called him over to the back. I insisted I didn't have any more money and he said I'd have to find it somewhere. He said he had big expenses, mainly his wife. If I didn't pay him, he'd turn me in. I was so mad. He wouldn't listen. He was very cold-hearted about it all. I just grabbed a small log and hit him on the head when he turned his back on me. When I saw him lying there, I panicked and ran. I knew he was dead. I didn't mean to kill him, just knock him out so that I could get away." She stopped for a moment and then blew her nose again.

"I couldn't believe it when I heard his body had been found in the water beside your houseboat. I didn't push him into the river you know, so he must have still been alive and maybe stumbled over the edge or something. I should have checked him more carefully. I hadn't thought he would do that. I'd just wanted time to get away." She closed her eyes and took a deep breath.

"I killed him, Shelby. And here I am trying to run away again, but I'm actually glad you've found out. I can't live with that much longer. It's been eating away at me, that's why I had to get out of Alexandria Bay. I don't have an aunt who needs my help. I just need to get away." Her voice quivered and she wilted against the stack of boxes, covering her face with her hands. "Go ahead, call the police."

She had started crying again. Shelby wanted to put her arm around her shoulders or squeeze her arm or something reassuring although she knew that didn't make sense. Nora was a confessed murderer. That would take a while to sink in. Instead, she pulled her phone out of her pocket and dialed Chief Stone. When the chief answered, Shelby spoke in a soft voice, giving her a brief account of what had happened and where they were.

She could hear Stone slamming what sounded like a drawer, then saying, "Don't say anything else to her. If she tries to leave, don't stand in her way. And in no way are you to ask her any questions."

Chapter
Thirty-Two

A couple of hours later, Shelby dragged herself inside the houseboat and sank into the nearest chair. She sighed as she stretched out, realizing that she felt totally deflated by all that had just happened. She still couldn't quite wrap her head around Nora's confession, more because she hadn't really been expecting one. Although she'd had some misgivings about Nora, she hadn't really thought she was the killer. Even when she'd confronted Nora, there was a part of her that had been prepared to apologize because she'd gotten it wrong. *Some investigator I am, so easily fooled.* But that wasn't important. What counted was that the killer had been found, bringing some closure for Hilary and her stepmom.

Shelby stood and walked over to the counter, plugging in the kettle. When the water started boiling, she fixed herself a cup of Earl Grey tea and then walked back to the chair. JT had arrived before her and she scooped him up, setting him down on her lap once she'd reclaimed her spot.

Nora must have put a lot of rage into her swing though, to topple and kill a man who had to be several inches taller and much stockier. In that case, Nora's claim that she hadn't meant to kill him didn't wash. It did allow her to run away, though. Although if she'd disposed of his body, she had no real reason to run, if that's what she had done. Shelby hadn't been allowed to be present for that part of the confession.

Shelby sat forward, mid-sip, causing JT to glare at her as he jumped to the floor. Nora hadn't said anything about getting rid of Nathan's body. She hit him and ran. That was her story. Was she playing games or was he actually not dead, perhaps just disoriented, and crawled looking for help and instead fell over the edge? That probably would have killed him or at least caused him to drown. She needed to run that by Chief Stone, but she realized her questions and thoughts would not be welcomed.

She felt totally frustrated, not knowing what was going on at the station. If only Zack were here, but that wouldn't have helped. He would not have been welcome at the police station either. She began pacing, wondering what she could do. Nothing, she realized sadly.

Or she could talk it over with Matthew. He might know if the second scenario was the more accurate one. She dialed his number, wondering if a walk over to Edie's might be just as useful.

When he didn't answer, she tried Edie instead.

"Matthew? Why yes, he's over here," Edie answered readily. "We were just going to sit down to eat. Can it wait? Or would you like to join us? Have you eaten yet?"

"No, I haven't and yes, I would. Thanks. I'll be right over."

Shelby practically ran but realized after a few blocks she'd have to dial it back. She just wasn't in any shape to keep up that pace, and it bothered her arm. She'd start jogging again soon, though.

She let herself in at Edie's and found her and Matthew seated at the kitchen table.

"I hope you don't mind," Edie said. "It was ready so I thought we'd just get started."

Shelby eyed the pork chop casserole with appreciation as she took her place. "Not a problem. This looks delicious."

She hadn't realized how hungry she was. In fact, she'd even wondered if she even had an appetite after all that had happened. It must have been the walk that had shaken off the exhaustion and awakened her appetite. She decided to stick with casual conversation until after dinner. Murder and mealtime were not a good combination.

When they'd settled in the living room with their tea afterward, Shelby finally broached the subject.

"I know you get tired of my talking about the murder, but a lot has happened and I just need to run something by you both, especially Matthew."

"We're all ears," Edie answered.

"Well, Nora Dynes, who's been working with us on the murder mystery event, has just confessed to Nathan Miller's murder."

Edie looked shocked while Matthew's face showed he was taking it all in stride, as usual. Shelby quickly filled them in on the details.

"I find that really hard to take in," Edie finally said. "I can't picture Nora as a murderer. Or even an embezzler. Boy, it just shows we don't really know others."

Shelby looked at Matthew who nodded. "That must have been a powerful swing."

"That's what I was thinking and then I remembered, she said he looked dead so she ran away, I assume to the dock and left on the next boat. But, if that's the case, how did he get into the river?"

Matthew looked intrigued. "She didn't say she pulled him over and pushed him in?"

Shelby shook her head. "She didn't add anything. She really did seem upset that she'd killed him. She said she just reacted and wanted time to get away." She paused to gather her thoughts.

"You know, somehow it doesn't feel right. Since she told me the details about their argument, why wouldn't she tell all about how she got his body over to the water? That would have been tricky and anyone could have turned up at any minute and seen her."

"Well, if she didn't confess to that because she didn't put him in the water herself, either he got himself over to the edge or someone else did," Matthew offered.

"Do you think he crawled over and, being disoriented or just about to pass out, ended up in the river?" Shelby persisted.

Matthew shrugged. "I have no idea. It's too bad you're not on better terms with the chief," he added with a small grin.

Shelby groaned. "So true. She'll never tell me."

Edie jumped in. "Well, you really have no need to know, honey. It's up to Tekla Stone to finish off the details. It really has nothing to do with you, and hasn't," she added, giving Shelby a pointed look.

Shelby was about to launch into an explanation giving her reasons for getting involved once again but thought it better to not get into it all. Just let it go. Besides, Edie was right. Nora had confessed, the killer was found, the family had closure. She wondered if she should call Hilary and see how she was but decided she'd better wait for Hilary to call her. Who knew when Stone would be ready to share this new information with Hilary and Giselle?

It was none of her business. She was finally starting to see that.

Chapter
Thirty-Three

S helby had just finished restocking the shelf of books by local authors, by far the most popular section in the store, when the door opened and she heard Hilary call out to her.

"I hope you've got some time to talk," Hilary said as she walked in. Giselle was right behind her.

"For sure." Shelby had been wondering about Hilary and how she'd taken the news about the killer being found. She'd wanted to call but had thought it best not to intrude but, rather, wait for Hilary to contact her.

"How are you?"

Hilary shrugged, but the sadness in her eyes seemed to have found its way to her entire body. She seemed even smaller in size. "You know, about the same. We've just come from talking to Chief Stone. She filled us in on everything she'd learned and what will happen now. I guess it's good that the killer has been found, but really, it doesn't make that much difference, does it? Dad is still dead."

Giselle let out a small sob and jumped in. "But it does matter, Hilary. We would have always wondered who had done it and why. So now we have closure."

"I'm so sorry. Do you know the why?" Shelby knew she shouldn't ask any questions. This looked to be hard enough for Hilary to handle, but she was curious how much the chief had told them. Of course, none of it was privileged in any way, unless the investigation was continuing.

"We do," Giselle answered. Her voice sounded strong, she stood straight and formidable. Shelby thought it a good thing that Giselle seemed to have enough strength to get them both through the next rough time. "That woman, that person killed him to protect herself. She's an embezzler and was taking the money from the library board, of all places. She should be ashamed."

Ashamed wasn't the word Shelby would choose. She was a murderer after all. Did they know about the blackmail? Nathan wasn't totally the wronged man, although he was the one who'd turned up dead. If he hadn't started blackmailing Nora, he might still be alive today. Shelby hoped neither Hilary nor Giselle could tell what she was thinking.

"Well, whatever," Hilary continued, "we just wanted to stop by and see you before we head home, and to thank you for everything.'"

"I was happy to help in any way I could."

"You offered your friendship and that really mattered to me. I saw her," Hilary added in a small voice. "Nora or Margo or whoever she is. I wonder how she managed to get the drop on Dad and have such power to kill him with a branch?"

"And to get him across the lawn and push him over the cliff," Giselle piped in. "That's a long way and quite the drop."

How do you know that? Shelby realized she had made a sound, although she wasn't sure what kind.

Giselle's gaze flew from Hilary to Shelby. Her eyes narrowed as Shelby tried to keep calm and act natural.

"I think we should be going, Hilary," Giselle continued. "We have a lot to do. Thanks again for all your help, Shelby."

Hilary hugged Shelby. "Yes, thanks so much, Shelby. Let's keep in touch, okay?"

Shelby nodded. *That would be nice.*

She had meant to finish shelving books but she couldn't stop thinking about Giselle's remark about the body being pushed into the water. How did she know about the logistics? She was certain Chief Stone would not have shared any of that. And how had Giselle known about the cliff and it being a long way down? A lucky guess? It didn't seem right.

She needed to tell the chief, even if she was all wrong about it. She tried calling but it went to voicemail so she left a message saying she needed to talk to her right away.

Since it was noon, she decided to take a quick lunch break. She hung the "closed for lunch" sign on the door, grabbed her bag, along with her cell phone, and headed out to her favorite picnic table, the one overlooking the strait, away from the tourist traffic. While she munched on an egg salad sandwich, she thought again about Giselle. What if? What if she was somehow tied to this? Nora had said she'd hit him and run; no mention of dragging his body to the edge. Was that true? Had she forgotten or just not shared that info? Shelby was tempted to call Chief Stone again and check it all out. If Giselle's comment was significant, Shelby couldn't just ignore it. She would do it.

She started to reach for her bag and her phone when she saw Giselle making her way across the lawn to her.

"What are you doing back here?" Shelby asked. "I thought you'd both caught the boat back to the mainland."

"Hilary went on ahead, but I had some things I wanted to go over with you." Her smile seemed friendlier than Shelby had seen it before.

"Sure. Like what?" Shelby hoped her voice didn't sound as panicked as she felt.

Giselle sat down beside her on the bench attached to the picnic table. "I'm curious. How do you think Nora managed to get Nathan's body over to the river? She's quite a petite thing."

Be careful, Shelby.

"I hadn't really given it any thought," Shelby finally answered, hoping she sounded calmer.

Giselle moved closer to her. "Oh, I'm sure you have. I believe you are much more attuned to what's going on around here. You're nosy, for starters, and from what I've heard, you've done some investigating in the past. I'm sure you've been looking around, as Hilary asked you to do, and have probably reached a few conclusions."

Shelby felt something hard poking into her side.

"It's a gun, Shelby, and although I'd be foolish to use it out here, you'd be foolish to challenge me. Now, I'd like you to stand up, very casual-like, and we two friends are going for a stroll over to the edge of the lawn back there, right around where poor Nathan went over into the river."

Shelby nodded and slowly stood, stepping over the bench. She didn't flinch when Giselle linked arms with her. She could still feel the gun poking into her side. They walked slowly in the direction Giselle had indicated, Shelby's mind racing, trying to think of what to say, what to do.

She glanced around, hoping Matthew would be in view, but no such luck.

"Stop it," hissed Giselle. "Eyes forward and walk a bit faster, too. I want to catch the next boat back."

Shelby's heart pounded and she tried not to think about what Giselle would do to her in order to make that boat. She heard its whistle at that exact moment and almost squealed.

"I don't know what you're planning or why," she tried, "but it most certainly won't work."

"The why is easy. I saw the look in your eyes when I mentioned getting Nathan's body over the cliff. I'm not dumb, you know. But I was stupid. That was a slipup I'll always regret."

Shelby took a deep breath. "Okay, so I'll admit that got me thinking. And what I'd like in return is to know why you pulled Nathan over to the edge and pushed him into the river. Were you working together with Margo?"

"With her? Perhaps you're not as smart as I thought. No, I followed Nathan because I was tired of his cheating on me. He'd done it before and although he promised never again, I knew he was lying. The so-called consulting contract here was perfect for that, and then when I saw him there with that Margo, I knew she was the one. I thought maybe they were arguing about his leaving me—she wanted him to and he said no. I thought that's why she'd hit him."

Giselle stopped abruptly, causing Shelby to stumble.

"I'd already decided I didn't want him back, but when I saw him lying there, I decided I did want his insurance policy, a nice big one that he'd taken out when we were first married.

That was long enough ago that it wouldn't attract attention as a motive. Getting rid of the cheater and getting rich at the same time appealed to me. She'd started the job, so I just tidied up and made sure he was really gone. I hadn't expected his body to be found that quickly, although, I guess, it didn't really matter."

She gave Shelby a nudge and they started walking again. They were getting close to the edge. Shelby tried slowing her pace. Giselle realized what was happening and gave Shelby another push.

Just what Shelby wanted. She pretended to stumble and went down on her right knee, taking Giselle down with her.

Shelby reached out to a pile of debris beside her. She grabbed a thick branch and swung around, smashing Giselle on the side of the head. Giselle fell, and the gun went flying.

Sharp pains shot through Shelby's injured elbow, which she tried to ignore. She sat there breathing deeply, staring at Giselle. It was hard to tell if she was breathing. Finally, Shelby snapped out of it and scrambled over to help Giselle. Next thing she knew, Matthew was kneeling beside her.

"Are you all right, Shelby?" He gingerly touched her shoulder. "Here, come sit here and just relax. I'll take care of this."

He helped Shelby stand up and walk the few feet to a log, then he moved back to Giselle. He knelt beside down to check her breathing, then pulled out his cell and called Chief Stone.

Shelby asked, "How is she? Will she be okay?"

"I'm sure she's just knocked out, Shelby." He stood and walked over to where the gun had slid, picked it up, put the safety on, and pocketed it. "You're sure your arm's okay?"

She realized she was cradling her elbow. "It's sore, but I'm okay. I can't believe what just happened. She was going to kill me, Matthew. She murdered her husband."

"Just try to relax, Shelby. It's been a shock, I know."

She closed her eyes for a few more moments and, when she opened them, one of the security guards came running toward them. Matthew went over to speak to him and they were soon joined by the second guard who was carrying the first aid kit. He knelt beside Giselle. The next thing Shelby knew, Chief Stone was standing in front of her.

Shelby lifted her head but, before she could say anything, Stone lifted her hand to silence her.

"I got your message, Shelby. And now it's really over. We're going to get you home."

"She is going to be all right, isn't she?" Shelby asked, her heart pounding as she thought of what could have happened. Nathan had been killed in the same way.

"She's okay. She'll have quite the bruise, I'd imagine, and a bad headache, but I don't think you could pack enough of a wallop for anything more, so put that out of your mind, young lady."

Shelby nodded but couldn't shake the sinking feeling. She'd actually clobbered someone.

Once again, Shelby had the feeling the chief might reach out and hug her but instead, Stone said, "This ends your sleuthing career, right?"

"Absolutely."

"Yeah, sure."

Chapter
Thirty-Four

"I can't keep driving back to the Bay at all hours of the night when you get into trouble," Zack said, pouring both Shelby and himself another cup of coffee.

She noticed there was a grin tugging at the ends of his mouth as he said it. Fortunately.

He'd arrived several hours earlier, at 2:00 AM, after hearing the news from someone—Shelby wasn't quite sure who his spy was—about what had happened on the island. She was surprised but delighted to have him back again, if only for a day. They'd been able to snag a few hours of sleep after Zack's arrival but Shelby felt a desperate need for caffeine. She cautiously rubbed her elbow and, although it still felt sore, an X-ray had shown nothing was seriously reinjured.

"You know, it wasn't my fault," she finally answered.

"It never is." He had a deadpan expression, but those eyes still danced. He looked so good to her.

"I mean, I wasn't actively investigating Giselle or anything."

"Maybe not, but you had been sleuthing for the past few weeks, right? And, I hope you realize how lucky you are that you didn't do anything more serious to your arm."

"I'm grateful for that but again, it wasn't my fault." She was sticking to it.

"Might as well admit it. Chief Stone is sorely ticked off at you again."

"You two are talking?" That surprised Shelby. That would certainly be a turnaround in the relationship between the two law enforcement officers. Was *she* his source?

"Why don't you fill me in? Where has your nosiness led you this time?" He sat down beside her at the kitchen island.

"You know, I think I'll just retire from being an investigator."

"Now why don't I quite believe that? But I'll play along. Why do you say that?"

"Because it took me so long to clue into the fact that Nora Dynes, the library volunteer, was the mystery woman. Okay, I did have an inkling that something wasn't right about her, especially when I'd heard about the mystery woman's skill at organizing events. That was a red flag but it came late in the game."

"Lots of supposition."

"I know. So anyway, Nora, or rather Margo thought she'd killed Nathan, but she'd just knocked him out. Giselle, his wife, had been following him, thinking he was having an affair. She assumed it was with Nora when she saw them together. And then, seeing Nathan knocked out, she decided to finish the job."

"The jealous wife?"

"And greedy. She wanted his insurance."

"So, if he wasn't having an affair with Nora, who was he cheating with?"

Shelby shook her head. "Nobody has come forward, as if they would. It might just have been Giselle's overly active imagination. She didn't like him staying overnight here when he was on business. Hilary thought he might have just been getting away from Giselle once in a while. Either way, the killer has been caught."

Shelby chewed on her bottom lip as she stared out the window. After a few seconds, she looked back at Zack, "But you know what also bothers me, Zack? I bashed her with a branch, exactly what Nora, I mean Margo, did to Nathan. I could have killed her."

"For starters, you did it out of self-defense. And Margo didn't kill Nathan, just knocked him out, which is what you did. You don't have the killer instinct, if that's what's worrying you. I do know anything like this can be hard to process, though." He gave her a quick kiss on the cheek and she felt her mood lighten.

"So, what do you think will happen to Nora?"

"I'd bet there's a list of charges starting with embezzlement and ending with attempted murder, or at the very least, assault causing bodily harm. But who knows what surprises Chief Stone might have up her sleeve? Now, enough talk about murder. Let's take our coffee out on the deck and talk. It's quite warm this morning."

Shelby nodded, a bit concerned about the "talk" part. Surely, he wouldn't expect her answer about moving right now, or would he? Today of all days? She sighed, still not certain what her answer would be.

JT dashed out ahead of them as soon as the door was opened, then sauntered down the steps and onto the dock.

"You'd better not stay out late," Shelby called after him.

Zack chuckled. "No, Mom."

Shelby smiled. "Okay, so I'm a little protective."

"That's not a bad thing." He grabbed her free hand and pulled her to a chair. "Now, sit. We have some things to discuss."

Her hand was shaking a bit as she took a sip of her coffee and watched Zack start pacing. This didn't look like a good start.

"I'm serious about you getting into trouble, Shelby. I don't know what I'd do if anything happened to you." He sat in the chair next to her.

"And I've been thinking a lot about the move to Boston. I know that was a lot to ask, and it must have been a total shock, coming out of left field like that. But I also know that what we have going is too special to give up. We need to follow this thing through, together."

He looked at her and she nodded. No argument there. And she knew in that instance what her answer would be. She'd go with him. He was the one.

Zack smiled, the look of relief on his face palpable. "So, I've decided there will be other promotions, other opportunities, and I'd be a fool to take this one. It's really asking too much of you to leave when you've just found yourself and your family. And I don't want to go where you aren't. So, I'm staying put. As soon as my secondment is over in a few weeks, I'll be back in the Bay."

Shelby dropped her cup and leaned over to kiss him.

"I'm so, so happy," she said, trying not to cry. She hadn't realized just how intensely she'd been feeling.

He gave her a quick kiss. "So, it's settled? We keep talking and figuring out where we're going, together?"

"Absolutely."

"But I'm really hoping that from now on, you'll stay out of any future police investigations."

He stood and pulled her into a proper kiss.

She knew this was the right decision for them both. A future here together.

But she wasn't so sure she could go along with the part about not getting involved in another mystery.

Acknowledgments

The wonderful thing about this space is that it allows the writer to acknowledge that putting together a book takes more than just one person with an idea. It starts with the emotional support of family and friends, and to that end I thank, as always my sister, Lee, who's always been there for me. As has my great friend and colleague, Mary Jane Maffini. We've shared a lot on this writing adventure. Being a part of the Ladies Killing Circle has also helped shape my path right from those early critiquing days, straight through our publishing successes.

Then of course, this wouldn't have happened without my savvy and helpful agent, Kim Lionetti from BookEnds Literary Agency. She's also a very nice person! Then, on to my most recent editor, Faith Black Ross, who has guided my writing from my first book with Crooked Lane Books. She has shown much patience and understanding along the way, and I thank her from the bottom of my heart.

And, although there are so many writers and readers I've met over the years, who have also played a large role in all of this, and to them I am indebted, I want to specifically thank you the reader. You are the reason why we as writers continue to do what we do. You cheer us on and you are quick to point out any errors, which help to achieve the goal of a well-written, and hopefully, well-loved book.

Also, thank you to the people and the amazing setting of the Thousand Islands. Who wouldn't want to write a book where you work in a bookstore, in a castle, on a romantic island? I love spending my days there.